"I want to try aga

Cody blinked, certain he heard wrong. "You what?"

"I want to try again."

"Jenna, I don't think that is a good idea," he said quietly, running his hand through his hair.

Jenna's face was streaked with tears. "I need to. I can't let that guy get in my head. He can't win. I need to do it again."

Cody heard the desperation in her tone. "I get it. But maybe we should wait and try again next week. Just slow it down. I told you, the last thing I want to do is upset you."

"I know that, and you aren't the one upsetting me. I appreciate what you are doing, and that is why I am counting on you to get me past the fear now."

"Did anyone ever tell you, you have a stubborn streak?"

"My dad, just about every day," she huffed. "Please, I need to do this."

Cody stared at her. Her tear-filled eyes ate at him. A lump caught in his throat. He wanted nothing more than to wipe away her tears and kiss those pouty lips, to make her forget about the attack. The training would do nothing but stir up the memories, but he could tell she wasn't going to take no for an answer.

24 to Life

by

DeDe Ramey

Dalton Skies, Book 1

24 to Life

Cover Art by *Kristian Norris*

The Wild Rose Press, Inc.
PO Box 708
Adams Basin, NY 14410-0708
Visit us at www.thewildrosepress.com

Publishing History
First Crimson Rose Edition, 2021
Trade Paperback ISBN 978-1-5092-3429-5
Digital ISBN 978-1-5092-3430-1

Dalton Skies, Book 1
Published in the United States of America

Dedication

To my husband Keith,
who encouraged me to try writing,
to my kids Drew and Leah,
who love me just as I am,
and to Jude,
who never fails to give me the best hugs.

Chapter One

The floor creaked beneath Jenna Corbett's feet as she shuffled to the kitchen with only the light from her bedroom lamp to break through the darkness. Clicks of her furry companion's paws echoed in the hallway as the large, white, fluffy mutt named Tucker followed her in close pursuit.

The clock on the oven emitted a golden light. Five a.m. Flipping the light on, she started her pot of coffee. Inhaling the rich aroma captured her senses.

Jenna tugged open the back door and Tucker escaped into the black void with the push of his nose against the screen door. The purple sky stretched above her as she stood on the porch and stretched and breathed in the freshness of the morning.

Stepping back inside, she poured a cup of coffee, sat on the sofa, and laced up her shoes. Tucker nudged her with his nose. He was ready to go. Pulling an elastic band from her wrist, she combed her fingers through her thick locks, securing it into a messy bun.

Running had become an everyday occurrence since Jenna rented the small farmhouse three months ago. Tucker recently joined her after she adopted him. The park trail, a mile up the road on the outskirts of Dalton, was perfect for their morning routine. The path took her through thick pine trees that emptied into Pinebrook Park. All total, she and Tucker could run just under five miles.

Finishing the last sip of coffee, Jenna set the cup in the sink, grabbed Tucker's leash, and latched it to his collar. She wrapped her wireless earbuds around her neck, open the door, and stood with Tucker on the front porch, taking a moment to view the twinkling stars. Life was sweet.

Jenna's dad, Will, had urged her to stay at their ranch. A large part of it had to do with losing her mom to cancer a little more than a year ago. It had taken its toll on the family. She loved her dad and knew he wanted to protect her. Guilt played a part in the reason she stayed for as long as she did.

Still, she yearned to explore what life outside the confines of the ranch had to offer. Her curiosity won the battle. She had finally found her independence and it felt good.

The heavy drumbeat of the music streamed through her earbuds and set the pace. The pair started slowly, then picked up speed until they found a comfortable cadence. Gravel crunched beneath her shoes. The humid July air quickly caused sweat beads to form along her hairline.

Darkness still blanketed the tiny town. Only a few well-placed streetlamps glowed. From where she was, at the top of a hill, she could just about make out the entire downtown.

Dalton, Arkansas sat in the middle of several small communities nestled in rolling hills about twenty miles south of Fayetteville. She loved her little town with its historic charm. Most of the townspeople treated each other like family and were always willing to help.

Jenna had spent her entire life living in the country

on the outskirts of town, devoted to working her family's ranch. She worked from dawn to dusk and no one could say she wasn't tough enough to handle the work.

On a whim, she applied for an office assistant job at Bruin's Veterinary Hospital after noticing the job opening when she took one of their barn cats in for a check-up. They hired her on the spot. It didn't hurt that her best friend, April, worked there. After three months, she had saved enough money to rent her little house.

So many things were falling into place. Jenna's head filled with thoughts of what might be in store for the day. Since getting accepted to a vet tech program at a local university, she had been corresponding with her advisor on her schedule for the fall.

Up ahead she could see the light at the 24 to Life Gym, the only business open at this time in the morning. It shined like a beacon, pointing to the piney woods, her favorite part of the run.

The gym sat across the street from the back entrance to the park, providing the only light on the trail, other than the moonlight. Pine trees flanked the long path that ran along the edge of a creek and opened into a grassy area with benches. Running through the trees, the aroma of the pine tar seeping from the bark captivated her senses. It always reminded Jenna of Christmas when the family would cut their own Christmas tree. She breathed deep the enticing scent. The trees parted, and she could just make out the opening to the park.

Hands grabbed her. Her feet tangled. The earbuds flew from Jenna's neck as her body collided against the rocky trail with such force, darkness invaded. Gravel and dirt embedded into her cheek as Tucker's leash jerked from her hand and he sprinted away. Searing pain shot through her and blood filled her mouth. The weight of her assailant crushed down on top of her and all the air escaped her lungs, leaving her unable to scream.

Legs straddled her. Jenna's fingers dug into the dirt, trying to pull away, but found no traction. A large hand gripped hers and rendered her immobile. Strained grunts escaped her throat as she tried to wiggle free, but the weight of her attacker had completely overpowered her. With one quick move, she was flipped over, giving Jenna her first glimpse at the assailant, who resembled an ominous shadow because of the dark clothing and mask he wore. He tore at her clothes, ripping her tank top, and pushing up her sports bra. His hands moved down her body and yanked her shorts down. She grabbed at them, but he was too quick and too strong.

Hot tears streamed down her face as his hands moved about her body. She felt his warm moist breath against her cheek while his body writhed on top of her. Again, his hands pinned hers above her head.

A snap of a stick in the darkness drew her attention. Tucker leaped at the masked figure, knocking him off balance. Jenna's hands slipped free from his grip, and with one hand, she struck him in the face. He chuckled sadistically and jerked his head to one side. His neck popped, and he let out a wheezy groan. Quickly regaining control, he backhanded her, sending her face against the gravel. A stabbing pain surrounded her cheek and eye, and a labored cry resonated from her throat.

Tucker released a low growl, baring his teeth,

ready to take a bite, and lunged at the attacker. The assailant swatted at him, but Tucker didn't back down. Within moments, the man fled into the woods.

Jenna lay on the ground, taking in short, ragged breaths. Tucker lay down beside her. Darkness surrounded her. She was alone. Panic set in. *What if he comes back?* She needed to move. Her head felt heavy and the ringing in her ears made her confused. She blinked slowly, trying to focus as blood poured down her face mixing with tears.

Dizziness caused Jenna to wobble as she carefully stood and pulled up her shorts that were halfway down her thighs. Once she regained some stability, she tugged at her tank top and sports bra that were scrunched up under her arms. Her hand rubbed her face, trying to clear her vision, but it was no use. She fought to stay upright and stumbled up the trail with Tucker's leash twisted around her bloodied hand. Her screams for help came out moans at first, then gathered strength when she saw the light of the gym.

****

Cody Spencer sat at the counter of the 24 to Life Gym wondering why he had agreed to switch shifts with his friend Joe. His brain refused to engage from lack of sleep, and he considered laying his head down and shutting his burning eyes.

The coffee he made when he came in at four thirty tasted burnt, so he only had a couple of swallows before pouring it down the drain. Even the southern rock music playing through the speakers had no effect on his drowsy state. *Seriously, would anybody notice if I fell asleep? There are only a handful of people here anyway.* Joe would be coming in around noon, but the question remained, would he find Cody asleep on the big bean bag chair in the kids' area? He pulled his cap over his eyes and sat back in his chair with his arms crossed.

A strange noise pulled Cody from his grogginess and drew his attention outside. His body straightened in the chair and he slowly tipped his cap back. There it was again. Louder now. The howl sent a chill up his spine. Jogging to the door to see where the sound came from, he spotted a young woman staggering up the trail across the street. A flood of panic ripped through him.

Cody's hands slammed against the doors. The gust of warm air prickled his skin. Bolting through the parking lot at full speed, he quickly crossed the darkened street. She continued screaming in a guttural cry, "Help me!" Terror filled her face as he approached her. Blood dripped from her nose, head, and mouth. Sticks and leaves were matted in her hair. Cuts and scrapes covered her body. Her clothes were torn and covered in dirt and blood. Gripped in her hand was the leash of a large white dog. Cody scanned the area wondering what had happened.

His hands circled her waist and her trembling body collapsed. The sudden shift in weight caught him by surprise and he stumbled but managed to lift her into his arms. The leash dropped from her grasp, so Cody chirped his lips, hoping the dog would follow, as he raced back across the street. Several members in the gym were standing at the door watching the commotion. An older man pushed the gym door open and Cody carried her into the office.

The room was dark, lit only by a desk lamp and the glow of the computer. Cody laid her down on the old leather couch across from the desk. After tucking a fleece jacket from the lost and found box under her head, he reached for his phone and dialed nine-one-one, then his dad. His heart pounded so violently he could barely breathe. He paced the floor trying to still his nerves.

From the window in the office, Cody caught a glimpse of some of the members standing outside talking and staring, so he closed the blinds to give her some privacy, and then turned his attention back to her. She was young, maybe around his age. Just the sight of her caused a lump to form in his throat. He knelt in front of her and she turned, studying his face.

Cody gently put his hand on her shoulder. "You're safe. You're going to be okay."

After checking her injuries, he took a rag from the storage closet, wet it, then gently dabbed the cut above her eye, trying to stop the bleeding. With his dad, Todd, being a retired police officer, he knew to limit his contact with her to preserve the evidence until they knew exactly what happened. Her eyes met his while he dabbed at the cut. "My name is Cody by the way," he said, trying to calm her fears. Though she said nothing in response, within a few minutes he noticed her trembling subside and the terror in her eyes fade.

The sound of sirens caught Cody's attention. He opened the office door and instructed one of the regulars from the gym to show the emergency crew in, while he stayed by her side continuing to hold the rag to her head.

The office filled with the sound of radio transmissions when the paramedics and police walked in. Cody moved behind the desk to give them room, but he kept his focus on her. The big white dog found a spot directly behind his chair and stretched out. Cody gave him a rub, then sat down. His mind raced, recalling the past few minutes, and watching the action unfold around him. *What in the hell just happened?* He took his cap off and ran his hands through his hair and down his face before he replaced it. *I'm awake now. That's for sure.*

Two paramedics moved around the girl, placing a blood pressure cuff on her arm and assessing her wounds. A female officer peppered him with a few questions about what happened, then squatted in front of the girl. After the officer's questions were met with silence, Cody noticed the girl's eyes lock on him. The terror reemerged. He made his way to the couch and sat beside her, hoping it would help quell her fear. A flutter filled his chest when she immediately gripped his hand and entwined their fingers. His eyes shifted to the officer who turned to him.

"Can you try asking her some questions?"

Cody nodded hesitantly, and the officer handed him a sheet of questions. His attention turned back to the girl. The room seemed to close in around them and all he could see was her. He hoped she trusted him. His hand gently squeezed hers.

"What's your name?" Cody asked softly.

The young woman clenched her teeth. Her lips trembled as she tried to speak. "Jenna. Jenna Corbett," she whispered.

Cody smiled. His thumb rubbed the back of her hand, coaxing her to stay strong. The officer jotted information down on a metal clipboard and he continued to help with the basic questions. When the questions became more personal, he stepped out of the office and nearly plowed into his dad.

"Geez, what took you so long? I was beginning to believe you weren't coming." Cody motioned for him to step over to an area outside of the office and out of earshot of the members.

"You woke me out of a dead sleep. What do you expect?" his dad said in a quiet voice. "What the hell happened?"

Cody's eyes wandered to the members milling around to see if they could hear them. "She was attacked in the wooded area behind the park." His voice remained quiet, just above a whisper. "I heard a strange noise outside, so I went to the door and saw her coming up the trail. When I got to her, she was all bloodied and banged up, so I brought her here."

His dad brought his arms across his broad chest and spread his feet apart, becoming an imposing figure. "Did she get a good description?" Cody knew, from years of living with his dad, the minute he went into cop mode. His salt and pepper hair gave the only indication of his mid-fifties age. He had always been very meticulous about his appearance, and it showed in his muscular build.

Cody tucked his hands in his pockets. "I don't think so. When the police were questioning her, she said it was dark and he had his face covered and was dressed in black."

"That's too bad. Well, it's a good thing you were here." A noise drew Cody's eyes back to the office. A tingle in his hand brought his thoughts back to her delicate fingers laced in his. "But where is Joe? I thought he had the early shift today."

The paramedics wheeled Jenna out on a stretcher. Cody's eyes stayed locked on her while he continued to answer his dad's question. "He did, but he asked me to fill in. He's been working with Becker Construction, and I guess he got too hot yesterday. Last night, when he came in, he said he had a migraine." His attention returned to Todd. "But he said he would be in at noon."

A paramedic interrupted their conversation and made eye contact with Cody. "The young lady is asking for you."

Cody's brows lifted in surprise. "Me?" The paramedic nodded and turned to walk away, so Cody started to follow him, then turned back to his dad. "Be right back."

Todd turned to walk with Cody as the police and paramedics continued to flow in and out of the office. "I think I'm going to go get some breakfast. It doesn't appear I can get in the office anyway."

"All right, sounds good. Can you bring me something back?" Cody called back to his dad as he pressed his back against the door.

"Sure."

Escorted to the back of the ambulance, Cody climbed in and smiled at Jenna, despite the fact he could see the damage of the attack. A bandage covered one eye and wrapped around her head. Bruises were already appearing on her face, shoulder, and arm. The unbandaged eye had nearly swollen shut, and her lip had swelled. Dried blood still stained her face and arms. A wave of sadness washed over him as he sat on the bench next to the stretcher and for the first time noticed his blood-stained shirt.

Jenna slowly turned to him. "Thank you," she

croaked, and tried to clear her throat, "you saved my life."

Cody rubbed his hands on his nylon gym shorts, his nerves still on edge. "Well, from what you told the police, I think your dog saved you, but I'm glad I was able to help." His cheeks warm with each word.

The growl of the engine caught his attention, and he surveyed his surroundings wondering what it would be like to have the job of a paramedic. Silence fell between them and felt awkward, so Cody asked, "Did they tell you what is going to happen now?"

Jenna nodded slowly. "They need to take me in to get processed, whatever that means. Then I think they said something about x-rays and probably stitches."

His nose wrinkled and his lip curled. "Yeah, that cut is pretty deep." Jenna turned her head away. Cody's chest tightened knowing she was probably playing the attack over in her mind. "Is there anyone you need me to contact or anything I can help with?"

She shook her head, not making eye contact, but then turned quickly back to him. Her eyes widened as her face filled with concern. She tried to raise up on her elbows but winced. "Where is Tucker?"

Confused, Cody tilted his head, then remembered the dog. "Would Tucker be your dog?"

"Yes."

He lifted the corner of his mouth and motioned over his shoulder. "He is currently sacked out in the office."

Jenna's hand patted her chest. "Oh, thank goodness." She let out a long breath, then met his gaze. "I hate to impose on you because you have already done so much, but would there be any way I could have

11

you drop Tucker off at Bruin's Veterinary Hospital?"

Cody hesitated. "Sure," he said slowly, "but he seemed fine. Do you think he might have gotten hurt?"

"Oh, no. I work there. They know Tucker."

Cody nodded. "Gotcha. I would be happy to drop him off."

Jenna's body relaxed. "I'll call and let them know you are coming."

"That would probably be a good idea."

A paramedic appeared at the back of the ambulance. "Are you riding to the hospital?"

Cody eyed Jenna, then responded to the paramedic. "No. I'm staying here." He stood and turned to her, "I will make sure Tucker is taken care of," then hopped out of the back.

Jenna called out, "Oh, hey!" He turned and leaned in to hear her over the loud engine. "You did say your name was Cody, right?"

"That's me." The paramedic closed the door with Cody's parting wave. He watched as the ambulance drove away, then jogged back inside the gym.

Chapter Two

A silver-haired officer flipped his aviators on top of his head and pulled open the gym door. Cody peered from above the computer and gave him a welcoming smile, but there was no response from the officer.

His brows creased and his lips thinned as he approached Cody. "I'm Sergeant Gallagher." He pointed to the blood stains on Cody's shirt. "I'm guessing you are the gentleman who took care of Miss Corbett."

Cody examined his shirt, then leveled his eyes at the officer, who appeared much younger than his silver hair implied. "Yes sir." He extended his hand and noticed more dried blood on his arm.

Sergeant Gallagher put his metal clipboard on the counter and shook Cody's hand without smiling. "What is your name?" He scanned the paper on his clipboard and picked up his pen. The harshness of his tone set Cody's nerves on edge.

"Cody Spencer, sir."

Sergeant Gallagher jotted down the information then laid the pen down. "Did anyone talk to you about your statement, or getting samples from you?"

Cody's eyes darted. "A female officer spoke to me briefly, asking what happened, but that's all." He swallowed. "I'm sorry. Did you say samples?"

The sergeant flipped through his papers and

continued with his questions. "The victim said you carried her. Is that correct?"

"Yes. I heard her scream and saw her running up the trail with her dog. When I got to her, she collapsed, so I picked her up and brought her into the office."

The sergeant motioned to his stained shirt. "I'm going to need your clothes so we can collect any evidence transfer."

Cody's body stiffened. "All right. I think I have something I can change into in my Jeep, if you have a minute."

The sergeant nodded, then held his pen up. "Before you do that, let me go ahead and get an evidence swab from you." Quickly scanning the room, he asked, "Do you want to go to your office?"

Cody's brows drew together. "What does it entail?"

"Swabbing the dried blood."

"Nah, I'm fine here."

The sergeant took a cotton swab and tube from his pocket and swabbed the dried blood from Cody's arm, then did a cursory check for other places of dried blood. Once he was done, Cody stepped from behind the counter and jogged out the door. He quickly returned with clothing in his hand and disappeared into the men's room. Within a few minutes, he returned wearing a yellow hoodie and a pair of navy wind-pants with slip-on sandals. The sergeant handed him a bag to put his clothes in and jotted down information on his clipboard.

His serious demeanor eased as he continued asking Cody questions. "I don't want to take up your time here, so do you think you could stop by the station later and give me your full statement?"

"Oh, absolutely. I have to take her dog to the vet anyway, so I can run by on my way."

"Dog?" A frown crossed the sergeant's face as he thumbed through his papers again. He rolled his shoulders as if he might be stiff, then let out a deep sigh. "The dog doesn't appear to have been processed either. Would you have a few minutes for me to do that now?"

"Yeah." Cody could see the frustration on the sergeant's face and moved out from behind the counter. "Follow me. He's in the office."

The squeak of the door caused Tucker to stir. He raised his head, smacked his lips a couple of times, then slowly sat up. Cody sat down on the sofa and patted his legs. "Tucker." The dog wandered over to sit at Cody's feet, wagging the tip of his tail.

Sergeant Gallagher donned a rubber glove. His focus landed on a photo on the wall of Cody and a man in a police uniform before he examined the dog. "Got someone on the force in your family?" His hand skimmed over the back of the dog.

"My dad. He was an officer in Montclair until he retired and bought the gym a couple of years ago."

The sergeant nodded, continuing to search for evidence in Tucker's fur. Reaching into his pocket, he retrieved a container with a small pair of scissors and trimmed several places where blood had spattered. Cody held a bag while the sergeant dropped the fur in. He continued to remove leaves and other items, dropping them each in separate bags. Next, he pulled a tube from his pocket, then a swab, and ran it along the dog's mouth.

Once he had that sample, he took a folded piece of paper out of his pocket. "Can you hold his paws while I scrape his nails?"

Cody lifted each of Tucker's paws while the sergeant took a metal blade and scraped his nails, collecting the residue into the folded paper. Tucker panted and smacked his lips while the officer took his samples, then wagged his tail and licked Cody once they were all done.

Sergeant Gallagher patted Tucker's head. "Friendly dog," he said, then stood. Noticing the bloody leash still attached to the dog's collar, he pointed. "Oh, I will need that too." After unhooking the collar and leash, he dropped it into a bag. "Okay, I think I got everything I need."

Cody rubbed Tucker's face, and it garnered a quick lick from the fluffy dog before he stood and followed the sergeant out of the office.

"Ask for me when you stop by."

"Sure. It may be after lunch if that's all right?" Cody pushed the door open for the sergeant.

"Yeah, that's fine. I should still be working up the case. If I'm not there, make sure you speak to Sheri at the window, and tell her who you are. She will be able to set up a time we can meet."

Cody's eyes squinted from the bright sunlight now coloring the peach and purple clouds. "All right, I will."

Sergeant Gallagher held his hand out, and Cody grasped it. "Thanks." He smiled this time, put his sunglasses on, and headed to his cruiser.

Once Cody returned to his spot behind the counter, it wasn't long before his dad returned with a large bag and a couple of Styrofoam cups.

"It's quiet," Todd said with a smile while surveying the gym.

"They all left like five minutes ago."

Todd set the items down on the counter. Cody immediately grabbed one of the cups and took a drink, letting the hot liquid slide down his throat. "You have no idea how much I needed this." He tipped the cup back again before setting it down and digging through the sack. "I am starving." He dug out several rolls of foil. "Oh, my gosh, you went to Tia Luna, didn't you? They have the best breakfast tacos in town." Rolling back the foil on one, he shoved a large portion of taco into his mouth.

The explosion of flavor caused a low rumble to form in the back of his throat, and a smile curled on his lips. Cody continued to inhale two more tacos before wadding up the foil and tossing it into the trash, right where Todd was standing. He chuckled, putting his fist to his mouth while still trying to swallow the last bite of food.

Pointing at the pair of purple and gold sneakers with a white bird emblem on the back that Todd was wearing, Cody snickered, "Where in the world did you get those sneakers?"

Todd inspected his shoes. "These? I have no clue. They're old. I wear them in the garden. I was trying to hurry to get down here, and I couldn't find my good ones. I found these in the garage, so I shoved them on."

Cody chuckled again. "I guess I never have seen you wear them."

Todd quickly scanned Cody from head to toe. "Hey, it's better than what you're wearing."

Cody eyed his outfit. "They had to take my clothes

for evidence. It's probably not a good idea to work the front desk with blood all over me anyway." He wiped his mouth with a napkin then dusted his hands. "Speaking of evidence, do you mind hanging out here for a little bit? I need to stop by the police station, then drop off Jenna's dog at the vet. I shouldn't be too long, probably back by lunch."

"She has a dog?" Todd wadded his foil up and tossed it in the trash.

"Yeah. A big one. He's in the office," Cody said hitching his thumb over his shoulder. "She said he jumped on the attacker and may have bitten him. He was the reason the attacker took off."

"Oh, really?" Todd chuckled. "You left that part of the story out. Sounds like he is the hero, not you."

Cody put his hands up. "I never said I was a hero. I was just there to get her to a safe place."

"Oh, trust me, once the news hears about this, you will be." He leaned his elbows on the counter and laced his fingers. "Why are you going to the police station?"

"I need to give them my statement."

Todd groaned and rubbed his hands down his face. "Yeah, I can hang out." He puffed his cheeks and let out a long breath. "You go do what you need to do."

The sudden shift in his dad's demeanor had Cody concerned. "Everything okay? I mean, I can wait for Joe to get here if you have other things you need to do."

Todd shook his head. "Nah, I'm good. I just don't like that you are being dragged into all of this." He waved him away. "Go ahead and go."

Cody scratched the back of his head and scanned the gym. There were still only a handful of customers. "All right, if you are sure you're good with hanging out here for a while, I'm going to take off. I shouldn't be too long." He moved out from behind the counter and jogged across the gym to the office.

When he reappeared, he had Tucker by his side. Todd briefly peered up from the computer. Tucker slowed his gait, sniffed the air, and let out a low growl. He tugged at the rope Cody had looped around his neck as a make-shift leash to get closer to the counter, but Cody nudged him toward the door.

"He must smell the tacos." Raising his hand to the bill of his cap, he saluted toward his dad and popped open the door. The sunlight blinded him as he walked to his crimson-colored Jeep. Tucker jumped into the driver's seat when Cody open the door, then showered him with dog kisses before Cody gently shoved him into his seat. Sliding in, Cody gave Tucker a few pats, retrieved his sunglasses from the visor, and headed out of the parking lot.

After making a stop at his house to change into cooler clothes, he headed to the station. An older lady with plump pink cheeks and wire-rimmed glasses smiled at Cody when he entered, then diverted her attention to Tucker and the smile faded to confusion.

"I'm here to see Sergeant Gallagher?" A loud buzz sounded and then a click from the door to his left. The jarring noise made Cody jump, and he realized how nervous he was.

"Go down the hall." She pointed. "He's the first door on the left."

He pulled open the door and entered the brown paneled hallway. The musty odor was indicative of the old building that appeared to have never been updated since it was built in the fifties.

The door was open a crack, and Cody noticed the sergeant was on the phone, so he knocked softly. Continuing with the call, he motioned Cody in and then stood. When he hung up, he walked around his desk and shook Cody's hand.

"Thanks for coming by so quickly. I didn't expect to see you until this afternoon." He shut the door behind Cody and walked back to his seat.

Cody sat in a chair across from him. Tucker lay down at his feet. "I hope you don't mind me bringing Tucker. I'm supposed to drop him off at Bruin's and the station was on my way."

The sergeant shook his head while he located the folder and dropped it on his desk.

Cody reached down to pat Tucker trying to calm his nerves. "So how does this work?"

"First, I will take your verbal statement. Try to recall exactly what happened. Start with what you were doing at the gym, and finish when help arrived. Include anything you may have observed around you, sounds, smells, movements, anything that might be pertinent. Be specific. At certain points, I may ask you questions. After that, I will have you write down what you remember."

Cody took a deep breath and rubbed his hands together.

"You good with that?" the sergeant asked, setting a yellow pad in front of him.

"Let's do this." Cody sat back in his chair and focused on the gray walls of the office trying to replay the incident.

"Ok, we are recording. Go ahead."

As Cody spoke, the memories flooded back; the

tone of her cries for help; the blood on her face; the rips in her clothing. His chest hurt recalling the terror in her eyes. All he wanted to do was get her to safety.

The sergeant rifled through the papers in the folder while Cody finished the verbal and written process. "How many people work at the gym?" he asked not making eye contact.

"Four regulars and then a few that come in on a part-time basis. Why?" Cody asked rubbing his hands on his shorts.

Taking a pen from the holder, the sergeant asked, "Who are they?"

"Me, my dad, Joe Cortez, and Sam Adelson. Do you want part-time too?"

"Not now," the sergeant said, scribbling on the pad, then continued. "Do you always work the early shift?"

"No, not regularly. My shift usually starts around noon. I was filling in."

"Who works the early shift?"

Cody's pulse ticked up. "Joe or my dad."

The sergeant continued writing. "You said your dad is a police officer?"

"Retired."

"And Joe?"

"He's my age. We have been friends for years."

"So, who were you filling in for?"

"Joe. He came in last night with a migraine and asked me to switch with him."

"You live together?"

"Yes, we're roommates." Cody let out a long breath. "Sergeant, I know where you are going with this. Trust me, Joe—"

The sergeant's eyes leveled with Cody's. "Just

following leads. The gym is on the path where Miss Corbett ran." His attention returned to his paper. "Can you get me the current member list?"

"Yes. Do you want just the ones that actually come?" Cody stood from his seat and paced. "I just—"

"I need those who are active members. Also, I need those who were there today. I have statements from several, but I want to make sure we didn't miss anyone." He paused, obviously sensing how uncomfortable Cody was becoming. "I'm just gathering the information that might help the case. We need to check with everyone. You never know who might have information. You should know this since your father is a police officer."

Cody scratched the scruff of his beard. "I do."

After thumbing through a few more papers, the sergeant closed the folder and urged Cody to give him a call if he remembered anything else.

Within a few minutes, Cody was back in his Jeep headed for Bruin's. His mind traced back through the questions the sergeant had asked. *I need to remember to talk to Joe and Dad.*

When he arrived at the vet, a slim blonde woman with a bright smile held the door for him. "I'm guessing you are Cody?" she said and held out her hand.

He grasped it and smiled. "How'd you guess?"

She pointed at Tucker. "Big white dog." Her eyes quickly made it back to Cody's face. "My name is Tracy. Jenna said you were coming." They made their way to the main lobby. The pungent smell of antiseptic wafted through the air. Several employees came out to play with the dog. Tracy knelt, staring at Tucker and digging her fingers into his fur, then lifted her focus to

Cody. "Jenna said you saved her."

Cody chuckled and pointed. "Well, actually Tucker here, saved her. I was just in the right place at the right time." He shoved a hand into his pocket. "Did she say anything about how she was doing?"

Tracy nodded. "She said she was okay but sounded tired. Her cheekbone is cracked around the orbital socket, which, she said, hurts the most. But other than that, she said she has just a bunch of cuts and bruises. They are keeping her overnight because they suspect she has a concussion. If everything goes well, she will go home tomorrow." Tracy stood and wiped her hands on her scrubs.

"I feel so bad for her," Cody said, "but I am glad Tucker was there to scare the guy off, or it could have been so much worse."

"Yeah, I agree." A smile crossed Tracy's face. "And I'm glad you were there to get her to safety."

The corner of Cody's mouth kicked up, and he brushed his hand in the air. "Eh," he said and shrugged. "Well hey, I need to get back to the gym." He smoothed Tucker's fur and handed Tracy the rope. "I think I am leaving him in good hands."

Tracy giggled. "If you aren't, then we are in the wrong business."

Cody chuckled, pushed open the door, and waved goodbye. His mind flipped through the events of the day once again as he hopped into his Jeep. Everything seemed to take him back to the same scene. The terror she had in her eyes. It continued to haunt him; how helpless and scared she was; how tightly she gripped his hand. It again made his heart flutter thinking about it. He knew she was needing some semblance of security, but the touch of her hand sent a ripple of chills through his body like a winter breeze. Cody brushed it off, thinking it had to have been the emotional temper of the moment but, suddenly, he found himself pulling into the hospital parking lot.

What am I doing? What would I say? I need to get back to the gym.

Cody stared straight ahead wondering what to do. Sucking in a deep breath, he closed his eyes, shut the engine off, and exited his Jeep.

After a quick stop at the admissions desk for the room number and directions, he headed up to room two-sixteen, and softly rapped on the door. An attractive slender woman with short-cropped jet-black hair, like something from Japanese animé, pulled it open and ushered him in.

Cody peered around the curtain to see Jenna propped up against several pillows, staring down at the covers of her bed, with a phone pressed to her ear. He ducked back behind the curtain to give her some privacy, and to steady his pulse he could now hear drumming in his ears. Out of the corner of his eye, he caught the dark-haired woman checking him out.

Stepping behind the curtain with him, she whispered, "Are you Cody?"

He nodded.

The woman gave him a sultry smile letting her eyes roam up and down his body once more. "Sorry, Jenna neglected to tell me her knight in shining armor was so handsome. But I guess I should have assumed."

Heat rushed up his neck, setting his face on fire.

"I'm Jenna's friend, April, by the way."

Jenna let out a growl. Cody peeked through a slit in

the curtain just as Jenna threw her phone on the bed and gripped the covers. "I am not a child!" April stepped back outside the curtain and turned to face Jenna. "I swear, my dad makes me so mad. Why is it when I was under his thumb, he trusted me? He had me doing everything Ben was doing, plus all the housework, and never batted an eye. Now that I live on my own, Dad thinks I am completely incompetent. He is acting like this is all my fault. I should have never called to tell him what happened."

April lifted her chin to speak but Jenna interrupted. "Do you know what my dad said? He wants me to move back home." Her hands flew up. "It's not happening." Cody's brows shot up when April peeked back at him, surprised Jenna hadn't run out of breath, and then Jenna continued. "He can't make me. I am twenty-three years old." April opened her mouth, but Jenna went on. "I mean I know my dad means well but, geez."

Clamping her lips together to stifle a giggle, April shot Cody a "do you think she's done" look before turning back to Jenna who was now silent, with her arms crossed, eying her.

"What? Why are you laughing? What is going on?"

April twitched her head, and Cody stepped out from behind the curtain wearing a sheepish grin. He raised his hand slightly to wave, then tucked both in his pockets.

Jenna's mouth dropped open. "Oh, my gosh. April, why didn't you say something?"

She shook her head and put her hands up. "I tried. But, geez, woman, you didn't even take a breath to give me a chance."

Jenna rolled her eyes, then shifted her gaze to Cody. "I am so sorry. My dad is frustrating the hell out of me right now."

"Don't apologize. You should hear me talk about my family." He then thought about what he heard her say. "You do know, your dad has a point though, right? I mean, I know it's none of my business, and I don't want to scare you, but if you are living alone right now, it might be safer to live with your family for a little while. At least until they can get this guy off the streets."

Her face sobered. "I know. I just like having my freedom. My dad means well, but he can be so overbearing." Jenna's voice softened. "But you're right. It might be safer not to be alone for right now."

Cody smiled, and suddenly he forgot why he was there. His fingers tapped on the footboard of the bed trying to remember, and then it came to him. "I was on my way back to the gym but thought I should stop by to let you know, I got Tucker dropped off at the vet."

Jenna's face brightened and she tried to smile, but it came out a bit one-sided, due to the swelling and bandages. "Thank you so much. Tucker is my baby."

"He's a great dog. It's a good thing you had him this morning."

"I know." She paused. "The funny thing is, he is such a sweetheart, I haven't heard him growl once since I got him. I can't believe he attacked the guy, especially since I haven't had him long."

"Really? Well, it's obvious he is attached to you." The room went silent. "Anyway, I am going to have to run. Let me know if there is anything else I can help with." He gave her a shy smile. "You know where to find me. I'm at the gym practically all the time."

"Okay. Thanks for everything. I honestly don't know what I would have done without you."

"Happy I could help." He tapped on the footboard once more and turned to leave. His hand reached for the door when he heard her voice again.

"Hey, Cody?" she said softly. Hearing her say his name made goosebumps explode all over his body. He popped his head back around the curtain. "You wouldn't have any self-defense classes at your gym, would you?

He grinned and nodded. "Yes. We do." Pausing for a moment, he said, "I can't remember off the top of my head what nights. But if you stop by the gym later this week, I can get you a schedule."

"Okay. I will do that," Jenna said while she adjusted herself in the bed.

"Great. If I'm not at the desk when you go, ask for me."

"I sure will."

Cody waved at Jenna and then turned to April. "Nice to meet you...April." She winked. His brow tipped up and he nodded once and open the door.

****

A wave of nausea hit Cody like a bomb went off in his stomach as he drove into the gym parking lot now filled with local TV station cars and vans. He took a deep breath and ran his hand across his mouth. "Geez, what have I gotten myself into?" After popping his sunglasses on top of his cap, he hopped out of his Jeep. When he walked through the door, he locked eyes with Joe, who was sitting behind the counter. "Feeling better?"

"Yeah, nothing a good night sleep won't cure."

"You looked pretty rough last night when you came in."

"Eh, just a bad headache. I took meds, and it was gone by this morning."

Cody eyed the reporters sitting in front of the smoothie counter. "What's going on?"

Joe turned, following Cody's focus, and glanced at the reporters. "You tell me, they're here for you."

Cody grimaced when he looked back at Joe. "Geez, what did you do to your neck?" Joe wiped his hand across the jagged gash.

"I wasn't paying attention and ran into a low branch this morning on my run."

"Did you run in the park?"

"Yeah. Why?"

He motioned to the reporters milling around. "I think that's what this is all about. A girl got attacked this morning. I heard her screaming and saw her running up the trail. She was hurt pretty bad, so I brought her in here and called the police."

"You saved her?"

"Well—"

Joe tilted his head with a sudden realization. "That's why part of the trail was cordoned off. I saw some police cars over there."

Cody crossed his arms. "My dad didn't talk to you?"

"Nope. Todd was in the office when I got here. I let him know I was here, and he told me you would be back around lunch, then left. Then the reporters came in asking for you. When I told them you would be in after lunch, they asked if they could wait. I was thinking you and your dad were doing a special promotion or something. I figured you would clue me in when you got here."

"How long have they been here?"

"About twenty minutes."

Cody let out a long, audible sigh. "I guess I just need to get it over with." He walked toward the group and was immediately surrounded.

Chapter Three

Cody strolled through the gym door preparing for the new day. Sleep had escaped him most of the night. His mind continued to flip through the events that had occurred. He hoped today would prove to be more normal.

Securing his sunglasses on his cap, Cody searched for Joe, scanning the room, the people, and the busy equipment. The welcome counter was unmanned, so he figured Joe had a piece of equipment he was working on, but he didn't see him. He headed to the office, and Joe met him with a pensive scowl. His normally laid-back best friend barely made eye contact with him as he moved past him.

Confused by the encounter, Cody stepped behind the counter and tried to tread lightly. "How was it this morning?"

Joe sat down on the stool barely acknowledging Cody's question. "Fine." His tone told Cody things were anything but fine.

"Did you have some trouble with a member?"

"Nope. They were all great." Joe's eyes focused on the computer, his fingers tapping the keys so hard, Cody worried the keyboard wouldn't survive.

"You got another headache?"

Joe took a deep breath and shook his head. "Nope. Head feels great. Now can we stop playing twenty questions before I get one?"

Cody's eyes popped open and he released a frustrated breath. "No, dammit. Not until you tell me what's got you so pissed?"

"Nothing. Absolutely nothing."

Cody could count on one hand the number of times he and Joe had a falling out. Every time there was a disagreement, they managed to talk it out. So, to have Joe obviously ticked at something he did, to the point of barely speaking to him, had Cody stumped.

He stood up and jerked his head, motioning for Joe to follow him. They both headed into the office. He flipped on the light and shut the door. His hand reached for his cap and sunglasses and tossed them on the desk before walking around it and throwing himself into the chair. "Obviously, I have done something to piss you off, so why don't you clue me in, so I can at least defend myself."

Joe flopped on to the couch and narrowed his eyes at Cody. "You don't know? Seriously?" His head twitched. "You throw me under the bus, and you are going to sit there and tell me you have no clue what I am mad about?"

"Throw you under the bus. For what? Joe, seriously, I don't know what the hell you are talking about."

Joe jumped to his feet and paced. "Well let me help you then. Officer Gallagher paid me a visit bright and early this morning. The gym was full. I had two pieces of equipment fail, and Polly Sanders was trying to kill herself on the rowing machine again. But I couldn't do squat because Sergeant Gallagher was peppering me with questions about where I was yesterday. He said you told him you were filling in for me and asked if I had ever seen Miss Corbett running in the mornings."

Cody closed his eyes, threw his head back against the chair, and rubbed his hands down his face. "Crap!" He turned and leveled his eyes with Joe's. "He asked me a bunch of questions when he took my statement. Scared the shit out of me." Setting his elbows on the desk, he pinched his nose with his thumb and forefinger. "He asked if I normally worked the morning shift and I told him I was filling in for you."

Joe's tone softened. "We spent all afternoon together yesterday. You didn't think to let me in on this tidbit of information? By the time he was ready to leave, I figured he was going to handcuff me and escort me out. I was petrified."

Cody's heart sank. His head lowered and his fingers dug into his hair. "Shit. I am so sorry." He raised his head to make eye contact with Joe again. "I planned to. Honest, I did. But with taking the dog to the vet, stopping by the hospital, and being accosted by a bunch of reporters, I forgot."

Joe sat silent on the edge of the couch for a moment. "I know you had a lot on your mind yesterday." Frustration now laced his voice. "I get it. And anyway, if you had said something to me, I don't know that it would have changed the outcome. I just felt blindsided. I think I am their prime suspect now, and I have no alibi. Hell, Cody, with everything they have against me, I'm not sure I am innocent."

Cody chuckled. "Oh, you can't be serious?"

"As a heart attack. I ran the trail yesterday. Remember? Sergeant Gallagher asked about the scratch on my neck and took DNA samples. I don't know what that was all about. And he wants the clothes I wore to check for evidence. I'm sure it will have dirt from the trail on it since I fell when I hit the tree branch."

"Did you tell him that?"

"Yes. And he became even more suspicious of me."

"Are you kidding me?"

Joe let out a breath. "I wish I were kidding. He told me not to leave town. Spent nearly an hour here asking questions and snooping around." Joe stood again. "Oh, and I'm sure we are going to get paid a visit to the apartment."

"Why?"

"I. Am. A. Suspect!"

"But you didn't even know about it until I told you."

"And if you told the police that, they would think you were trying to cover for me."

"I'm going to give my dad a call. Maybe he can help."

"Oh, the sergeant was asking about him too."

"Why?"

"He's here in the mornings."

"Crap. That reminds me. I am supposed to get the sergeant a list of members too. We do have some regulars who are early morning. Can you make me a list?"

"Yeah." Joe stopped pacing. Worry washed over his face. "But Cody, do you honestly think any of our members would do—"

"No. Not any more likely than you would. The sergeant is simply investigating the leads."

"I don't have anything to hide. Let him investigate

all he wants."

****

Cody pulled into the apartment complex parking lot after his shift at the gym and watched in horror as two officers exited his apartment with Joe in handcuffs. Anger engulfed him. *So much for today being a better day.* He bounded out of his Jeep and jogged up to them.

"What's going on?"

A female police officer extended her hand. "Mr. Spencer, please step away."

Cody stayed in stride with them.

Joe peered over his shoulder. "They found my hoodie and sweats I wore at the construction site the other day when we were pressure washing. They said it was enough evidence to take me in." The officers towed him along. "The place is totally trashed."

Cody's chest tightened. "Dammit." His hands flew to his hips trying to decide what the best course of action was.

"They said they need to take me in for further questioning." The officers stopped at the cruiser and opened the door. "But I don't have money for bail if they put me in jail."

"Don't worry about it, Joe. I will get you out. I'm calling my dad right now."

Cody watched as they placed Joe in the back of the patrol car and drove away. He stood at the bottom of the steps with bile creeping up his throat until the car disappeared. When he made it upstairs to the apartment, he realized Joe wasn't joking. The place was destroyed. The sofa cushions were flipped. Pots and pans were removed from the cabinets. Bed covers were on the floor, and drawers were left standing open. Cody had his phone to his ear waiting for his dad to answer. He continued to scan the rooms. Nothing was left untouched.

His mind played through the chain of events. *There is no way Joe could have attacked Jenna. Could he?* Anger filled him at even the fleeting thought that his best friend could be capable of harming anyone. Joe didn't have a mean bone in his body.

Cody had been best friends with Joe since junior high school. With two parents who worked, Joe spent most of his time at the Spencers' home. When Cody decided to go into the military, the plan was for Joe to join with him. But Joe changed his mind, deciding to remain in Montclair so he could get a job and help his parents out. He was hired as an apprentice at Becker Construction, and had been there six years mastering every aspect of the construction business, when Cody offered him a job at the gym and a place to live. Joe jumped at the chance. The flexible hours at the gym allowed him to continue working his construction jobs and help his parents even more.

The phone went to voicemail. "Dad, call me back. It's important." He picked up the cushions and shoved them back where they belonged and sat down. His elbows bore into his knees as his hands clasped together and banged up against his lips.

By ten p.m., three hours had passed since they took Joe in. Cody had tried calling his dad at least a dozen times with no response. He couldn't decide if he should head up to the police station or continue to wait for his dad to call him back. His gut ached, feeling like he somehow was responsible for Joe getting pulled into the mess.

His head jerked with the sound of a key in the lock. The door swung open and Joe appeared. Cody hopped up and gave him a quick hug.

Joe backed away and stared down at the floor, running his fingers through his thick hair. "You got the place cleaned up."

"I was waiting for my dad to call back to see what we could do, but I still haven't heard from him." He sat back down on the sofa but kept his focus on Joe. "So, what happened?"

Joe sat in the reclining chair adjacent to the sofa. "At the station or here?"

"All of it. All I saw was them escorting you out in handcuffs. How did you get home?"

Joe leaned the chair back and propped the feet up. "Oh, Sergeant Gallagher gave me a ride." Cody's brows shot up. Joe glimpsed out the window and bobbed back and forth then turned to Cody. "I was on the phone with Bill Becker about a construction job we are getting ready to bid, and someone started pounding on the door and hollering 'Police. Open up.' I hung the phone up, opened the door, and they came barreling in. They showed me the search warrant and started tearing the place apart. I was following them around, and they headed into my bedroom. The hoodie and sweatpants were lying on the floor. I wore them the other day when we were pressure washing at the job site. They were covered in mud. I told them what it was from, but they weren't having any of it and said it was enough to take me in for more questioning."

Cody shook his head, still shocked at seeing Joe. "So, what happened at the station?"

"They took me to an office and started bombarding

me with questions. Some I had already answered with Sergeant Gallagher, and some I think they asked just trying to rattle me. It's nothing like you see on TV. Sergeant Gallagher came in about halfway through the questioning. He seems like a decent guy. We sat and talked for a little bit. He asked about my family." His mouth tipped up on one side. "Did you know he grew up in a trailer park?"

"No. We haven't talked much other than the case."

A full grin crept across Joe's face. "I guess you get to know a little more about the police when they are trying to pin a crime on you. They try to win your trust and then stick it to you." Joe chuckled but it had a twinge of nervousness in it.

"So how did you get out of there?"

"After talking to the sergeant for a little bit, he decided that they didn't have enough to keep me. He said they would have to wait for all of the evidence to come back from the labs before he would know if they had enough to charge me with a crime."

"I don't understand why they put you in handcuffs then, if you weren't technically arrested."

"Well, that I don't know. Other than, maybe, my size had something to do with it."

"Possibly. You are a bit intimidating."

"All I know is, I plan to stay squeaky clean from now on. I would rather not wind up there again."

The phone rang, and Cody snatched it up from the coffee table. "Finally," he said with a huff, "it's my dad." He stood up and answered, putting it on speakerphone.

"Where have you been? I've been trying to call you for over three hours," Cody griped. "The police searched our apartment. Joe got hauled off to the station."

"They were here too doing a search," Todd responded. "I didn't realize you had called until now. I lost my phone in the commotion. It had fallen behind one of the end tables. Have you heard anything from Joe?"

"Yeah. He just got back." Cody rubbed the back of his head trying to release the pent-up nerves. "They took him in for more questioning, and then released him. I thought we were going to have to bail him out."

"Did they find something?" Cody could hear the concern in Todd's voice.

"Yeah. A black hoodie and a pair of sweatpants he wore at the construction site. They had some mud and dirt on them, and I guess the police thought they could be evidence."

Todd's tone turned harsh. "Cody, take me off speakerphone." The torment on Joe's face, hearing the comment from Todd, sent guilt reeling through Cody. He knew what his dad was going to say. He walked into his bedroom to protect himself from Joe's pain, hit the button, and sat on his bed.

Within minutes Cody returned to the living room wondering why he thought it was a good idea to call his dad. Joe sat in the same chair staring out the window and didn't make eye contact when Cody sat down.

"He thinks I did it, doesn't he?" Anguish filled Joe's face.

"I don't think—"

"I could hear what you were saying, Cody. Don't lie. He's suspicious." Joe's words were filled with despair.

"That's the cop in him." Cody couldn't believe how easy it was for his dad to turn on Joe. He had been a part of their family for over ten years. "Everything is circumstantial. Once they get all the evidence back, it will prove what you have said. We just have to wait for the lab—"

"And hope to hell they do a good job, and there isn't someone in there simply trying to close the case."

"Sergeant Gallagher is heading up the investigation, and I think he will do a good job. He doesn't seem like the type of person to just pin it on anybody. He wants to find out who did it."

"I hope so."

Chapter Four

The sun shot glittering rays of light through Jenna's window. She stretched and rolled over, checking the time on her phone. Her heart skipped. "Geez, it's almost eight." *Oh, its Saturday.* Staring at the ceiling, she finally threw the covers off and stumbled to the kitchen.

April sat at the dining room table in her Snoopy pajama pants and red tank top. Her eyes focused on her phone while she sipped a cup of coffee and polished off her bowl of oatmeal. Jenna smiled. Seeing her meant she had won the battle with her dad to stay in her house, provided, of course, April stayed with her for a while.

She knew April would be there for her. Since first grade, they had been there for each other no matter what. Even though their personalities were polar opposite, they were kindred spirits.

Jenna traipsed into the kitchen. "What are you doing up so early? It's Saturday."

"Couldn't sleep. It's too quiet out here. I'm used to the traffic sounds, I guess." April continued to scroll through her social media. "How'd you sleep?"

Jenna took a mug from the cabinet and poured some coffee. "Actually, I slept pretty well. I only woke up once, but it wasn't from nightmares this time. I got too hot with Tucker sleeping up against me. I'm glad you suggested going to your counselor Bekah."

Walking from the kitchen with her mug and a paper plate, she continued, "I think she is really helping." Jenna set her mug on the table and knelt to ruffle Tucker's fur.

"Bekah's a little out there for me, but she knows her stuff." April lifted her focus from her phone making eye contact with Jenna, who was still rubbing Tucker's fur, before returning her attention to her phone. "By the way, I already let Tucker out and fed him."

"Thanks. He is used to getting up early for his run."

A wave of sadness flooded Jenna's chest and obviously showed in her expression.

"Give it time," April said, genuinely sympathetic.

"I know." She sat down across from April with a Strawberry Pop-Tart and a handful of grapes and gazed out the window. "I enjoyed taking Tucker running. It was so peaceful."

"Hopefully, they will catch the guy soon. Sounds like, from the newscast, they have stepped up the manhunt."

"I saw that." She took a sip of her coffee, then popped a grape from the stem and bit into it. "Speaking of newscasts, they called me about doing a story on Tucker." She captured a glimpse of the dog who was sound asleep, taking advantage of the warmth of the sunbeam shining on the floor.

April followed Jenna's focus. "How do they know about Tucker?"

"Cody said something about him in his interview, I think." Fingers of heat climbed up her neck. "What did you think of his interview?"

"He did great. A bit nervous maybe, but I can't

41

imagine how he felt being interviewed." April stirred her oatmeal. "I am guessing they all ambushed him because I saw a couple of stations with the story."

"He was like a deer caught in the headlights." A smile slowly crept across Jenna's face. "He seems kind of shy, don't you think?" She wrinkled her nose picturing him.

April took a sip of coffee. "He did seem kind of shy when he came by the hospital."

Jenna pictured his face when he peeked around the curtain. "He's a cutie. I love his hair… and that smile. I've never seen anyone with a smile like his. It's kind of upside down."

April rolled her eyes. "Yes, he is adorable, and I have a feeling someone has a bit of a crush." She paused, with her brows raised at Jenna. "Actually, I did think it was nice of him to stop by to let you know about Tucker."

"Hey, that reminds me." Jenna shifted in her chair. "Do you want to go to the gym with me to see about the self-defense classes?" She yanked another grape from the stem and popped it into her mouth.

April shrugged. "Sure, as long as you don't expect me to take the classes with you." She picked up her bowl, walked around the counter, and placed it in the sink.

"Why not?" Jenna turned around in her chair. "You might like it."

"Well, one, when do I have time? I am either at work or in class." She stopped for a second then turned directly to Jenna. "And two, can you seriously picture me at a gym?"

Jenna knew anything that made her sweat was not

exactly April's cup of tea. "Not really, but you don't have classes right now and I don't want to go by myself. Besides, I think it would be fun, and it is something good to know."

Even though she didn't have the best home life growing up, April was born into money. The Westermans gained their wealth in the oil fields in Oklahoma. Their company dated back several generations. With some of the oil money, her great-grandfather purchased hundreds of acres of land in Arkansas which the family had slowly sold off, piece by piece, when the price was right. Now, they were considered one of the richest families in the area.

April joked about being a bit of a diva when it came to anything that would make her sweat, and for the most part, it was true, unless she thought her friends needed help, and then she was there right beside them.

Jenna shoved a piece of Pop-Tart in her mouth and dusted her hands. "To be honest, I don't think they will have classes that will fit with my schedule for the fall either, but at least we can take some now. Some is better than none."

April stood beside the table with a fresh cup of coffee. "Did you get your schedule worked out?"

"Yes, finally. I have Mondays, Tuesdays, and Thursdays, until nine, Wednesdays until eight, and," she tapped her hands on the table like a drum roll, "Fridays are open." April didn't say a word but donned a Cheshire cat smile and wiggled her brows.

After a few moments of silence, April let out a huff, threw her hand in the air, and quirked her face. "If we are going to do this gym thingy, then let's go!"

Jenna tipped her nose up. "Okay then. Let me get a

quick shower and throw some clothes on, then we can head up there and see what they have available." She pushed her chair out, piled the rest of her Pop-Tart in her mouth, wadded her napkin up, and threw it and her plate into the trash.

April turned to head to her room. "For some reason I think you have an ulterior motive for wanting to go to the gym."

Jenna yelled from the bedroom, "Shut up, April."

****

Jenna and April pulled up in front of 24 to Life. Several people were milling around, from what Jenna could see through the glass entrance. She squinted to see who was behind the desk, but the counter appeared empty. The doors of the silver, crew cab Ford pickup squeaked when Jenna opened it. April opened the door to the gym and a chime sounded as they stepped inside. The counter was empty, so they waited for someone to help them. Jenna hoped that that someone would be Cody.

The gym was full. Everybody seemed to be engrossed in their workouts, with only a few who were working out their mouths more than their bodies. The weights clinked as Jenna took in the scene. Techno music thumped through the speakers. News and sports filled the televisions. The smell was citrusy which surprised her. She figured it would smell more like her brother's pickup after a hard day's work at the ranch. It was odd that she didn't remember any of it from her first encounter with Cody.

She turned to April, who had become mesmerized by a guy bent over a piece of equipment helping an elderly woman. His tanned skin set off his dark brown hair that was almost shaved on the sides and longer on top. His muscles bulged out of his tight emerald green tank. He turned and caught April staring. Jenna giggled watching April's cheeks take on the color of a ripe strawberry. He stood and headed toward the counter. His height and build gave him the appearance of a Greek god.

"Hey, sorry." He peered right at April with beautiful blue eyes. April smoothed her top, apparently regretting wearing a T-shirt and faded blue jeans. "I hope you weren't standing here long." His eyes moved to Jenna and a slight grimace crossed his face. She combed through her side-swept ponytail. It evidently had not succeeded in covering her injuries. "I had a piece of equipment freeze up," motioning behind him and then pausing, "I'm Joe Cortez." He held out his hand. April slid her hand into his first, then Jenna. "Now, how can I help you?"

Jenna batted the air. "No need to apologize. We just came in. Is Cody around?"

"Ah, no, he had to run to the bank." Joe's eyes popped open, and a smile captured his face. "I hope you don't mind me asking, but are you Jenna?"

Her pulse skipped. *Cody has talked to him about me. But how could he not? It was all over the news. But how did Joe know it was me?* Skimming her teeth over her swollen lip, she suddenly remembered the injuries to her face... again. *I will be so glad to have my face back.*

A sigh escaped. "I guess I can't hide this." Jenna motioned to her face and chuckled in embarrassment, which still didn't keep Joe's cheeks from turning red. "I'm so sorry. You told us your name, but I forgot to introduce us. Yes, I'm Jenna, and this is my friend April. Cody said you guys have self-defense classes."

Joe's eyes moved to April and remained long enough for April to give him a quick wink. He let out a chuckle and shook his head. "Um, yes we do have self-defense classes. Let me get you some schedules." He reached his hand toward April, who again gave him a flirty smile while she played with her necklace, but he didn't find the schedules he was searching for. He leaned over the counter to visually check. "It appears all our schedules have been taken. Give me a minute and I will print some out."

Jenna nodded. "Take your time."

His fingers danced across the computer keyboard then he hopped up from his stool. "Be right back." April watched him take off across the gym and disappear around the corner.

"Mm mm mm." April took a deep breath and let it out as a sensual smile crossed her face.

Jenna rolled her eyes and grinned. She was used to April being a bit of a flirt but knew she seldom let guys close enough to date her, always joking that no man could handle her diva needs.

A chime from behind them made them both turn around. Cody walked through the door. Sunlight cast a glow around him, and Jenna's breath caught in her throat. His red T-shirt stretched across his shoulders with the name of the gym emblazoned perfectly over chest muscles that were outlined through the shirt. Gray wind pants fit low on his hips and accentuated the best part of his backside. A pair of aviators were perched on top of a black and red ball cap that covered most of his hair except a few curls that escaped out the back. His phone was pressed to his ear and his attention was solely on the conversation at hand.

"I should be able to make it by this afternoon."

Jenna turned to April with her mouth open.

Cody tapped the screen, finishing the call, and noticed them. A smile spread across his face. "Hey." His dimples dug deep into his cheeks. He dropped his phone in his pocket and stepped up to the counter. "I am so sorry. Have you guys been here long?"

His voice wrapped around Jenna like a soft blanket, and her body tingled. "Oh, no. Joe is helping us. He had to print off some schedules."

Cody ducked behind the counter and then skimmed the top. "I just printed off a bunch," he said, somewhat talking to himself. Checking a nearby table, he pursed his lips, which sent heat coursing through Jenna's body. "I guess Joe will be back in a second with the schedules." Another smile crossed his face as his gaze met Jenna's, and another wave of heat hit.

"How are you doing?"

"Pretty good actually." Jenna tipped her head toward April. "I took your advice. She agreed to hang out with me for a while."

Cody pointed his finger at April. Squinting one eye and lifting the other brow, he said, "April, right?"

"Yes! Good job." April gave him a high five.

He returned his attention back to Jenna. "Great idea." His eyes twinkled.

"I really didn't want to move back home, so this seemed like a good compromise. So far so good. Although, a few of our nightly Scrabble games have gotten a little heated."

Cody laughed. "Yeah, those can be brutal. I never

win because I can't spell to save my life." Pausing, he said, "I'm glad you are doing better. How's Tucker?"

"He's doing great." Her mouth tipped up realizing he was trying his best to make small talk. "And how are you doing?"

Cody hesitated. "Me? oh, I'm fine."

"I saw your interview," she quickly lifted a finger to correct herself, "sorry, *interviews* on TV. You did great."

He playfully winced and turned away. "I was terrified, if you couldn't tell."

She pinched her fingers together. "Maybe a little bit." Tiny wrinkles appeared around the corners of his brown sugar-colored eyes when he smiled back at her, causing her to forget to breathe. "They called me. They want to do a story about me and Tucker. I told them Tucker was available but if they wanted to interview me, they would have to wait until I've healed a little more."

Cody's face filled with sympathy, then his focus moved past her. Joe approached with a stack of papers. "Where did that pile I printed go?"

Joe shrugged and slapped the papers on the counter. "I have no idea." Picking up two of the sheets, he handed them to Jenna and April who scanned the classes.

"Oh, yay! They have them Tuesday and Thursday at seven." April's face beamed. Jenna cocked her head and her mouth dropped open in disbelief.

"What was that you were saying this morning about not wanting to take—"

April shot her a glare and pinched her thumb and fingers together, signaling her to stop talking. "I don't remember."

Jenna turned back to Cody. He motioned over his shoulder. "Can I give you a tour?"

April batted her lashes at Joe, whose grin lit up his eyes, and she nodded happily. Jenna shot her a quizzical expression and chuckled, then nodded to Cody. He stepped from behind the counter and escorted them through the weight machines, cardio center, and CrossFit area, giving them brief descriptions of each.

Walking through the free weight area, Jenna pictured Cody curling one of the heavy weights, causing his biceps to bulge more than they already did. Her teeth dug into her lip trying to keep the heat from flooding her cheeks.

"We have a smoothie bar over there." He pointed. "The classroom where self-defense is taught is in here." Pushing the door open, he said, "There should be a class coming in a few minutes."

A portion of the floor was covered with thick mats. Pushed up against the back wall were a dozen spin cycles with a full wall of mirrors opposite them. Against another wall hung several heavy bags for boxing. Medicine balls, lightweights, and other equipment sat on racks in the corner.

Jenna flipped the sheet from one side to the other. "So...how much?"

"If you are only wanting to do the class, it's normally five for each class. But you can take it free for a month." Cody then turned to April. "Dad is giving her a special...sorry."

April crossed her arms and lifted her eyes to the ceiling, waving him away, and feigning irritation for a minute, then smiled. "Don't worry. I get it."

Jenna studied the paper. "Do you teach the class?"

"No, it's a lady named Debra Oliver. She teaches several of the classes."

April piped up, "Why don't you or Joe teach the class?"

Cody's face filled with color. "Well...she is a better instructor for that class. Joe and I mainly manage the gym and do personal training."

Jenna turned to April, who was staring off toward the front counter where Joe was working on the computer. "What do you think? You want to take the class?"

"Wha..." She slowly shifted her attention back to Jenna. "What?"

Jenna rolled her eyes. "Do you want to take the class?"

"Sure," she said surprisingly quickly.

Cody's eyes sparkled and his mouth kicked up at the corner. "Great. I will take your names and pass them on to Debra, so she is expecting you." They headed back to the front. Cody stepped behind Joe and grabbed a pad and pen from beneath the counter. April dug in her purse.

"All right, Jenna...Corbett?" Cody said, hesitantly.

"Oh, good memory," Jenna responded, surprised.

"...and April...?"

"Westerman," she answered, pulling her phone out and holding it up.

Joe's eyes tipped up from his focus on the computer for a second, and he chuckled at April's obvious flirting, but then they widened when he heard a click.

"Did you take a picture of me?"

April smiled and shrugged, then returned her phone to her purse. Joe's mouth tucked in on one side and he shook his head.

"You guys are all set," Cody said. "April, you will pay each time you come in. Jenna, you have eight free sessions." He tapped the pen on the paper. "Oh, I should have asked you this earlier. Are you medically cleared to take the class?"

"Yes, the doctor said I could resume normal activity. Do I need to bring that paper with me?"

"You might, as a precautionary measure. That way I can make a copy of it."

"Okay." Checking the schedule one last time, Jenna said, "I guess we will see you on Tuesday," then folded the schedule and turned to leave.

April fluttered her fingers at Joe, and winked, then followed Jenna out the door.

Chapter Five

Cody backhanded Joe in the arm as Jenna and April left the gym. Pointing his finger at April, he said, "You are in trouble with that one, my friend. I think she has a thing for you."

"You think?" Joe chuckled rubbing his arm. "I am fairly certain she does. She made no bones about it. Hell, she took a picture of me." He dragged his hand through his hair and sighed. "Yep, I am in deep trouble." He paused, then snickered. "I don't know that I'm too upset about it though."

Cody put his elbows on the counter and laced his fingers together. He pictured Jenna and the smile on her face when he talked to her about the classes. "That's not to say I'm not in a little trouble with the redhead. There is something intriguing about her." His chest warmed. Even though she was still banged up, Cody was taken by her dark auburn hair. The V-necked sapphire blue T-shirt she wore hugged her figure and brightened her blue-green eyes. The mere thought of her made a zing of electricity shoot through his body.

"Jenna does seem sweet," Joe said, slapping Cody on the back, and Cody narrowed his eyes.

"Don't even think about it."

"Nah, I'm definitely more into the edgy, in your face type."

"Yeah." A smirk curled on his lips. "Jenna is

sweet....but she does have a feisty side. I saw it when she was in the hospital. I have a feeling you would be on the losing end of the stick if you got into a fight with her." He adjusted his cap and repositioned his sunglasses, then noticed Joe squint and rub his temple. "Got another headache?"

Joe pushed the heels of his hands in his eyes. "Yep. I don't know what's going on. I used to never get them, and now I can't seem to get rid of them." He rubbed the back of his neck.

"Maybe you should go to the doctor," Cody concluded, concern lacing his tone. "I'm kind of getting worried about you."

"Nah, it's nothing. Probably just the junk I'm eating. I'll be fine. It's more of an annoyance than anything."

Cody studied Joe's face. "If it hangs on for much longer, make an appointment and go in. It's been, what, going on a couple of weeks now?"

Joe nodded. "Yeah, I guess, something like that." He rubbed the back of his neck again and shook his arms. "I'll be all right."

"Are you sure? I was needing to run an errand, but I can hang out here if you need to go home."

"Nah. I'm good. Where are you going?"

"Sergeant Gallagher called and said I can pick up some of my clothes I had to turn in for evidence."

"Did they take anything else of yours from the apartment?"

"No. It's just the stuff I was wearing the day of the attack. What all did they take of yours?"

"The stuff I was wearing on the run, and the black sweatpants and hoodie. I wonder if they will come back destroyed?"

"My shirt is probably toast anyway since it is covered in blood, but I think the rest of my stuff was fine."

Joe's face fell, solemn. "Have you heard anything else about the case?"

"Nothing, other than what has been on the news, but I am going to talk to the sergeant and see if I can get some more information when I go up there." Cody hopped off the stool and stretched his legs. "You sure you got this? I can wait."

Joe waved him off. "Nah, I'm fine. You go ahead." Cody plunged his hand in his pocket, retrieving his keys, and grabbed his sunglasses off his cap.

The door chimed as he pressed his back against it. Turning to Joe, he asked, "Do you need anything?"

"Nope. But let me know what you find out." He laced his fingers and flexed his wrists to stretch, then continued his work on the computer.

****

Cody made the short drive to the station still so focused on the encounter with Jenna he nearly missed his turn. When he arrived, he met Sergeant Gallagher in the foyer. "Perfect timing." The sergeant escorted him back to the dingy office with boxes piled in the corner and chipped linoleum on the floor. A stagnant, musty smell mixed with food lingered in the air. On one chair sat a plastic bag.

Sergeant Gallagher motioned for him to have a seat, so he moved the bag and sat down. The sergeant tipped back in his chair behind his desk. "You are on the ball. I didn't expect to see you this quick."

"Eh, Joe has the gym covered so I thought I would

go ahead and come by." He removed his sunglasses and cap and propped them on his knee. "Do you live up here? Is there a cot in the break room or something?" He hitched his thumb pointing out the door. "You're here all the time."

"No. No cot," he chuckled, "but that isn't a bad idea. This case just requires all my time right now. One of the drawbacks of a small police force. If you have a big case, you get no sleep." Sergeant Gallagher motioned to the bag. "You gave me the shirt, shorts, socks, and shoes, correct?"

"Yes." He paused, remembering the envelope he held in his hand. "Oh, here is a list of all of our active members. Joe highlighted the ones that come in during the early hours."

"Great." The sergeant added it to a stack of papers on the corner of his desk, then pulled a piece of paper from a folder and pushed it to him. "I need you to sign this. It states you picked up your shoes, socks, and shorts. We have retained the shirt in evidence."

Cody scooted the chair closer to the desk, causing a high-pitched scraping noise, then picked up the paper. The sergeant handed him a pen. Scanning the paper, he scribbled his name on the bottom and pushed everything back.

The Sergeant put the folder back in the tray. Cody scanned the room. His nerves were causing his whole body to buzz. He wanted to ask the sergeant about the case, but he didn't quite know how to approach it. Scratching his face and crossing his ankle over his knee, he decided to attack it head on and cleared his throat. "So, have you had any leads come up so far?"

"No. Nothing other than what you already know.

We have Mr. Cortez's statement, and his clothing is being checked for evidence. We also have your dad's statement and have made a visit to his residence.

"So, what can you tell me about the case that I don't know?" Cody pried.

Sergeant Gallagher got comfortable in his chair. "What have you heard?"

"Basically, just what you stated on the news. There are similarities between her case and four others?"

"Yeah."

"So, this is a serial rapist? What are the similarities? I didn't even hear exactly what happened to Jenna. I stepped out when the officer started asking her personal questions."

"They were assaults, not rapes. So far, the information that has been released in the case is pretty much all we have. There have been five victims dating back five years. The towns involved are within a fifty-mile radius. All the victims were attacked in a remote area. They were approached from the back, knocked to the ground, had their clothes removed or partially removed, and groped but not raped."

Cody was relieved to hear that last bit of news. He had wondered.

"The assailant was always dressed in dark clothing with a mask and hoodie, and always wore gloves. The victims said he pinned them down where they couldn't move. Two attacks were in broad daylight, and three while it was dark.

"We are fairly sure it's the same guy, but with what we have so far, we can't even say that definitively. He hasn't left much at the scenes except a couple of sneaker tracks, but they aren't the same."

The Sergeant paused and then waved his finger in the air like he remembered something. "We do know, Miss Corbett made it a habit of jogging that same trail, about the same time during the week. So, it could be someone who has watched her and knew her habits." Cody's stomach clenched as the sergeant shared the information. *What if the attacker lived in Dalton? What if he had figured out where she lived?*

"We sent in the samples from the dog and are hoping we get something from that. But other than that, and Mr. Cortez's clothing, everything has been released to the news." He sat up and rubbed his hands together. "We are thinking about gathering the victims to see if their stories trigger any other memories that might be helpful. Have you been in contact with Miss Corbett?"

"Yes, but only on a professional basis. Miss Corbett asked about self-defense classes. She hasn't said anything about the case. I'm only interested because I was somewhat involved, and because my dad was on the police force in Montclair, so stuff like this always interests me."

"I remember you telling me that. Did he work the case? Two of the attacks were in Montclair."

"Not that I'm aware of, but my dad was pretty tight-lipped about the cases he worked on."

"Well anyway, you probably know how this works if your dad is a retired police officer. It's a wait and see process. Right now, we are waiting for the lab to respond."

"I know it takes time. I actually planned on following in my dad's footsteps at one time."

"Oh…you decided against it?"

"Not so much. I kind of got it decided for me."

Sergeant Gallagher's face twitched. "How so?" He leaned back in his chair and put his hands behind his head.

"I've got a pending assault charge against me for a bar fight."

"Yep, that will do it every time." The sergeant smirked. "So, what were you fighting for? No, let me guess. A girl?"

"Well, yes and no. More along the lines of defending a friend."

He nodded. "That's honorable. So, are you still interested in law enforcement?"

"Yes sir. But I have to wait for my case to be heard." He rubbed his hands on his pants. "I've still got a while. If they drop the charges, then I can reapply, otherwise, I have to wait out the designated period. Then, it depends on if they will accept me."

"Well, if you ever want to do a ride-along, let me know."

Cody's head jerked up. "Seriously?"

"It will at least give you an idea of what it would be like to work with a small-town police department. It's not for everyone."

A jolt of anticipation filled him. "That would be great."

Sergeant Gallagher reached in his drawer and wrote on the back of a business card, then handed it to Cody. "This is my direct line. Give me a call during the week if you decide you want to, and I will get you set up. Also, let me know if you talk to Miss Corbett and she remembers anything."

"Yeah, I should be seeing her more often since she is taking the class." Cody stood and picked up his bag.

"Thank you so much, Sergeant. Oh, and if you ever want to work out at the gym, let me know. We give all law enforcement, fire, paramedic, and military a discount."

"I might take you up on that offer. I have some equipment at the house, but it doesn't help when it's used primarily to hang clothes."

"I've heard that more often than you can imagine." Cody stepped forward and shook the sergeant's hand. "I will give you a call about the ride along for sure."

The sergeant stood and walked around his desk. "Great. I look forward to it," he said, then escorted him up the hallway. "So, you and your dad own the gym?" He pressed the button to release the door.

"Yes, sir. My dad actually owns it, but we took it over together."

"How long have you had it?"

"A little over two years."

"You said your dad retired from Montclair?"

"Yes, sir."

"I have some friends over there. How long was he on the police force?"

"I think around thirty-eight years?"

"I bet they would know him."

Chapter Six

"So, what did you think?" Jenna hollered to April. She finished getting ready in her bedroom and walked into the living room pulling her hair up in a high ponytail. Tucker brushed up against her legs and she knelt and dug her fingers in his furry face. "I know you made everyone fall in love with you." Tucker sat, begging for even more admiration by putting his paw on Jenna's knee.

April padded up the hallway pulling at her tank top. "I thought you did great. I don't think I would have been able to be that calm. I can do live video posts on the internet all day long, but I'm just talking," she said, walking into Jenna's line of sight. "No one is asking me a bunch of questions."

"Good grief. What are you wearing?" Jenna blurted. April's leggings were a mottled mix of blue, yellow, and purple hues. Her sneakers were blue and pink, and her top was neon yellow.

"Too much?" April questioned, holding her arms out, giving herself the once-over.

Jenna continued to gawk at her outfit while she sat on the sofa to lace her shoes. "Well, let's just say, if Joe is there, he definitely will see you."

April's forehead creased. "I didn't think it was that bad."

Jenna didn't want to hurt April's feelings, figuring

the outfit probably cost more than what she got paid in a month. "It's not bad, it's just...bright."

April had always been one to take chances with her fashions, and normally, her style sense worked out well. This time, a certain guy with piercing blue eyes might have clouded her judgment.

"Do I look okay?" Jenna asked, standing and holding out her arms, sporting a lime green tank with black trim and plain black Capri leggings.

April let out a sigh. "You're lovely, as usual, but you are used to wearing this stuff," April responded, sounding disheartened.

"Your outfit is fine, and honestly, you don't have time to change since we waited to watch the news, so grab your water bottle and let's go."

Jenna slung her purse across her body and reached for her water. April stepped out of the door behind her, obviously still bugged by the comment from the frown on her face.

"I knew I shouldn't have agreed to go to the gym with you."

"You didn't. In fact, you only agreed to go with me to get the schedule. You told me not to expect you to take the classes, but once you got to the gym, something changed. Hmmm...I wonder what that was? I think it had to do with a certain someone named Joe."

"Okay, okay." Jenna glanced at April, who didn't make eye contact but was pinching back a smile.

After a short drive, they pulled into the gym parking lot. Jenna noticed Joe behind the desk and smiled at April.

Joe sat up when the door chimed. His eyes widened, and a big toothy grin spread across his face.

"Wow, nice outfit, April," he said with a wink.

April's entire face lit up. She wrinkled her nose at Jenna in satisfaction. Jenna rolled her eyes. Joe turned to Jenna and smiled at her.

"Saw you on the news a little bit ago."

Her lip curled. "I was so scared."

"So, you have had Tucker only a few weeks?" His focus momentarily returned to the keyboard.

She nodded. "Yes, I think it's been about six weeks now. He came into the vet as an injured stray with no collar or chip. We treated him, then put the word out that he was with us on social media, and the newspaper, but had no response. The lady who brought him in already had two dogs so she couldn't take him.

"I fell in love the minute I saw him. He was so sweet. I would go in and talk to him and keep him company during his recovery, and then took him for walks. I couldn't let him go to a stranger, so I adopted him, and now I am glad I did."

"No kidding. He's a hero."

"Yes, he is." She searched for her other hero who seemed to be MIA. The gym was filled with people, so she scanned the area hoping he was out on the floor and hadn't seen them come in.

Giving up on her search, Jenna balanced her purse on the counter and dug through a pocket. Pulling out a yellow piece of paper, she unfolded it and placed it on the counter. "Here is the medical release form. Do we have to sign in or anything?"

"Not here, but Debra may have a sign-in sheet in the classroom." He picked up the paper. "Let me make a copy of it, and I will get it back to you."

She waved her hand. "That's fine."

"And I have my money. Do I give it to you?" April asked in a sweet, innocent voice, batting her lashes as she held out the cash.

"Yes, ma'am, I will take that." Joe turned. His hand slowly caressed hers as he retrieved the money. April's lips parted, and she let out an audible gasp. Her face turned a rosy pink. Joe winked and leaned in close to her. "Two can play this game, Miss Westerman." He stepped back and gave her a wolfish grin, then gave Jenna a smile. "I hope you girls enjoy the class."

Jenna tried to stifle a laugh, watching April completely unable to form words. It was so unlike her. "Come on, April, the class is about to start." Jenna's eyes remained locked on her while she turned to head to the class, and slammed into Cody's muscular chest.

"Hey, you made it," Cody said enthusiastically, gripping Jenna's arms to stabilize her. His eyes searched her face. After a week, there was a marked improvement in her injuries. The swelling had disappeared around her eyes and mouth, and the only thing that remained was a tinge of discoloration and the cut above her eye. "You look great."

The feel of his body against hers and the deep rich chocolatey scent of his cologne made her knees weak. She couldn't peel her attention away from him.

Cody looked like he stepped right out of a magazine, dressed in a violet button-down that hugged his arms and chest perfectly. His dark gray tapered jeans fit right at his hips and sat at the top of his lace-up black boots with one cuff. Best of all, his dark brown hair was in full view. No cap. It appeared he had run his fingers through it a couple of times to get it moving in the right direction. Perfectly messy. Top it off with a bit of a five o'clock shadow and...*Mercy, could he be more gorgeous?*

Jenna tried to divert her focus. Her face flooded with heat, and she could only imagine what shade of red she might be. Now, it was her turn to be speechless. "Uh, th-thank you." Her hand flew into her hair, nervously trying to make sure it was in place. "I am so sorry. I am such a klutz. I, I...."

When Jenna's eyes met his, it only made it worse. They had that same warmth as they did when he rescued her. She didn't remember much about the attack, but she remembered those eyes. Brown. Like two pieces of smoky quartz with flecks of gold surrounded by a million long lashes. Every time she gazed into them, they melted her insides like warmed caramel.

She knew she probably sounded like an idiot trying to talk, but from his lopsided grin, he enjoyed her embarrassment. After a moment he let her off the hook.

"I saw your story on the news."

Jenna peered out from beneath her lashes. "Now I know why you seemed to be a little scared. I was terrified."

Cody chuckled. "Tucker was cool as a cucumber."

She gave a sarcastic laugh. "Well, they only came to interview him anyway."

"Yeah, I thought he had a stellar interview, and I guess you didn't do too bad."

Jenna glared at him with her face scrunched but she couldn't hide the smile.

A voice echoed from the classroom. "All right everybody, let's warm-up."

Her eyes darted to the classroom. "Sounds like they

are getting started, I better get in there."

She tried to step past Cody, but he moved the same direction, and they danced back and forth a couple of times before they both smiled. Cody stood still and let her and April pass. She noticed April giving him the once over and suddenly wondered why he was so dressed up. *Could he be going on a date?*

"You look nice tonight by the way. Any occasion?" *Geez, could I have been more obvious? Please not a date, please not a date.*

He climbed up on the stool behind the counter. "I am going on a ride-along with Sergeant Gallagher tonight. Should be quite interesting."

"Oh, that sounds exciting." She let out a breath, relieved it had nothing to do with a girl.

"Stop by after class and let me know what you think. I should still be here. I'm not supposed to meet him until eight thirty."

"Will do."

Chapter Seven

Cody pulled out of the gym parking lot wondering what it was about Jenna that made his body turn up the heat to high. He hated the way they had met, but he was sure glad they did. There was something about her that was so sensual, yet so innocent. Her outfit tonight was nearly the death of him. Every curve of her body was accentuated with that tight-fitting tank top and leggings.

His body tingled like it was being stung by forty thousand bees the minute he laid his hands on her, and just thinking about her made his blood rush south.

Even now, Cody couldn't wipe the grin off his face if he tried, thinking about how flustered she got when she ran into him. She made his life much more interesting. He had to admit, he was excited he would be seeing more of her since she told him she liked the class.

Cody turned into the police station's parking lot. His pulse ticked up as his thoughts turned to the ride-along. The phone call between him and Sergeant Gallagher went well, and he had easily passed the security protocol needed.

The sergeant's demeanor toward Cody had done an about face since the first time they met, and he was excited to see the job up close.

He walked into the station and was buzzed through to the back. The sergeant was engrossed with something on his computer screen, so Cody knocked on the door frame and the sergeant motioned him in.

"Good to see you again." The sergeant stood and shook his hand. "Are you ready to go?"

"Yes, sir. I appreciate you letting me ride along this evening."

"Well, I hope you have the same enthusiasm at the end of the night. I have to admit, sometimes being a cop in a small town can be a bit boring." Sergeant Gallagher dragged his keys off his desk, and they headed out of his office up a long, dark hallway. "I know you may be hired in a larger city, but, with all the smaller communities around here, chances are good that you will wind up in one of them, if you want to stay in the area."

"I'm good with whatever."

"I figured, since you said you were interested in police work, it might be a good idea to show you what it's like." He pushed open the door that spilled out into a gated area holding the patrol cars. "But then again, you might already know, since your dad was a cop."

"He never took me on a ride-along. I only saw his job from the office standpoint, and that wasn't very often."

They walked up to the police cruiser. Sergeant Gallagher chirped the key fob and unlocked the doors. "Well, good, then this should be a great learning experience."

Heading down Main Street on the backside of the old town square, they passed many of the buildings that were hundreds of years old. Until recently, they had fallen into disrepair. The town's population had dwindled, and businesses were leaving for better locations.

With the discovery that the area was perfect for growing grapes, wineries started to pop up. That led to buildings being restored and turned into wine shops, coffee shops, art galleries, ice cream parlors, restaurants, and ladies' boutiques.

In the center was the county courthouse. The stately building, with its carved columns, copper dome, and lush green lawns on all four sides, had stood as a county seat for close to two hundred years. It was the main gathering place for Saturdays on the Square. During the winter months, it was decorated with thousands of twinkling lights that brought many out for Christmas strolls.

"So, have you talked to Miss Corbett this week?" Sergeant Gallagher asked over the noise of the police radio.

The mention of Miss Corbett caused a stir in Cody's core. He cleared his throat. "Actually, Jenna and one of her friends took their first self-defense class this evening."

"That's great," Sergeant Gallagher paused, then continued, "how is she doing?" His eyes stayed focused ahead, turning up Post Street by Stokes Hardware store.

"She seems to be healing well." Cody shook his head holding back a chuckle, remembering the run-in they had earlier. "She even did a couple of interviews for the TV stations that aired earlier today."

"Well, I'm glad to hear that she is still getting out, even though the case hasn't been solved yet. It will though."

"She's pretty tough." Cody paused. "I know you may not be able to tell me, but have you gotten anything back from the lab? Joe is worried."

"Does he have a reason to be?"

"Well, it does seem like you guys think he's a suspect."

"Not any more than you, or anyone else."

"But he doesn't have an alibi."

"Neither does your dad. They both said they were asleep. I'm simply covering all the bases. We have little to go on right now, so, like I said, we have to follow every lead.

"As for the labs, we've gotten back the clothes, and there were no connections with Miss Corbett in the preliminary findings. Some had dirt consistent with the trail, but no blood other than his. But we will hold on to everything until we can rule out conclusively his connection.

"We are working on contacting all of the victims to bring them in and share stories, to see if we can get any more information."

"So, have you gotten any other possible leads?"

"Not really. Whoever it is, is calculating. He covered his tracks well."

A voice broke through the noise on the police radio. "All units, we have a silent alarm at fourteen fifty-two Elm Street. Repeat we have a silent alarm at fourteen fifty-two Elm Street."

Sergeant Gallagher picked up the mic and responded, "Four twenty-nine en route." He flipped a couple of switches, firing up the lights and sirens. "All right, you have to stay in the vehicle. It's a triggered silent alarm at a business. Usually nothing."

When they arrived at the scene, Sergeant Gallagher quickly exited the vehicle. Cody watched him walk the property and tried to picture what it would be like to be in the sergeant's position. Within a few minutes, he returned to the vehicle and keyed his mic. "Four twenty-nine is ten eight, location secured." He drove away from the scene. "Those...are our usual calls."

"So, what are you telling me? Do you like the job?"

"I do because I love the community. If I didn't, I wouldn't have stayed for fifteen years. But I want to make sure you get the fact that it's a small town. There aren't very many 'damsel in distress' calls. Miss Corbett's assault was an anomaly.

"We get our occasional domestic assault, but most of the calls are checking buildings, checking abandoned vehicles, garbage complaints, and stray animals, and on and on. I answer all of them. Heck, I have even been a plumber when need be. I enjoy it but I would have liked to have had someone tell me what it all entailed when I was considering the position...the exciting and the boring parts.

"I am betting your dad didn't come home talking about the barking dog calls, or the calls he got about the wheelbarrow in the middle of the street. What's crazy is, those calls could still kill you. I don't want my kids to lose their dad because he got hit by a car while he was pushing a wheelbarrow out of the street."

"So, what would you have done if you weren't a police officer?"

"I don't know actually, probably a paramedic. I've always wanted to be in a position that served the community."

"Really? I was considering that path if I didn't go the law enforcement route. It fascinated me when they were working on Jenna and got me thinking about that line of work instead of law enforcement."

Again, the dispatcher's voice cut through the static of the radio. "All units, we have a suspicious person at one-zero-zero-one-two East Garden View, wearing black pants, black hooded sweatshirt. Repeat, all units, we have a suspicious person at one-zero-zero-one-two East Garden View, wearing black pants, black hooded sweatshirt."

Sergeant Gallagher's body visibly stiffened. He keyed his mic. "Four twenty-nine is en route." The sound of the siren filled the unit. Red and blue lights sent a strobe effect onto the trees and buildings surrounding them. The cruiser increased speed.

Black pants, black hoodie. The address is close to the park. What if it's him? Cody could feel his heartbeat in his throat with the thought of taking down the guy who hurt Jenna.

"Do you think it's him?"

"Who knows. There are plenty of people who have those clothes including your buddy Joe." He pulled up to the house and threw the door open. "Stay in the car." The sergeant stepped out and was approached by an elderly gray-haired woman in a cotton floral dress and house slippers. She gestured up the street and Sergeant Gallagher nodded.

After a short time, he returned and eased back into the street, driving slowly, his eyes darting from side to side. "She indicated the guy was heading this way and seemed to be stumbling. She saw him lying in her yard, and when she hollered at him, he got up and took off."

Cody scanned the area out the window hoping to see movement. Following the curve in the road, he focused his attention between cars lining the curb and noticed a shadow ahead.

"Could that be him?" He pointed to a barely visible moving blob. The sergeant narrowed his gaze and craned his neck over his steering wheel to get a better view. His foot hit the gas pedal and the patrol car picked up speed. Within seconds they were behind someone in a black hoodie and black pants. The guy turned and stopped.

The sergeant keyed his mic. "Four twenty-nine checking suspect," then turned to Cody, "stay in the car."

He knew the drill by now but appreciated Sergeant Gallagher protecting him. The sergeant approached the suspect, and Cody watched the confrontation through the windshield. He couldn't hear the conversation except when the sergeant keyed the mic on his uniform. When he gave dispatch the name of the suspect, Cody's stomach boiled. Irritation set in.

Brant Ellington had been a thorn in Cody's side for a while. He was an arrogant, rude human being, and the sole reason he had to put off going to the police academy. Could he possibly be the person who has been attacking all these women? He watched as Brant pushed his hoodie off his head, placed his hands on the patrol car, and spread his feet, while Sergeant Gallagher patted him down. There was a satisfaction watching it happen, and with the bright lights shining in Brant's eyes, Cody figured he couldn't see him sitting in the front seat, but if he were arrested it might be awkward.

Within a few minutes, Sergeant Gallagher motioned ahead, and Brant walked away. The sergeant's voice came through the radio as he returned to the car and put it in drive. Brant hung his head when the car passed.

Cody, thoroughly confused, couldn't hold in his concern any longer. "Why did you let him go?"

"Didn't have anything I could charge him with. Yes, he was drunk, but he said he was walking back to his house from a party. The house was within visual distance, and the address on his license matched with his story. I had nothing else on him, so I had to let him go."

"But he matched the description of the attacker, and if he lives in that house, it's close to where the crime happened," Cody countered.

"True, but again, there are plenty of people who have black pants and black hoodies in their closets, you can't jump to that assumption."

"But it's July! Why would someone be wearing a hoodie in July, and at night?"

"Who knows. But it's not a crime. I patted him down, he had nothing on him other than his phone and wallet." He paused. "Trust me, I will be doing some more investigating." Cody's eyes narrowed. "I know. I want to solve the case too, but you can't arrest every suspicious person out there merely because of what they are wearing. You have to have a little more to go on than that."

"I get it, but it's frustrating. Plus, that guy is a real ass."

"What? You know him?"

"Yeah. He is the reason I had to put off going to the academy. My buddy Joe and I were having some drinks at a bar in Cimarron. Joe was talking to a girl that he knew, and apparently, Brant thought she was a girl he had gone out with or something and didn't like that she was talking to Joe. Brant slugged him out of nowhere. Knocked him out cold. He was reared back, ready to continue, so I jerked his arm, spun him around and popped him once. The police were called, of course. He got brought up for assaulting Joe. I got brought up because my punch, he said, was unprovoked. I wasn't going to let him wail on Joe. The worst part about it was the girl said she didn't even know Brant."

"Damn, that sucks."

"Oh, it gets even better. He is a member of the gym. Works out all the time."

"Why don't you revoke his membership?"

Cody laughed, realizing the conversation had come full circle. "Well, he hasn't exactly done anything to warrant it. The guy is just broody. He never has a kind word for anyone, but actually hasn't broken any of the rules." Cody smirked and shook his head.

Sergeant Gallagher gave a half-hearted laugh. "Frustrating, isn't it?"

"You're telling me."

"You've probably told me this before, but how long have you and your dad had the gym?"

"Dad bought it two years ago after he retired, right before I got out of the army."

"Which job does he like better? I mean, it sounds like he would have some long hours he'd have to put in at the gym."

"He did when we first opened. But after the traffic picked up, he was able to hire more staff. He's the office manager now. He did love being a cop, but there were some circumstances that came up that pushed him to retire."

"What was that, if you don't mind me asking?"

Cody let out a breath, trying to come up with a way to evade his question. "It's a long story."

"Okay, you don't have to tell me, but we are going to be in the car for a while longer."

He sat silent, wondering if opening up about his past might garner the sergeant's help. Cody cleared his throat hoping his gut feeling was right. "Well, about a year before I got out of the army, I got called up to go to Afghanistan. While I was there, I got a phone call from my dad. He said my mom was missing. He came home after work and her car was there, but she wasn't. No one had seen her.

"He made some phone calls, went through all the protocol with filing a missing person report, and they started an investigation. They searched the house, searched the car, searched the area. Nothing. They called the cab companies and airlines. Nothing.

"Of course, they suspected my dad, but they couldn't find any evidence to charge him, and everyone they talked to, except my sister, sang his praises. He was a good cop and well-liked around the town."

"So, they haven't found anything?"

"No. Nothing at all. No blood, no fingerprints. She just vanished. We don't know if something happened to her or if she left to be with someone else."

"Well, what did your sister have to say?"

"She basically said she thought my dad could have had something to do with it. My sister never got along with him. I don't know what the deal was. She is ten years older than me and, when she hit eighteen, she moved out and said it was because of him.

"But, in the end, it was just her statement and didn't hold any credence because she couldn't give them anything to back it up."

"So, do you think your mom could have left with someone else…like had an affair or something?"

"I guess it's possible. It seemed to me like my mom and dad loved each other. They showed affection to each other. Of course, I can remember a few times when they argued. They never got physical though, and from the way my dad reacted to the whole thing, I know it affected him."

"In what way?"

"He's changed. Dad was hoping the police would find her. He was on the news and everything. As it dragged on, I think Dad blamed himself and the department that the case went cold. He thought they missed something. That was pretty much the reason he quit. He had lost his confidence in doing his job."

"Yeah, it's frustrating enough to not be able to crack a case, but when it's personal it has to be on a whole other level. How long has it been?"

"She's been gone for about three years."

"Well, I'm sorry to hear that."

"Yeah, it's crazy. It's one of the reasons I applied to the academy. I wanted to work on the case. I figured I might be able to get some help if I was in law enforcement. You know? I honestly don't believe she ran off because I would think she would have contacted her kids at least by now." Cody's mind wandered, and his throat tightened thinking about it. He knew his voice was going to crack, so it was time to change the subject. "Anyway, how exciting is your life?"

Sergeant Gallagher snickered at his obvious change

of subject. He paused and sighed. "Don't worry, it's about time to head back to the station."

Cody smiled. "You're not getting off that easy. Turnabout is fair play."

The sergeant eyed him and chuckled again. "Well, okay. I'm a single dad with two kids. Brandon is eight and Georgia is six. Got married too young but thought we could handle it. The marriage became a victim of the job. She wanted something different. I don't blame her. It's not easy. The good thing is, we are still friends."

"That's hard to come by these days. Especially since you have kids."

"Yep. We have joint custody. All the jobs like law enforcement, fireman, paramedic, military, and others are hard on a marriage because of the stress. You are hailed as a hero by some. Others think you are the scum of the earth, and the latter is growing in popularity. It messes with your mind. You were in the military; you know what I'm talking about. Every day you leave your house wondering if it will be your last day. It can wear on you, and with some of the more difficult cases, it's hard not to bring them home."

"What's the worst case you have ever had to deal with?" The sergeant remained silent, staring at the road ahead but his mouth scrunched to one side. "Have you ever had to shoot anyone?"

"We've come across a few assault cases that were pretty bad. Had some gruesome accidents. Suicides." His eyes darted to Cody. "No. I haven't shot anyone. Have you?

"No. I was lucky. My tour in Afghanistan was crazy at times but I never had to pull the trigger."

The sergeant nodded. "But it's hard not to get obsessed with certain cases. Like this case with Miss Corbett, I keep going over what we have and wonder what we've missed."

"Yeah, I do the same thing. I wonder what it is that will break the case wide open. It's out there. I know it is."

"You said she is taking a class at your gym, right?" Cody nodded. "Every time you talk to her and she brings up the attack, listen closely. Write down anything that might be pertinent and let me know."

After a few other minor calls, they arrived back at the station and headed into the building. Sergeant Gallagher walked Cody up to the foyer.

"Thank you so much for the opportunity to ride with you, Sergeant Gallagher."

"How about you call me Mitch. Any time you want to go again, let me know. We can set it up. And, like I said, if you hear anything that might have something to do with the case, give me a call. That goes for your mom's case too."

Cody reached out his hand and Mitch grasped it. "I sure will." He turned and pushed open the door. "Thanks again, Mitch."

Chapter Eight

The damp heat of the stagnant mid-August air burned Jenna's nose. Her peach colored capris and floral tank stuck to her skin like cellophane wrap. No matter how high she set her air conditioner, it didn't ward off the beads of sweat forming on her neck. Her hair was up in a high ponytail with tendrils of curls that framed her face. Large, colorful earrings dangled from her ears. A small pink scar above her left eyebrow was the only remnant of the attack last month.

Grabbing her purse and books, she popped her hip against the door of her truck to push it shut. Perched on her nose were white sunglasses with purple watercolor flowers, but they failed to shade her from the sun that sat right at eye level, rendering her nearly blind. *I hope today isn't as boring as the other classes this week.*

Massive columns flanked the heavy metal doors of the Newman Science and Engineering building that stood in front of her. Having to take generic classes was a pain, but tonight's biology class was at least in her field.

This week marked a big change for Jenna since she and April decided things needed to go back to the way they were. She had been meeting with Bekah, her counselor, for six weeks, along with taking the self-defense classes, and was ready to take back her independence. The self-defense classes had been fun, but due to her college classes, they no longer fit into her schedule. The worst part was not seeing Cody. She thought about asking him for other options but couldn't work up the nerve, so she hoped he and Joe would take April up on her invite to go to TopHops Brewery Friday. Her heart skipped thinking about seeing him outside of the gym.

The white walls and plastic plants in the hallway gave off a sterile feel, but the scattered dusty artwork on the walls implied otherwise. Students were already milling around when she finally found the room, so she located a seat in the back and sat down. Jenna thought taking college classes would be reminiscent of high school, until she realized on the first day, she felt much older than most of the other students. This class proved to be no different.

The professor, Mr. Hastings, an older heavy-set man with thinning hair and a striped button-down that appeared to be a bit too small, toddled in within a few minutes and shut the door. He introduced himself and started to delve into the syllabus but was interrupted by a tap on the door. Pushing the door open, Jenna's heart tumbled when Cody appeared. His jeans and navy T-shirt were casual but fit perfectly, and his hair was messy, but she could fix it if she could run her fingers through it. Her breaths came so quickly she got light-headed. Sitting up, she cleared her throat, hoping he would notice her.

Cody scanned the room, then spotted Jenna, and a smile lit up his face. An empty seat sat next to her and he slid in.

Without breaking his smile, Cody leaned in and whispered, "I guess I have my answer to why you weren't there yesterday." His eyes roamed over her. "You look great by the way."

Her body tingled all over. *Heaven help me, even his whisper sounds sexy.*

The professor continued with his instructions, but she couldn't hear him speak over the thumping of her pulse.

"Thank you. You're pretty great yourself." She paused a beat hoping he couldn't read her thoughts. "I thought April told you, when she invited you and Joe out to TopHops, that we had to quit because the semester was starting." Jenna hoped the reminder didn't sound too obvious.

"April may have told Joe. But if she did, I wasn't there for that conversation. I'm just glad it wasn't because of something dumb I did. I do remember the invite though." He focused on the professor but continued talking. "Isn't that bar kind of a dive?"

"No. Not since they remodeled it a couple of months ago. It got bought out. They pretty much gutted the place. It's nice now. They've enclosed an area in glass where you can see their whole brewing facility. Their menu is totally different too. Still bar food, but now it's edible. They even have special nights like karaoke and game night."

"Really? I had no idea. I guess we will have to check it out."

A squeal escaped from her excitement, which garnered a frown from the professor. Cody snickered and wiggled his eyebrows at her, and she slid down in her chair. Maybe it was more like high school than she thought.

Throughout the fifty minutes of class, Jenna tried

to pay attention, but she continually noticed Cody's gaze boring holes through her, causing butterflies to take up residence in her gut. She turned to him when the class ended and noticed a scowl on his face while staring at the syllabus. "Why so gloomy?" she pried, keeping her voice low.

He immediately changed his expression. "Oh, it's nothing."

They walked toward the door and Jenna turned to him. "Hey, I have something I need to talk to you about. Would you want to get something to drink?"

Cody pushed the door open. "Sure. I saw a smoothie place in the Commons next door."

"That sounds perfect, except I have no idea what to order." They walked along a path across a small courtyard.

"Do you trust me?" He lowered his head and peered at her through his lashes.

Jenna raised one brow and lifted her mouth to one side. "Hmm, should I? I'm kind of picky."

"I've got some favorites."

"All right." She pointed her finger at him. "But don't put anything weird in it, like kale or that grass stuff." She turned and motioned with her hand. "I'll go find us a place to sit."

The sun had set, and there was a nice breeze, so she found a table on the patio. Glimpsing through the glass door, she watched Cody while he waited for their drinks to be done. A smile crossed her face. *I must be caught up in some crazy dream.* Tilting her head back, she closed her eyes and listened to the faint sound of crickets filling the air.

"Should I get you a blanket and pillow?" The deep

voice startled her, and Jenna opened one eye to see Cody's dimples making an appearance.

"No. Listen." She danced her finger to the sound of the crickets chirping. "I love being outside." Cody tilted his head, listening, and continued to smile. He handed her the drink and waited. She took a sip while he studied her as she swished it in her mouth. Fresh fruit collided with a creamy vanilla flavor. "What's in it?"

"Do you like it?" He searched her face, grinning from ear to ear.

"Yes, it's delicious. But what's in it, so I know what to order next time."

"It's a secret." He gave her a playful smirk. She could tell by his expression he was enjoying his little game with her. "It's my own concoction. I make it at the gym all the time."

"Well, does it have kale in it?"

"Maybe not kale," he confessed teasingly, making her continue to wonder about his secret potion. She studied him, and he continued to smile while silence took over. He finally scooted his chair back and sat down. "So, what was the question you needed to ask me?" He picked up his drink, leaned back in his chair, and crossed his ankles.

Jenna took a long sip on her straw, pushed it aside, and tried to clear her throat which had frozen from the gulp she took. "It's about classes at the gym." Her fingers threaded through her hair. "I enjoyed the self-defense class, but—" she jerked her gaze away trying to choose her words carefully.

Cody's smile disappeared. "But?"

Jenna let out an audible breath. It seemed like her life currently revolved around one thing. "But all of the classes taught responses when attacks were from a standing position. When I was attacked, he knocked me immediately to the ground and had my hands pinned. Are there any other classes I could take, like Tae Kwon Do, or something that would cover—"

"The self-defense class does progress to some floor moves later, so it's unfortunate that you had a scheduling conflict." He scraped his teeth across his lip while he thought. "Most of the different martial arts classes are in the evenings and may not offer what you need. But maybe—" He stopped and tapped his fingers against his mouth.

"What are you thinking?"

"Well…what do you have after this class?" he asked hesitantly.

"Nothing, this is my short night."

Cody continued to stay silent, pursing his lips and staring off into the night sky, which sent goosebumps up her spine. He finally sat forward and took a deep breath. "I have an idea but I'm not sure it's a *good* idea." Jenna took a long draw from her drink and tilted her head. He focused on her and continued.

"I was a wrestler in high school. I know some wrestling moves I can teach you. It's not self-defense per se, but I think it would probably be as good, if not better."

Her brows raised and a smile slowly spread across her face. "That would be great."

"Wait." Cody held up his hands. "Let me finish. There are a couple of problems with this idea, and it comes at a cost." Jenna crossed her arms on the table and leaned in.

Cody rubbed his hands on his pants, and his eyes

narrowed. "Okay, here's the deal. We don't normally have men teaching the self-defense class for one reason. Most of the clients are women, as you know. In order to teach the moves, it requires the instructor to get extremely close to the clients. That is even more so when the class progresses to the floor moves. The same thing goes for the wrestling moves. So, think about whether you would be able to handle me teaching you the moves before you agree to anything."

Jenna was suddenly, brutally aware of what he was saying. Panic surged through her body. She peered up at him. His expression filled with concern, but he continued. "The second issue is location. The classroom at the gym is out, it is booked solid."

After hearing everything, she sat back in her chair and took in a deep breath, then let out a heavy sigh. She glimpsed at Cody from beneath her lashes, thinking about what he said. It hadn't been that long since the attack. *He's right. Would having him that close, and having his hands on me, trigger memories? He wasn't the one who attacked me though. Could I handle it? Would I panic?*

She studied him again. He was staring at something off in the distance, and she noticed his cheeks had a bit of a rosy tone from the heat of the evening. Her insides quivered as she watched him take another sip of his shake. *Who am I kidding? The real question is, can I keep from throwing myself at him?* She noticed he now sat with the lid off his smoothie, eating it with a spoon and staring at the syllabus they had gotten in class. Her insides turned to mush, and a firestorm enveloped her when he licked the spoon. *Mercy!*

Jenna captured his eyes and knew her cheeks were

probably as red as a cherry but tried desperately to sound professional.

"I understand your concern, but I at least want to try the wrestling moves. I know now how important it is to be prepared." She paused and drew in a deep breath. "As for location, my place is only a couple of miles from here. If you would be good with that, I think it might work. But I need to know what you would charge."

Cody lifted the corner of his mouth. "Oh." He chuckled. "I was thinking we might do a trade. I would teach you wrestling, and you could help me with this." He held up the syllabus.

"Ah, I'm guessing that's why you had such a frown in class." He nodded. "That absolutely works for me. But are you okay with going to my house?"

"I'm fine with it, as long as it's okay with April."

"Oh, April moved out last weekend."

"Are you sure you are ready for that?" he asked, his tone turning serious and his mouth pulling into a straight line.

"I had extra locks put on the door and a high-tech security system installed." Jenna picked up her phone from the table and shook it. "I can see everything from my phone." Her attention was drawn back to the paper in Cody's hand. "Why exactly are you taking Biology?"

"Well, I had planned to go to the police academy a while back but got into a little trouble and had to put it off. But after watching the EMTs and paramedics with you, I decided to check into it."

"What made you change your mind?"

"Sergeant Gallagher. Remember me telling you about me doing some ride-along shifts with him to get an idea of the job?"

She nodded.

"Well, it became clear law enforcement wasn't what I wanted to do. My dad was a police officer, and I knew I wanted to do something to serve the community. But I don't know, now that I've done the ride-along, that's not where my interests lie. What the paramedics were doing fascinated me. So, I'm going the paramedic route. That is, if I can handle the classes." He lifted his eyes to hers and smiled. "So why are you?"

The corner of her mouth tipped up. "Well, I started working as an office assistant at Bruin's about eight months ago. I love animals. Always have. So, when I found out they would help pay for college classes in the veterinary field, I jumped at it."

"Yeah, I can go to college under the G.I. bill. That's a big incentive."

"You are in the military?"

"Was. Army. Got out a couple of years ago." He crossed his ankle over his knee and brushed his pants off.

"Somehow I can't see you with short hair." She wrinkled her forehead trying to picture him that way.

"Trust me," pointing to his head, "you don't want to see this without hair." She clamped her lips together trying to stifle a giggle.

Realizing she didn't know that much about him, curiosity set in and she decided to dig a little deeper. "So, you're military, you know how to wrestle, you like to help people...what else?"

He squinted one eye and remained silent for a moment. "Well, I will only answer if I can ask the same of you."

Jenna stirred her smoothie. "Sure. But you go first. Start at the beginning."

"Okay." He let out a long breath and stared down at the table, letting his finger trace the design on the top while a slow, crooked smile formed on his face. "Cody Spencer, twenty-four, I like long walks along the beach—"

Jenna giggled. "What's your full name?"

He lifted his eyes. "Cody *James* Spencer. I grew up in Montclair. Wrestled and played football in high school and went into the military once I graduated. When I finished my commitment, I started working for my dad at the gym, and now I'm going to school to be a paramedic." He crossed his arms and nodded then continued. "Oh, and I taught myself how to play the guitar."

"Cody James," she said slowly continuing to stir her smoothie, "you are going to have to play something for me some time."

He shook his head. "I'm not any good."

"Let me be the judge of that." She paused. "I like that name, Cody James. Is it a family name?"

"Yes, my mom's dad was named James. I was named after him. He was a good guy. Worked for the county, paving roads and putting up signs and stuff."

"That's dangerous work." She stirred her smoothie. "Do they live around here?"

"No, he and my grandma lived in Missouri but they both have passed away."

Her voice softened. "Oh, I'm sorry." She paused. "Well, tell me about the rest of your family," she said, brightening her tone. Cody's face turned solemn, and he took a deep breath. Jenna immediately realized she had hit on a sore spot. "I'm sorry." Humiliation filled her. "I seem to be asking all the wrong questions. You don't have to tell me."

"No, no, it's fine." He studied the table and played with the design on the top again. "My dad was a police officer for several years until he bought the gym. I was always close to him. He kind of pushed me to follow in his footsteps. He wrestled in high school, was in the army, and then became a cop.

"I strived to be like him but was never quite as good at any of it. I appreciated how much he pushed me, but at times, it almost felt like I was competing against him, and I seriously messed up with the police academy." His attention was drawn away, but his hand still traced the design on the table. "I'm sorry," his eyes meeting hers again, "I don't know why I just spilled all my troubles on you."

Jenna could hear the raw honesty in his tone. "I don't mind. You know, maybe it was simply that those things really weren't your passion," she said nonchalantly. "I mean, I get you wanted to make your dad happy, but maybe they didn't make *you* happy."

Cody quickly met her eyes and swayed his head back and forth, considering her comment.

"Can I ask what happened," she asked quietly, "to keep you out of the academy?"

"A guy got pissed at Joe when we were at a bar and sucker-punched him. So, I punched the guy. He filed an assault charge against me. Can't get into the academy if you have an assault charge against you."

"Sounds bogus to me," she said, stirring her straw around in her smoothie.

"It was. He attacked Joe, and I was defending him.

But now that I have done the ride-along shifts, I am kind of glad it happened."

"So, how about the rest of your family."

His gaze drifted. "I have a sister, Hillary. She is ten years older than me and a bit of a free spirit. Left home at eighteen to spread her wings and get away from my dad. She knew how to push his buttons. Now she's married, has a couple of kids, and settled down. Her husband, Jack, does something with computer programming. Kind of an odd pair but good for each other."

His eyes went back to his fingers tracing the design on the table. "I've never met their kids." Jenna tipped her head listening intently, and a heaviness filled her chest. "She had my nephew, Joel, when I was in the military, then my niece, Hallie, right after I got out. At that time, the gym hadn't been open long, so I was working night and day, and our schedules just never worked out."

"Awe, that's sad."

"As for my mom," Cody sat up in his chair, "she disappeared while I was doing a tour over in Afghanistan."

Jenna's throat tightened. Was she hearing him right? She could feel the tears filling her eyes. "Cody. No. Really?"

"Yeah, the police never found any clues as to what happened. It was the reason my dad finally left law enforcement."

Jenna didn't know what to say. Every time she saw him, Cody came off being happy and carefree, but his life was anything but that.

He leaned back and tipped his chin up. "I'm done.

Your turn."

Her eyes focused on him, trying to study his face. His story made her heart ache, but the smirk he was giving her made her smile.

"Jenna Rose Corbett. I'm twenty-three. I also like long walks on the beach." She slowly leaned her head to one side. "Well, I think I would. I have never been anywhere other than the lake. I was raised here in Dalton. My family owns an eighty-acre ranch west of town. We have an assortment of animals. I love to ride horses." She paused a beat and asked, "Have you ever ridden?"

"No, it's something I have always wanted to do though," he confided.

"I'll have to bring you out one weekend. You would love it." He nodded, and a grin spread across his face. "Anyway, I worked at the ranch until February when I got the job at Bruin's." She paused recalling what she had said. "I have one brother, Ben, who is twenty-eight and still lives at the ranch along with my dad. He was kind of annoying growing up. Always picked on me, but I knew he had my back. Oh, and as far as talents, I don't play any instruments, but I can whistle really loud."

Cody's mouth dropped open. "Do it," he whispered loudly.

Jenna scrunched her face. "Here?" He nodded.

Jenna sat up, scanned the area for a second, then wrapped her lips around two fingers and took a deep breath. The high-pitched noise reverberated off the building and out to the parking lot.

Cody's dimples dug deep into his cheeks. "Dang, girl," he sang, drawing each word out.

Her heart fluttered seeing his expression. "It comes in very handy when you work at a ranch."

Cody leaned back, crossed his ankles, and rested his hands in his lap. "Your family owns a ranch. You mentioned a dad and brother. I kind of don't want to ask…but…mom?"

"Passed away about eighteen months ago from a long battle with cancer." She could see in his eyes that he knew the hurt.

"What was her name?"

"Karen…and yours?"

"Mary." He paused. "Miss her?" he asked not making eye contact.

"Terribly." A sharp pain radiated through her. "We were extremely close. Dad and Ben can be kind of gruff, so she was my go-to person when I couldn't handle them anymore." She squinted at something off in the darkness, then brought her attention back to Cody. "Were you close to your mom?"

"Yeah. My mom was one of those people you meet and immediately know they are kind." He lifted his eyes to Jenna's. "You know? She was always willing to help where she could."

"You must take after her then," Jenna broke in.

A smile rose on his lips, but then Cody's focus shifted away from her. "My mom was at every event I was involved in and always cheered me on. Embarrassed the hell out of me at times but made no bones about how much she loved her kids." He rubbed his hands together. "That's what makes it so hard. If she ran off with someone, I would think she would have at least let me or Hillary know."

Jenna turned away, feeling the sting of tears. She

was usually good at keeping the tears at bay, but now, hearing Cody's story made her feel her pain at a new level. She couldn't imagine not knowing if her mom was dead or alive. A glimpse of Cody's glistening eyes pushed her over the edge and a tear trickled from the corner of her eye.

She quickly wiped her cheeks. "Okay, enough of that. So, what's it like running a gym?" She could tell from his relieved expression he welcomed the change of subject.

"It's not bad. I enjoy getting to know the members." His face brightened again. "We are kind of like a family. You wouldn't believe some of the stories I have been told."

"So, do you train everyone?" Jenna balanced her chin on her hand and sipped the last of her smoothie.

"Not everyone. Some come in to use the equipment, some the classes, most I train until they get used to the routine and they go off on their own, and a few have the money to have me train on a continual basis. In those cases, there are some that use it more as a counseling session than a training session."

"Do you have girls hitting on you a bunch about training them?"

"A few." Cody paused. "I kind of know most of the time if they are serious," his dimple appeared on one side, "and try to avoid those that aren't."

"Would you train me?" The words flew out of Jenna's mouth before she realized she was speaking them out loud.

"Seriously?" Cody cocked one brow up.

She hesitated, feeling the familiar rush of heat to her cheeks. "Yeah. I mean, when I lived on the farm, I got plenty of exercise doing the daily chores. After I moved to my house, I picked up running in the morning with Tucker. Right now, I don't feel comfortable doing that, so I need to do something else. I figure it would help to build my strength."

"Well, I can help you, but…" his voice drifted.

"But what?"

He rubbed the back of his neck and sat up. "I can't do it for free."

"Can we do a trade?" Jenna asked coyly. A glint sparked in Cody's eyes and a tingle shot through her.

He sat back with a devilish smirk. "I don't know, what did you have in mind?"

Jenna gaped at him as the flames from her cheeks engulfed her body. "Well, I, I don't—"

Cody let out a sigh and waved off her response. "No, no trading." He chuckled. "This one you have to sign up to be a member."

"I can handle that," Jenna fired back quickly. "So, if I sign up, would you train me if I come in early?"

"How early are we talking?"

"Well, I'm used to being up around five and go on my runs around five-fifteen so…" Her voice trailed off as her mind flashed through her memories.

"I think I could swing that. When do you want to start?"

Cody's smooth voice brought her back, and nerves took over when she realized she would be seeing much more of Cody. "Let's get through this first week of classes and then start next week. Would that work?"

He stood up, darting his head back and forth before walking over and throwing away his cup. "I think so. I will make sure everyone is good with the schedule change. Would you be able to come by sometime this week so I can get you into the system?"

Cody pointed to her cup. She took one last sip and handed it to him, then stood and retrieved her book and purse. "Yes, when will you be there on Friday?"

"Um...I think around eleven maybe?"

"Can I come by at lunch?"

"Sure." He picked up his book, and his attention turned to the parking lot. "Where are you parked?" She pointed to her truck and Cody grinned. "You drive a truck?"

"Yeah. Again, I lived on a ranch. I hauled stuff all the time. What do *you* drive?"

"I drive Rubi." He pointed to his Jeep.

"Rubi? You named your Jeep?"

"It's a Rubicon, and since it's red, I call her Rubi."

She smiled. "That, I have to say, sir, is adorable."

Cody's dimples made another appearance. "Does that lower my man points?"

"No, not a bit. I think it's rather attractive honestly."

"Well, then, maybe I can take you for a ride in her some time."

"That would be fun." They stopped at her truck. "Now I'm thinking maybe he needs a name."

Cody gave the truck a once over, rubbing his hand against the dents and dings. "How about Rusty?"

Jenna immediately frowned and stuck her lip out. "Awe, he's not that bad." She turned and patted the edge of the hood. Cody chuckled and shook his head. She tilted her head and the corners of her mouth lifted. "Thank you for hanging out with me, I enjoyed it. My smoothie was delicious. I will have to hit you up for another one sometime."

"Thanks for the invite. I enjoyed it too. I'm glad you liked my secret recipe." He paused and squinted his eyes, almost in a grimace. "I hope you don't mind me asking, but would there be any way I could get your number...just so I can let you know, if I have a problem setting up the training?"

The flutters in her tummy turned into an all-out swarm of wings taking flight. "Oh. Sure. I should have thought about that, it's—"

Cody held up a finger. "Hold on." He quickly retrieved his phone from his pocket, then nodded.

"It's six nine seven, four two one, six eight six eight."

"All right, hang on and I will text you, so you have mine." He tapped on his phone and she heard her phone buzz.

"I think I got it." Jenna dragged her phone out of her bag. "Yep." She couldn't keep the huge smile from pulling at her lips. "Thanks again for agreeing to do this."

"Remember, you have to hold up your end of the bargain. I expect an A in the class."

Jenna smiled. "I will do my best."

Chapter Nine

Jenna shifted nervously in her seat, hoping someone would show up to cover for her lunch. But with no one else at the desk, she was forced to continue manning the phones and fielding the customers at the vet clinic. Cody had texted her earlier to make sure she was stopping by. Seeing his name pop up on her phone was enough to set off tingles all over her body.

With each passing minute, Jenna became more antsy to leave. She hadn't stopped thinking about him since their impromptu smoothie date. His openness about his life filled her with a warmth every time she thought about him. Yes, he was gorgeous, but there was something else about him that drew her in like a magnet.

April suddenly appeared from the back, and Jenna cornered her. "Hey, do you know where Tracy ran off to? I'm supposed to be going to lunch, and the phone won't stop ringing. Mrs. Jackson is waiting for Gonzo, and Mrs. Harrison is supposed to be bringing Hector and Otis in to be boarded."

"I think Tracy is waiting for them to release Gonzo. They are swamped back there." April fidgeted with her necklace. "Dr. Walker has surgeries stacked today, and the groomers are booked completely up." She stepped behind the desk and sorted through paperwork, then finding the sheet she needed, handed it to Jenna. "Here are Gonzo's papers. Go ahead and enter them in the computer and then all you have to do is process the payment."

"Oh, good idea." She took the papers and began to enter the information into the computer when the phone rang again. Jenna rolled her eyes and reached for it, but April beat her to it. She returned her focus to the computer determined to finish the entry before being interrupted again.

Tracy came around the corner with a large, fuzzy, black and white dog with floppy ears and placed a piece of paper on the counter with two bottles. Mrs. Jackson approached the counter and took Gonzo's leash from Tracy. Jenna went through the information on the sheet, took Mrs. Jackson's payment, and put the bottles in a plastic bag. As Mrs. Jackson trotted out the door with Gonzo, Jenna retrieved her purse and slung it across her body. Turning to Tracy, she said, "I'm going to get out of here before the lobby fills up again."

Within minutes, the vet clinic was disappearing in her rearview mirror, and Jenna's thoughts turned to what she was about to do. The sheer anticipation took her breath away. Not only would Cody be helping her in weight training but would be personally teaching her wrestling moves. Her body filled with goosebumps with the thought of his hands on her. How could he have gotten under her skin so quickly?

Jenna drove into the parking lot and parked right next to "Rubi". *I can't believe he named his Jeep. I really should come up with a name for my truck.* The creak of the door as she popped it open, and the rust around the edges, made her rethink the name he gave it. *With all the dents and dings and chipped paint, Rusty does fit.*

The door chimed when she entered the gym. With no one at the counter, she searched the area to see if she could spot Cody. She could hear a voice above the music blaring from the overhead speakers and turned her attention to where the voice came from. Her eyes landed on several people perched upon spin bikes, pumping their legs. Then, her eyes darted, and she was startled when three guys walked past her and nodded as they headed to another piece of equipment. A roar of laughter came from the other corner of the room where a group of men were standing. Her gut tightened. Would she be able to do this?

Jenna checked her phone wondering if she had missed him since she was running late. *Maybe I should text him. But if I do, would that appear desperate?* Her mind wandered. She let out a sigh and checked her phone again, then out of the corner of her eye she spied Cody exiting the men's room, pushing a cart of cleaning products. Her teeth scraped her lip as she tried to hide her smile.

"The not so glamorous part of the job."

Cody jumped, obviously startled from her comment, and chuckled. "That is an understatement," he responded sarcastically. "Especially the men's room." He pushed the cart aside. "Look at you, all cute and professional in your scrubs." She put her hands on her hips and posed. He stepped behind the counter, then squatted down and disappeared. "I didn't hear you come in. I hope you haven't been standing here long." His smooth voice rose from the counter depths.

"Nah, only a couple of minutes," she answered gripping the edge of the counter and pulling herself over to see what he was doing. He reappeared with a folder, retrieved some papers, and pushed them to her.

"Fill this out, and I will get you inputted into the computer." He snagged a pen out of a cup and handed it to her. She read through the form and began filling in the blanks.

"Do I need the medical release?" she questioned, continuing to examine the paper.

"No, I have your other release on file. It will be fine." The door chimed and Jenna turned to see a well-dressed man with a muscular build and pepper colored hair carrying a plastic sack. She stepped aside moving her paper with her so Cody could address the customer.

His focus shifted momentarily then returned to the computer. "Hey, Dad," he said monotoned.

"Hey, how's it going today?" Mr. Spencer stepped behind the counter. Jenna's eyes tipped up after their greeting. She discreetly glanced back and forth, comparing the two. Cody had several inches on his dad and a leaner frame. Although she could see a few similarities, she figured he resembled his mom.

"Good. We've been busy. Joe had the early shift and he said traffic was steady. Sam will be in at five."

"Great! And we have a new member?" Mr. Spencer nodded acknowledging Jenna.

She gave him a quick smile then continued to fill out the paperwork.

"Oh, yes. This is Jenna Corbett, Dad. She is going to be doing some weight training."

Her eyes met his, and she held out her hand. "Nice to meet you, Mr. Spencer."

He took her hand in both of his. "Call me Todd. Now, are you—"

Cody interrupted, "Yes, Jenna is the young lady I helped last month. She asked me to train her."

"Okay." Todd nodded.

She pushed the paperwork to Cody.

He studied it. "I think it's good. Now, all we have to do is take your money."

Jenna handed her credit card to him, and he entered the information. "Perfect. You are all set."

"Yay!" Jenna clapped rapidly. "I'm excited." After returning her credit card to her purse, she met Cody's gaze. "So, you and Joe are coming tonight, right?"

He continued to enter information into the computer. "Yes. We will be there. You said seven, right?"

She nodded. "Yes, seven." Slinging her bag across her body, she tapped the counter a couple of times. "All right, I need to go get some lunch and head back to work. See you tonight." She pressed her back to the door, then paused. "It's nice to meet you, Todd."

Todd tipped his chin up and waved. "You, too."

****

As the door shut behind her, a muscular man caught it. Brant Ellington strolled in wearing the same black hoodie and sweatpants he had on the night Mitch stopped him. He made his way past the counter, unaware Cody's eyes were locked on him.

Todd's forehead creased. "What's that glare for?"

Cody continued to watch him disappear around the corner while he responded. "When I did the ride along with Sergeant Gallagher, we stopped Brant on a suspicious person call. He was dressed in that black hoodie and pants, and very drunk. His clothing matched the description of the person that assaulted Jenna. I had to wonder if it was him."

"Did Sergeant Gallagher take him in?" Todd questioned.

Cody shook his head, still feeling the frustration. "No. He let him go. He was headed to his house up the street, and Mitch said there wasn't enough to hold him."

"I hate to say it, but I agree. I mean, it could be him, but you can't go off the clothes he wears." Todd peeked back at him as Brant did bench presses. "But I see where you are coming from."

Cody pressed his lips together. "The guy comes in here all the time and never takes the scowl off his face. I mean, I know I have a reason to have it out for him, but beyond that, he has always had an attitude, and I wouldn't put it past him to do something like that."

"Maybe so, but you would think the person attacking the women would be smarter than to wear the same clothes around in public."

A frown crossed Cody's face. He glared back at Brant again. "Yeah, you would think." His attention returned to the sack on the counter. "So, what did you bring me."

"I got some subs from Hanson's deli." Todd quickly scanned the gym. "Why don't you get us a couple of waters out of the machine. I'll set everything out at the table."

The two stepped out from behind the counter. Todd set out the sandwiches on the table and scooted out a chair. Cody grabbed the waters and sat down.

"So where are you going tonight?"

Popping open the bag of chips, Cody reached in and grabbed one. "We are meeting Jenna and her friend

April at TopHops."

"That old, dilapidated building on the side of the highway? I thought they shut that place down."

"Jenna said it's been remodeled and is pretty nice. I am curious to see what they've done. It's a brewery now, not simply a bar."

"So, you are going out with her tonight, and then you have agreed to train her?"

"Well, it's not a date, Dad."

Todd took a bite of his sandwich. "Um-hum."

Cody didn't appreciate the interrogation and figured the details of the wrestling lessons didn't need to be discussed. "And yeah, she said she hadn't done any exercising since the attack, and she wanted to get back at it and build some strength, so she asked if I would train her."

Todd took another bite of his sandwich. "Well, I don't want to get in your business, but I hope you can keep this strictly business between you two."

Cody crossed his arms and sat back in his chair. "Why do you say that?"

"Two reasons. One, she is now a client, and getting into a relationship is never a good combination. It can cause other clients to feel like you are playing favorites, and if things go south, she might stir up trouble for you and the gym. And two, many victims and rescuers develop false feelings for each other. It's called White Knight Syndrome. It happens all the time to police officers and first responders. The rescuer and victim are drawn to each other from whatever tragedy they have faced together."

His dad's words stirred up a war within him. He couldn't deny he was attracted to her, and from what he had seen, the feeling was mutual. *Could it all be due to the incident?* But trying to dispel the feelings he already had wouldn't be easy, and even harder now that he would be training her. But as much as he wanted to explore a relationship with Jenna, Cody understood what his dad was saying. "Yeah, you are probably right. I need to keep it professional. I don't think she will need too much training before she can do the program on her own. I'll go tonight since I already agreed to, but after that, I will keep my distance."

Todd wiped his hands on his napkin. "Trust me, it's best for everyone involved."

"I'm sure you are right," Cody agreed, hoping his dad didn't hear the uncertainty in his voice.

Thoughts raced through his head of the wrestling training. Keeping it professional was going to be the biggest challenge. *Maybe I should cancel it. But I really think I'm going to need her help with the class.*

Todd wadded his paper up and threw his trash into the bag. "I've got some stuff to do in the office. Do you need me for anything up front?"

Cody stood and added his trash to the bag. "I don't think so, I'm just going to hold down the fort for a little while longer until Sam gets here."

"Sounds good." He threw the bag in the trash and headed to the office.

Cody mulled over the comments his dad made and let out a heavy sigh. Since he had met Jenna, his life seemed to be headed in a good direction. He enjoyed their conversation Wednesday night after class. Jenna was easy to talk to and had a great laugh. He respected his dad's insight, but his advice continually messed up the things that made him happy. Regardless, this needed to be a professional training session, nothing more. But he wanted more.

Chapter Ten

Cody and Joe pulled into the crowded parking lot at TopHops a little after seven. The exterior of the brewery, which at one time housed a large Mexican food restaurant, hadn't changed much, other than a coat of paint, so Cody didn't hold out much hope.

Walking through the doors, though, he couldn't believe the difference. The bar had been completely transformed. Several wooden tables and chairs surrounded a small parquet dance floor. Outside of those tables were round booths in red vinyl with wooden tables in the center. There were two bars, both in a stained hardwood with black granite countertops. One long, narrow bar stood at the front of the building, while another smaller one sat in a back corner, with a glassed-in area displaying the brewing facility. A raised stage sat off to the right.

The interior was awash in grays and purples, and colored lights were strategically placed around the room. Large TV screens sat in all four corners of the building and behind the bars, but from what Cody could tell, very few people were paying attention to them. Bruno Mars played through the sound system and put him in a good mood.

He stopped at the bar and got a beer while Joe got a glass of tea. They scanned the room, and his body thrummed when he spotted her. Jenna and April were sitting in one of the booths. Jenna's scooped necked burgundy top set off her wine-colored hair that was half up in a clip, letting her curls hang loose down her back.

Cody and Joe walked up to the booth, and Jenna smiled. "Hey, you made it." She and April scooted in together. The guys took the outside. "What do you think? Isn't this place cool?"

"I can't believe what they did to it." He hitched his thumb over his shoulder to the stage. "Do they have bands play too?"

"I don't know about bands, but they do have karaoke." Her grin caused tiny wrinkles to form around her blue-green eyes and drew Cody in. "They are going to get that started soon."

"Oh, you and April should get up there." Joe nodded to the stage then winked at April.

April's eyes widened, and she shook her head. "Ha! You're funny. There is no way I would get up there. I sound like a goose being dragged to its death when I try to sing." Her finger bounced between Cody and Joe. "But you and Cody feel free." Then she shooed them away.

Jenna turned to Cody. "You said you play the guitar, so I bet you can sing."

Joe picked up his tea. "He can. I've heard him." Cody's mouth dropped open. "He needs to get up there."

The beer Cody held hovered at his mouth. He turned and glared at Joe with his forehead wrinkled, feeling like his best friend had thrown him under the bus. His bottle hit the table with a loud clink. "No way. I've never been in front of a crowd, and I don't plan to start my singing career singing karaoke."

"Oh, it's fun. Just wait," Jenna chimed in. "There are all kinds of people that get up there. Some can sing great, and some can't, but they all have fun."

"Would you guys like menus?" a cheery voice inquired as a young lady dressed in a bright pink T-shirt sporting the brewery's name approached the table. She passed out glasses of water and handed them menus. "We have our loaded fajita nachos topped with chunks of tenderloin, peppers, onions, and cheese for eleven ninety-nine, and our Spanish hot wings, with jalapeno and onion fries for eight ninety-nine, on special tonight until eight."

Cody peeked above the menu with his brows raised. "Do you guys want to start with some nachos?" Seeing everyone nod, he turned to the waitress. "We'll take the nachos."

"I will get those started. Any other drinks?" After no response, she scurried off across the room.

Within a few minutes, a voice rang through the speakers. "All right, friends, it's time for a little karaoke. So, you guys need to warm up your vocal cords and get up here. We have lists of songs to choose from up here at the front. All you have to do is choose a song and fill out the sheet of paper. When your name is called, hop up here and sing your heart out. Remember, the person who gets the biggest applause at the end of the night will win five hundred dollars."

Cody's head jerked, and his eyes locked on Jenna with the announcement of the cash prize. People trickled up front and turned in their papers. First up, a thirtyish woman belted out the song "Crazy". After hearing her, Cody thought for sure he would never stand a chance up there. Next, a blonde with a short pixie cut sang "Wake Me Up". Jenna and April clapped along with the rest of the crowd. Once she had finished, a tall, dark-haired guy took the stage. Trying to relieve his nerves, he shook his body and took several deep breaths. A bright melody drifted through the air, and his mouth moved at lightning speed, singing "I Want You". Cody turned to everyone at the table who were all trying to sing along. He watched for a moment then joined in.

The more Cody watched, the more he wanted to try it. He loved to sing. As a kid, he and his mom would sing along to songs during his car rides to school. After begging his parents for a guitar, he wound up finding one on his own at a thrift store. He even signed up to be in the high school talent show, but when his dad found out, he talked him out of it.

The crowd continued to get more involved with each song, and after the nachos were dropped off and more drinks were ordered, Cody went up front and got a song list. His finger bounced from song to song until he found one that he knew well. He filled out the piece of paper and took it up front. His nerves kicked in as he walked back to the table. Jenna and April were both clapping enthusiastically.

Several others got up to sing, including a girl with dark brown hair and glasses, who appeared way too shy to sing. But when she opened her mouth and belted out the song "Titanium", everybody grew quiet. Her crystal-clear voice hit every pitch, and when the song ended, everyone clapped. Cody closed his eyes hoping he wouldn't have to follow her.

"Everybody put your hands together for...Cody Spencer." *Of course.*

His eyes darted from face to face at the table. "You guys gotta go up there and cheer me on. I want to win." He stepped out of the booth with the other three close behind. His throat slowly constricted with each step toward the stage. *God, I shouldn't have eaten all those nachos.* His gut rolled like it had been inhabited by a stirred-up den of snakes.

Standing in front of the mic, he scanned the room before focusing on the screen. He didn't think he would need the prompted words, but after seeing the sea of people standing at the stage, he was glad they were there. The familiar intro boomed through the speakers. Cody pumped his shoulders and belted out the first line of Bon Jovi's hit, "It's My Life". The crowd's roar caused every hair on his body to stand at attention. Cody smiled and drank it in.

The more Cody sang, the more the song took over. He relaxed and leaned into the mic, egging the crowd on to join him on the chorus. Moving with the beat, he pumped his fist in the air. His voice thundered with the anthem as his eyes took in the crowd.

Jenna stood front and center. With her arms above her head, her whole body moved to the music while she sang along with him. She gazed up at him and her face was lit up with a grin from ear to ear. April stood right next to her snapping photos. When he finally sang the last note, the crowd roared again. He took a bow and jumped off the stage.

His heart pounded like it was about to explode. He grabbed Jenna without thinking and wrapped her in a hug before heading back to the booth with a huge smile spreading across his face.

Jenna scooted in to make room for him. "You were

incredible. The best so far."

Cody tried to act as blasé as possible but his whole body hummed with excitement. He picked up some nachos and put them on his plate.

"You have got to do another song," Jenna insisted.

He lifted one brow and chuckled. "I think I should end on a high note. Next time I might get booed off the stage."

Cody shoved a nacho in his mouth and took a swig from his beer. Watching the next few singers, who were a bit underwhelming, his mind went back to the feeling he had watching the sea of faces singing with him. It excited him, he had to admit. He picked up the list again. "What song do you want to hear?"

Jenna's face brightened. "Are you going to do another one?"

"Maybe."

Jenna scooted in. Her body brushing against his arm sent prickles down his spine. "I don't know." A seismic wave shot through Cody's body when she pressed against him even more. His eyes darted to her, trying to gauge whether she might be feeling the same spark. A long breath escaped. When her eyes locked with his, the smoldering gaze she gave him was unmistakable. "What about something a little slower? Then you have the crowd pleaser and the tear-jerker."

"Okay." There was a song Cody had picked up recently on his guitar that he thought would work. He walked up to the front, filled out the paper, and headed back to the booth. Jenna rapped on the table, obviously excited to be able to hear him again. The next two singers were decent but only got moderate applause. When they called his name, he immediately questioned again why he signed up. His breath caught in his throat as he slid out of the booth and motioned for the group to follow.

The audience clapped and whooped before Cody stepped foot on the stage. He took that as a good sign. The first notes played. He cupped his hands around the mic, closed his eyes, and hummed. A loud roar went up as the audience immediately recognized the familiar entrance to Sean Mendez's song "Mercy". His voice was soft and breathy as he sang the first verse. He made eye contact with the crowd and told the story through his voice, expressions, and movements.

As his volume grew toward the chorus, Cody gripped the mic stand and leaned forward. The crowd clapped and sang along. With a cry in his voice, he clutched his chest as if he were in pain, and it set the crowd on fire. Yanking the mic from the stand, he gazed down at Jenna.

Jenna's face beamed, and Cody found himself suddenly singing every word to her. He dropped to his knees with the last chorus, letting the song completely consume him. With the ring of the last chord, the crowd again broke into a loud roar. His eyes swept the room. Spotting Mitch, he pointed. Mitch nodded.

Cody's eyes drew back to Jenna in time to see a tall muscular guy, with ash blond hair, place his hand on her back. He moved her hair and whispered something into her ear. Brant Ellington. Cody's mind shot back to the ride along with Mitch when they found Brant dressed in black walking near the area of the attack.

Cody stepped off the stage and tried to continue to smile, but he was seething. Jenna was obviously uncomfortable. He could tell by the fear creeping into her eyes, but she smiled politely. Cody walked up behind her. Wrapping his arms around her, he pretended he didn't see Brant standing there. She flinched and turned in his arms.

Pulling her tight, he winked at her, hoping she would follow his lead. "How did I do?"

Jenna smiled, wrapped her arms around his neck, and ran her fingers through his hair. Her touch sent an explosion of sparks throughout his body. "You were absolutely fabulous." She batted her eyes at him, and they strolled back toward the booth. Brant tapped Cody's shoulder, but he ignored him and continued walking. When Brant attempted to grab him, Mitch appeared. As Cody and Jenna reached the booth, he turned to see Mitch escorting Brant out of the building.

His brows creased and he leaned into Jenna. "What did he say to you?" His tone was full of indignation.

"Who was that guy?" Jenna motioned toward the door.

"Brant Ellington. He is the reason I am not at the academy. Tell me what he said." His whole body was shaking with anger but he tried to steady his voice so he wouldn't scare Jenna.

"I'm not sure. There was so much noise. I may not have heard him right. He mumbled something, said I was beautiful, then I think he said I smelled like pine." Confusion filled her face, but Cody's gut clenched. Could Brant have been taunting her about the attack? He rubbed his hands against his legs. The door opened and Mitch walked toward their table. Cody stood up and met him halfway.

He didn't give Mitch time to say anything. "I think Brant taunted Jenna."

Mitch's forehead creased. "How so?" He leaned in to hear him better.

"Brant spoke to her during the song. Flirted with her, then told her she smelled like pine." Cody could see in Mitch's expression that he thought it was far-fetched. "I know it sounds trivial, but don't you think it's suspicious since the attack occurred in the pine trees?"

"Cody, I don't think Ellington is the attacker. Plus, it could be her perfume, her shampoo, her drink, his drink. The guy was stumbling drunk. I saw him outside, and I followed him in here. I'm surprised she understood anything he said. The minute I got him in my car he passed out."

"Why do you think he isn't the one who attacked her?"

"I don't want to get into it now. I did some checking, and I will fill you in later. I know you want to find the guy, no more than I do, but I think you are getting so close to the victim that it is affecting your judgment."

The words stung. The conversation he had with his dad earlier was ringing in his ears. His stomach churned. *Professional. Keep it professional.*

"I'm worried about her. She told me she is living alone again, and you said it's possible that this guy has been watching her."

"Do you know where she lives? I can step up patrol in the area."

"Yeah." Cody retrieved his phone and pressed his finger up the screen. "Here is her address."

Mitch took out his pad and pen and wrote the address down. "I know where that is. I will keep an eye out." He put the pad back in his pocket. "I better get the drunk in his bed for the night."

"Thanks, man." He gave Mitch a pat on his back.

Mitch turned to leave, then turned back with a smirk on his face. "By the way, you weren't too shabby."

Cody brushed his hand in the air dismissing the comment, and Mitch chuckled. Shoving his hands in his pockets, Mitch turned to leave. Cody watched as he disappeared out the door and then returned to the booth, scooted in next to Jenna, and something wet brushed up against his arm.

"Did you spill your drink?" he asked with a smile, as he tugged at her shirt.

"No, I don't think so," Jenna said confused, her eyes following his. She felt the side of her shirt. "I guess I bumped someone."

Joe and April slid into the booth speculating about what had happened between Cody and officer Gallagher.

Joe leaned on the table and peeked back at the door as Mitch left. "What was that all about?"

Jenna turned to Cody. "Yeah, what's going on?"

Cody's eyes bounced from Joe to Jenna trying to figure out which question to answer first. "Oh, Mitch was asking what he said to you. He was very drunk, and he is taking him to the drunk tank."

April and Joe had missed the whole scene. "Him, who him?" April asked.

Cody made eye contact with Joe and mouthed 'Brant' to him. Joe rolled his eyes and shook his head.

Jenna turned to April. "This guy came up after the song and started trying to talk to me. Very weird. Cody dragged me away." Jenna shook her head then yanked on her shirt to see if she could smell anything.

The DJ's voice came over the speakers ending their conversation. "That's it for tonight's contestants. Our semi-finalist with the most applause for the night are Vicky Peterson, John Ford, and Cody Spencer. You guys come up on stage."

Cody's mouth dropped open. The other three yelled. He stepped out of the booth, motioned to the others, and jogged up to the stage. The DJ walked in front of all the finalists motioning down the line.

"We are going to determine who will get the cash award by your applause. Those of you who thought Vicky's spot-on rendition of "Titanium" was the best of the night, let me hear you."

A round of applause went up, and Cody figured he didn't stand a chance. He hung his head and put his hands behind his back.

"All right, those of you who think John's rapid-fire rendition of "I Want You" was your favorite, let me hear you." Another round of applause went up.

Cody chewed on his lip, feeling like the snakes that were in the pit of his stomach were about to crawl up his throat. He wanted the win, not only for the money, but to prove to his dad once and for all that all the hours he spent sitting in his room playing guitar weren't wasted. He glanced at the crowd from beneath his lashes. His pulse thumped in his ears and he closed his eyes.

"Those of you who think Cody's performances of "It's My Life" and "Mercy" were off the charts, let me hear you." The crowd erupted in a deafening roar. Cody jerked his head up, surprised at the volume. "We have a

winner! Cody Spencer, you just won five…hundred…
dollars."

Electricity shot through him, lighting up every cell
in his body, as he took in the moment. A grin spread
across his face. He patted his heart, lifted his hands, and
waved to the crowd who continued to cheer, then he ran
his hands down his face, still not sure he heard right.
The DJ handed him the cash and shook his hand.

As the roar died down, a voice came from the
crowd. "Hey, I'm a little short on cash for my tab."

Cody scanned the crowd and pointed at Joe, then
turned to see Jenna jumping up and down, beaming
from ear to ear.

Chapter Eleven

Cody tipped back his cup and let the last of his coffee trickle down his throat, trying to get enough caffeine in his bloodstream to wake him up. His years in the military trained his body to be used to the early hours, but those days had long gone, and his body evidently forgot.

It didn't help that all weekend long his mind kept playing Friday night over and over. Watching the crowd sing along with him and winning the contest had renewed his spirit. Jenna's smile and feeling her silky skin in his arms was icing on the cake.

Cody leaned over to place the cup under the counter. The door's chime caught his attention. There she was, dressed in black athletic shorts that fit snugly to her muscular legs and a pink and black tank that dipped low in front and hugged her waist, which accentuated her chest. Jenna resembled a decadent piece of candy that Cody couldn't wait to taste. From the curve of her lips down to her perfect butt, the minute that he laid eyes on her everything about her caused his heart to beat outside his chest and heat to pool in his gut.

"I'm here," she sang. Her merlot curls, in a high ponytail, danced with each step she took.

Oh, this is going to end bad. Very very bad. He stretched, trying to act nonchalant, except for the fact he couldn't wipe the smile from his face. The words his dad said played in his mind. *Keep it professional. Keep it professional. Keep it...damn, those eyes.* They seemed greener today. Dark lashes encircled them, and her brows continually gave away her thoughts.

The more he gazed at her, the more his body ignored his chants. He let out a breath, stood up from the stool, and clapped his hands together. "Are you ready?"

"I think so." Jenna took a deep breath and followed him into the gym.

Gesturing to a row of lockers, he instructed, "Go ahead and put your stuff in one of the lockers and I will meet you at the cardio area." Jenna trotted off and Cody made his way to the machines, thankful for the minute he had to calm his pulse and focus before she returned.

He handed her a small card when she stopped next to him. "This is your workout routine. It probably will make no sense to you now, but it will become clearer as we go through all of the pieces of equipment and program." He pointed to the card and kept talking. "This week we are going to get familiar with the equipment and the routine I have designed for you. We are not going to do all of the full sets and reps." He had completely stepped into his trainer presentation.

Jenna studied the card, then lifted her head with her lips pinched together. Noticing her amused expression, he stopped mid-speech and studied her. "What?"

"Nothing. You are just really cute when you go into trainer mode," she said smiling.

"Are you going to be one of *those* girls?" he said, crossing his arms. Jenna shook her head trying to hold back her smile. He narrowed his gaze, pretending to be irritated, but then smiled and continued. "Next week we will start the full program. There will be four days of training, each working different areas of the body, along with core exercises. We will be working the back and biceps today, then legs, chest and triceps, then hips and shoulders."

Cody stood at the treadmill with his hand on one of the handles. "I like to start all the training sessions with twenty minutes of cardio to get the muscles warmed up. I figured since you are a runner, you might feel comfortable on the treadmill. You can do intervals, if you like, or do the full twenty minutes. I also like the elliptical. It's easier on the lower joints. Do you have a preference?"

"Before we get started, I need to ask you a question." Her fingers threaded through her hair.

Cody tapped his hands on the bar of the treadmill. "Okay, shoot. Am I going too fast? If it's about the equipment or the program, I can—"

Jenna waved her hand. "No, no, everything is fine. I need to ask what you charge for your training." She stepped up on the treadmill and continued. "I've paid for the membership, but you never told me what you charge to do your personal training sessions."

His lips pressed together, trying to hide his smile. "Well, since you got me to sing Friday and I won a fistful of cash, let's call it even. I don't think you are going to need that many sessions before you can do it on your own anyway."

"Really? I mean, I don't want to take up your time, if you can be earning money training someone else."

"Oh, trust me, I don't have many people seeking me out to train them at five in the morning."

Jenna laughed. "Okay, if you are sure." She quickly scanned all the equipment and turned back to him. "I guess, until I feel comfortable running through the park again, I would choose the treadmill. So, how does this thing work?" She examined the digital display, then turned to Cody.

"Hold on to this bar." He tapped on the handgrips in the front then moved to the buttons. The belt moved and Jenna's feet stuttered. With the press of a button, her pace increased, and she fell into a comfortable stride. Her mahogany ponytail bounced behind her. Heat crawled up Cody's neck as Jenna's ivory cheeks bloomed into a dusty rose. He swallowed hard and focused on the equipment.

After a couple of minutes, he reduced the speed. "If you need to stop, hit this red button." The belt slowed to a stop, and she stepped off.

Cody pressed her card against his leg to write on it. "I'm keeping track of the settings and weights we work with."

Jenna followed him when he turned and moved to another piece of equipment.

"Next we build your core. We will do this exercise every session." He stopped and rested his hand on the armrest of the equipment.

"This is for your abdominal muscles." Cody placed his arms on the pads, raised his body into position, then moved his legs, showing her the different exercises. Once he had gone through all the positions, he moved and let her try. "Put your arms on the pads and lift your body up."

Jenna followed his instructions.

His hands gently moved her legs to different

positions. Each time his fingers skimmed her soft skin, lightning pulsated down his spine. *Keep it professional.* Cody closed his eyes briefly, trying to steer his mind away from the thoughts he was having. His body wasn't listening. He cleared his throat and pointed to her card.

"Once you have completed a set of twelve on each exercise," Cody motioned, and she followed him to the next piece of equipment, "you will work on pull-ups with this machine." Cody demonstrated the exercise. When he released, he caught the smolder in Jenna's eyes and knew she was probably having the same hard time focusing he was, which made trying to keep it professional virtually impossible. The corners of his mouth lifted into a quick smile, then Cody positioned Jenna on the bar. He figured he would have to give her a little support, but he was wrong. To his surprise, she completed three with no assistance.

"Wow, I'm impressed." He raised his hand up and gave her a high five. "You said you thought you were weak, but most girls don't have the upper body strength to do one pull up, let alone three."

Jenna gave him a sassy smirk and flexed her arm to show him her bicep. "I guess ranching is good for something."

Cody's cheeks puffed with air, and he let it release slowly. *That sass is going to be my undoing.* "I would have to say so." He turned his attention to the next area before he spontaneously combusted. "Okay, we are going to do stretches next to finish getting warmed up." They strolled over to a small open area with thick mats."

"So, have you spent your winnings yet?" Jenna asked wiping her brow with a towel.

"Not yet, but I have it burning a hole in my pocket," he said with a smile. "I still can't believe I won."

"You were incredible. You seriously haven't performed in front of an audience before? I mean, you seemed so comfortable up there."

"No. Never. It was such a rush seeing all the faces singing with me. I had so much fun."

"Me, too."

"Oh, and I got a call from the manager yesterday asking if I would come back and sing at their next Karaoke Night."

"How cool! You will have to tell me when so I can go cheer you on." He nodded and set his water bottle down on a table next to the mat. "And I definitely want to hear you play your guitar sometime," she added.

Cody's face filled with heat. His mom had been the only one who had ever listened to him play other than Joe, and that was an accident. "I told you I'm not very good."

The plastic chair chirped as he pulled it out and sat down.

Jenna lowered her chin, darted her eyes to him, and scowled. She sat down in the chair next to him and put her hands on her knees. "And I told you, let me be the judge of that."

He rolled his eyes, and then changed the subject by pointing to her card. "Is this making sense to you?"

Jenna's attention remained on the card. Cody studied her face until she let her eyes drift back to his. "I think so." Every time she spoke, he could feel his breath catch in his throat. There was nothing he could do. He had been completely swept up in her spell. Her hand moved to her hair to tuck some stray strands behind her ear. She was sitting so close he could smell the lemony scent of her shampoo. Cody felt his body come to life and he tugged on the legs of his shorts.

"Okay let's go to the mats." He walked her through each motion before they moved on to the different exercises with the equipment and free weights.

Once they had finished, Jenna retrieved her stuff from the locker and headed to the counter where Cody had positioned himself behind the computer. He caught her out of the corner of his eye and took in a shaky breath, noticing the sweat beads glistening on her face and chest. Clearing his throat, he returned his gaze back to the computer. "So, what do you think?"

"I think you are going to whip my butt into shape in no time." Jenna wiped her forehead with the back of her hand and took a sip of water from her bottle.

He captured her gaze and smiled. "Well, from the looks of things, you are in pretty good shape already."

"Oh, so you noticed?" she teased and shimmied her shoulders playfully.

His pulse pounded in his neck and heat blasted into his face. *If you only knew.* "No," he lied. "I mean, the weight you were lifting…" His chin dropped knowing he couldn't recover, and he squeezed his eyes shut.

Jenna snickered and then broke into laughter. "You stepped right into it."

The way her face lit up, and the easiness of her laughter, completely consumed his heart and pushed him dangerously close to losing control of his actions.

His eyes narrowed. "You are in so much trouble." Cody tore a piece of paper off the scratchpad, wadded it up, and threw it at her. Jenna ducked while continuing to double over in fits of laughter.

After dodging a few more wayward wads of paper, she put her hands up in surrender and fanned herself, trying to settle down. "Okay, okay."

He pressed his lips together trying not to smile.

"So, tomorrow same time?" she asked breathlessly.

"Same time. Be ready."

"Cool." Jenna held up her hand, and Cody gave her a high five.

Once Jenna was out of view, Cody let out a long breath, wondering if he would ever be able to keep his mind and body in control while training her. Somehow, he hadn't anticipated the magnitude of the reaction he would have around her when he discussed the training. He was right telling Joe "He was in trouble with this one." He was, and there wasn't anything he could do about it.

Within a few minutes, the door chimed, and Cody peered up to see his dad enter, carrying a bag. "What did you bring me today?"

"Breakfast sandwiches from Arnie's."

"Did you get the Jalapeno tots?"

"You know I did."

"What did their sign say today?"

Arnie's was one of the most popular places to eat in town, not only for the food, but for their crazy sidewalk signs.

"Eat here, or we'll both starve."

Cody chuckled. "They never disappoint. I wish I knew where they came up with all their signs."

"And they never repeat," his dad responded. "At least I've never noticed it if they have."

Cody hopped off the stool and headed for the

tables. They unpacked the sack and sat down. "Didn't see you this weekend?"

"I did some work around the house, got the yard mowed." Todd tossed one of the tots in his mouth. "How did your date go?"

The question immediately set Cody on edge. Something told him the conversation was about to turn ugly. He kept his tone light and forced a smile.

"It wasn't a date. I told you, Joe and I met Jenna and her friend April up there." His mind suddenly flashed on her expression when she wrapped her arms around his neck after he sang.

"Doesn't matter how you got there. I still think it's a bad idea for you to hang out with her. Hell, I'm being investigated again because of her."

Cody's muscles tightened. How could he blame her? She was brutally attacked.

His agitation rose. "It's not like Jenna asked to be attacked, Dad. It wasn't her fault. It was the jackass that attacked her."

Todd quieted his voice. "I know it wasn't her fault, but that still doesn't change the fact that our business and employees are being subject to an investigation because she was attacked, and I think it's a bad idea for you to get involved with her."

"I am involved already because I rescued her."

Todd motioned with his hand. "And that is where it should have ended."

"But it didn't. What did you want me to say? She asked if we had self-defense classes. Did you want me to tell her, yes, we do, but not for you? You, yourself gave her a discount. Jenna is a client, like everyone else, and as for the *date*, it was innocent. We were just out blowing off some steam. Nothing happened."

"You say that, but now you are training her."

"She signed up to be trained before we went out."

"Cody, don't be stupid. The writing is on the wall. She has a crush on you."

"So, what do you want me to do? She asked me to train her so she could get some exercise until she felt comfortable running again."

"You already accepted and signed her up, so you might as well train her, but you are playing with fire. She is a beautiful young woman, and she obviously likes you. I'm worried you are digging a hole for yourself, and if anything happens, it might not only be you who gets thrown in it."

Cody's teeth clenched. His dad's comments had a kernel of truth to them, but he was sick of him always playing the "you screwed up" card. He tried to do the right thing, and his dad still made it sound like he was nothing but trouble. He was fighting a losing battle if he didn't play by his dad's rules.

"I know the consequences. You have made that crystal clear. But again, I am keeping it professional. Friday was simply a night out, nothing else."

"Good." Todd took another bite of his sandwich. "So, you said you went to TopHops?"

"Yeah. Jenna was right. The place has been completely updated. It hasn't changed much from the outside, but inside was totally remodeled. It's a microbrewery now, and they have a great pale ale."

Cody thought about the night and the extra cash in his wallet. He contemplated continuing the story. Todd's expression told him he didn't care. But he was proud of his winnings. "They had a karaoke contest."

He paused a beat. "Jenna talked me into entering it." Cody again paused to see how his dad would respond and caught his raised eyebrow, but he still didn't speak. "I won." He tried to suppress his grin but failed. "Five hundred bucks."

Todd nodded lightly, pinched his lips together, then wiped his mouth with his napkin. "Way to go," Todd said, somewhat sarcastically. "That's probably more money than most musicians make in a month trying to have a career in that field."

Cody took a deep breath. His grin faded. Nothing had changed. He didn't understand why his dad was so against his passion for music, or anything that made him happy for that matter. "They want me to come back in two weeks to be the opener for the next contest."

His dad barely acknowledged the comment, and it wasn't worth continuing down that road, so Cody took a bite of his sandwich.

"Well, keep in mind, you are bound for the police academy, not Nashville…if you can ever get the assault charge dismissed."

The growl in his dad's voice caused a rock to form in Cody's stomach, as well as a stabbing pain in his chest from his dad's obvious insult. Cody had always respected him, but he had had enough of feeling like he was a constant disappointment. His dad would not approve of the decisions that he'd recently made, but it was time to step out from under his shadow.

He leaned back in his chair and crossed his arms. "I decided not to go to the academy." The words spilled out easier than he thought, and it felt strangely freeing.

Todd stopped mid bite of his sandwich and threw it down. Cody finally had his full attention.

"You what?" Anger filled Todd's voice.

"I'm not going to the police academy," he said with more confidence.

Todd glared at him and crossed his arms. "That's the most asinine decision you will ever make. What do you think you are going to do, run the gym? It's great for a single person, but you can't make enough money here to support a family."

Cody sat up and snagged a tater tot. "No, actually, I am studying to become a paramedic. I've already started classes."

"What made you decide to go down that road? Oh, wait, let me guess. It was that red headed girl wasn't it?"

"No, it wasn't Jenna, Dad. It was Sergeant Gallagher."

"So how did he change your mind?" Todd let out an exasperated breath.

"I told you, he let me ride along on a couple of his shifts to give me a good idea of what is involved in the job." Cody took another bite of his sandwich and wiped his mouth with his napkin. "I respect the time you put in as a police officer, but I don't think it's what I want to do."

"And what makes you think being a paramedic is what you want to do?"

Cody straightened in his chair, resolved to the idea that his dad would not be on board with any step he took away from his direction for his life.

"The day Jenna was attacked I watched the paramedics and EMTs work on her. It fascinated me. I sat in the ambulance, and there was something about it that felt right. I like the idea of helping people who are sick or hurt. When I rode along with the sergeant, most of the calls were silent alarms or barking dogs. I think I would get bored. I feel like my time could be better served as a paramedic."

Todd leveled his eyes at Cody but sat in silence for a minute. "Fine. But I don't think you know the half of what you are getting in to. You never were that good at school. I hope you can handle those classes." Todd picked up his trash and stood up. "And don't come crying to me the first time you aren't able to save a child's life." He dropped his trash in the can and turned to walk away.

"I promise I won't."

****

Cody fought to keep his focus on the discussion of the biology class Wednesday evening, but sitting next to Jenna and the thought of what was planned after class made it virtually impossible.

If he thought day one training with Jenna was hard, day two was ten times worse, and tonight they were kicking it up a few notches. Everything about Jenna, from the way she filled out her spandex, to her determination during training, to her infectious laugh, made his temperature rise along with other body parts. Not to mention the complete meltdown his body had every time her face flushed from the heat.

Jenna's hair was down tonight, falling over one shoulder of her plain white fitted T-shirt. She barely had any make up on, just a bit of mascara and lip gloss. She didn't need any. Her face was flawless. Jenna stood, and Cody got the full view of her fringed blue jean cut offs. He bit down on his lip, trying to will the thoughts he was having away.

The more Cody thought about it, the more he wondered if teaching her wrestling moves was such a good idea. The line between professional and personal relationship had become razor edge thin and was steadily disintegrating. But he couldn't call it off. He needed her help with biology if he stood any chance at becoming a paramedic.

Peering over at Jenna, he watched as she gathered her binder and book.

"Are you ready?" Jenna asked as she slung her purse across her body.

Cody stood and adjusted his shorts. "As I'll ever be. Are you? Remember, I need an A in this class."

Their words echoed as they stepped into the hallway. "I think you will do fine. You probably don't even need my help."

"Trust me I do. I had a one-track mind in school. I was an athlete."

They exited the building and headed for the parking lot.

Jenna searched for her truck and then motioned with her hand. "I'm over there. Do you want to follow me?"

"Yeah, give me a minute, and I will pull up." Cody jogged off in the opposite direction while she headed for her truck. He hopped into his Jeep, backed out, and pulled up behind her beat up silver ford.

Chapter Twelve

The pink and purple sky was filling with stars as they arrived at the small farmhouse. Cody crawled out of his Jeep and took in his surroundings. The house was in decent shape but needed a coat of paint. A large porch spanned the front. To one side was a picture window with a planter box filled with colorful flowers. On the porch were two hanging baskets filled with ferns, a dark stained rocking chair, and a floral wreath that hung between two windows. Cody could imagine Jenna sitting in the rocking chair sipping on some sweet tea. It all seemed so comfortable.

An outcropping of pine trees filled one side off the back where it sat at the top of a hill. The view took in miles of a colorful valley. He could see the last of the sunset over the pine trees from the side of the house. "Wow, how did you find this place? The view is spectacular."

"You should see the sunrise!"

Cody remembered the comment she made to him a few days back and he decided it was time for a little repayment. "Is that an invitation?" he said, donning a wolfish grin.

Jenna turned with her mouth gaped open and swatted him across the arm.

Cody recoiled. "What? You stepped right into it."

Her brows lowered, but a knowing grin slowly

spread across her face, and she released a soft laugh. "Actually, this was April's grandma's place."

He surveyed the old architecture. "So, why didn't April take it?"

Jenna scoffed. "Have you met April?"

Cody nodded, but still didn't quite understand.

"Let's just say, rustic farmhouse wasn't quite April's taste."

"Yeah, but I mean, April could probably live here rent free." His hand ran along the railing, and he plucked at a piece of chipped paint.

"I know, or she could have bought it outright. I don't get it either." Jenna bounded up the stairs. "It's perfect. It sits on fifteen acres. I would buy this place in a heartbeat if I had the money." She dug for her keys in her purse. "But you should see April's place. It is high-end chic. Of course, I'm sure she pays out the nose for it, but it fits her to a tee."

The door opened with a loud squeak, and Tucker came barreling to her legs. "Let me take him out really quick. There is some iced tea in the fridge, and glasses are on the left of the sink."

Cody sat his book and spiral on the island and retrieved the pitcher from the fridge. Spying the cabinet with the glasses, he grabbed two and filled both while his eyes took in the area.

The place smelled of apples and had a warmth to it that reflected Jenna's personality. It wasn't huge, but it was laid out well. The walls were painted in a light taupe with white trim and decorated with brightly colored accents. To the left of the kitchen was the dining room, which held a white pedestal wooden table, with a dark stained top, and four ladder-back chairs. To the right sat the living room. A thick, off white, fuzzy rug covered the floor in front of a navy micro suede sofa. Yellow accent pillows and a red fuzzy blanket sat at one end. Off to one side of the sofa was a small table with a lamp. On the other was an over-stuffed navy and tan pin-striped chair, with a matching ottoman. Cody sat down on the sofa and placed his glass on the side table.

"Did you get something to drink?" He heard Jenna's voice from behind him along with the click of Tucker's paws.

"Yeah, and I left yours on the island." Tucker suddenly appeared and placed his head on Cody's lap, then his paws, and before he knew it, he had all sixty pounds of white fur in his lap.

"Hello."

Tucker gave him a couple of sloppy kisses while Cody rubbed the dog's scruff.

"Thank you." Jenna came around the back of the sofa and laughed at the sight. "Tucker, get down." The dog gave her a woeful expression but slowly lowered himself to the ground and disappeared up the hallway. Cody dusted his shirt and shorts. "Sorry about that. He seems to really like you."

"The feeling is mutual. I would have a dog in a heartbeat if our lease would allow it."

Jenna sat down in the chair across from the sofa and folded her legs under her. "So, do you want to work on biology first or...*wrestling*?" She playfully growled and scrunched her face.

Cody chuckled from her comical voice and expression. "I guess wrestling, since there is no assignment for next week, except that quiz. But can I thumb through your notes?" he requested sheepishly.

"Sure, but if you want, I have a printer, and I can make copies for you."

"That would be awesome."

She rose from the chair. "While I do that, why don't you set up the living room."

"You got it." Cody's heart rate increased with the thought of what was about to take place. He pushed the chair and ottoman back, followed by the coffee table, clearing off the rug. After moving the side table, as if on cue, Tucker appeared, lay down next to Cody, and pushed a toy in his direction. Cody grasped the toy and waved it in Tucker's direction until he latched onto the other end. The tug-of-war match went on for a couple of minutes, until Cody relented with a rub through the dog's fur. Jenna returned to see Tucker on his back, with his tongue hanging out the side of his mouth, and Cody sitting cross-legged with a smile.

"I think you have made a friend for life." Jenna giggled and held up the papers. "I'm going to put the notes at the front of your spiral.

"Perfect." Cody continued to scratch Tucker's belly until she returned.

"Okay, Tucker, enough for now." Jenna tapped the big dog's collar and he sat up, then slowly stood. She ushered him to his bed and then returned.

"I honestly think Tucker understands every word you are saying. I've never seen a dog respond to their owner the way he does to you."

"In a way, I think Tucker knows we saved him. He was pretty banged up when he was brought in. To be honest, there was a point when we weren't sure if he was going to survive. But the minute he opened his eyes after surgery and I saw him, we connected. When I brought him home, it was like Tucker knew this was where he belonged. But what shocked me the most was how he reacted when I was attacked." Her voice trailed off, and Cody saw a spark of fear in her expression. He could tell the ghosts of the past had paid a visit.

She waved her hand in the air. "Okay, I think I'm ready."

Cody's muscles tightened. He could feel his heart pulsing in his neck, and he wondered how she would handle the training. She was obviously still affected by the attack.

"First, have a seat on the rug with me."

Jenna sat down and ran her fingers through her hair, gathering it in one hand. She grabbed a hair band from her wrist, wrapped it around her hair, and secured it in a messy bun. Cody couldn't pull his attention away from the whole process. Her hair was filled with natural curls and waves and was the color of red wine. It had fascinated him since the first day he met her.

"What?" She grinned, noticing him staring.

"Sorry, you just did that so quickly," Cody lied. He was totally lost in his own fantasies of running his fingers through those deep auburn curls. Breathing deep, he knew it was time. "All right, I need to address something before we get started." He chewed on his bottom lip and locked eyes with her. "I have to be honest. I came awfully close to calling this off. The more I thought about it, the more I wondered if you were ready to do this…or me for that matter."

"Why?" Jenna questioned, pulling at the rug, her eyes fixed on him.

"Well, it hasn't been that long since you were

attacked, and the last thing I want to do is reopen the wound. Plus, I have never taught wrestling moves to a woman." He gazed at her from beneath his lashes. "Let's just say, the close proximity of the bodies can do things." He swallowed hard and waited for her to react, but her expression didn't change. "Just please let me know if I make you uncomfortable."

She pinched her lips together. "I promise I will."

Cody stood up and held his hands out to help Jenna up. "First, I am going to show you the takedown. I think you have already worked on fighting out of this, so we aren't going to spend a lot of time on it. But I do want you to show me later what you have learned. Stand with your back to me."

Jenna timidly turned to face away from him. Cody scooted in behind her. Her body stiffened. Slowly grabbing her, he swept his leg in front, causing her to lose her balance. His arm held her tight, so she didn't fall. "See how easily I could have taken you to the ground. It's all about balance and shifting weight." She nodded.

Cody could feel Jenna's breath becoming shorter, and his mind drifted. She fit so perfectly in his arms. Her skin was so soft and smelled like lemons and lavender. *How am I going to get through this?* She shifted her weight and his mind cleared.

"Before we go any further, show me some techniques you learned if you are attacked from behind in a standing position."

Jenna pretended to stomp Cody's foot, elbow him in the stomach, and then punch him in the throat.

"That's good, but you have to remember, if you get in a real situation, you have to do it with force." He wrapped his arm around her again. "Okay, now we are going to go all the way to the ground. When you get down on your stomach, I want you to wrap your hands around the back of your neck. That's the first rule. Protect your neck, because it is extremely easy for an assailant to break your neck in that position. When you feel my weight on top of you, try to pull your knees to your stomach. Got it?"

She nodded.

His arm dropped. "You aren't talking. Are you sure you are okay?"

Jenna turned to face him. "I'm good." Her voice sounded fine, but her eyes told him a different story.

"You tell me the minute you feel uncomfortable." Cody reached his hand around her shoulders, swept his leg in front of her and slowly let her fall to the ground. Jenna moved her hands awkwardly to grasp her neck. He sat on her legs and leaned against her putting his hands on her shoulders. Her body shifted once and then again. After a couple more times her legs flailed.

Her breath came in short pants. "Get off me. Get off. Get off." The panic increased with each word.

Cody moved off her onto the rug. Jenna rolled over, propped her knees up, and draped her arm across her face. He could see her shoulders vibrating and then heard her sniffle. This was exactly what he didn't want to happen.

Cody wrapped his arms around his knees and bowed his head on top of them. Tucker appeared and licked Jenna's hand covering her face, then moved over to Cody's hand, then back to her, licking her face. "I know, buddy, I tried to warn her."

Jenna turned her face away from the dog. Tucker

moved in closer, thoroughly covering her face with wet, sloppy licks. She pushed him away and sat up. "Tucker, back to your bed." She motioned with her hand, and Tucker padded off. Wiping her face of her tears and dog slobber, she softly said, "I want to try again."

Cody blinked, "You what?" certain he heard wrong.

"I want to try again."

"Jenna, I don't think that is a good idea," he said quietly, running his hand through his hair.

Jenna's face was streaked with tears. "I need to. I can't let that guy get in my head. He can't win. I need to do it again."

Cody heard the desperation in her tone. "I get it. But maybe we should wait and try again next week. Just slow it down. I told you, the last thing I want to do is upset you."

"I know that, and you aren't the one upsetting me. I appreciate what you are doing, and that is why I am counting on you to get me past the fear now."

"Did anyone ever tell you, you have a stubborn streak?"

"My dad, just about every day," she huffed. "Please, I need to do this."

Cody stared at her. Her tear-filled eyes ate at him. A lump caught in his throat. He wanted nothing more than to wipe away her tears and kiss those pouty lips, to make her forget about the attack. The training would do nothing but stir up the memories, but he could tell she wasn't going to take no for an answer.

Cody shook his head. "I have a feeling I am going to regret this, but all right." He slapped his hands to his legs, stood up, and motioned for her to give him her hands. "How much do you hate this guy?"

"Dumb question," Jenna snapped back, irritated.

"Use that when you are on the ground. I am that guy, and you aren't scared. You are angry. Remember, when you go to the ground, cover your neck. When you feel my weight, pop your legs under you. If you can't get both, get one then the other. Got it?" His eyes studied her, and she nodded. "Are you sure you want to do this?"

Jenna's lips pressed together. "Yes."

"All right. Turn your back to me." He again squeezed up behind her and wrapped his arm around her shoulders. His foot swept in front of her, and he slowly lowered her to the ground. This time she immediately put her hands around the back of her neck. He shifted his weight onto her and placed his hands on her shoulders. She wiggled her hips trying to bring her knees under her but was still struggling.

"Fight for it, Jenna. Bring one leg up," he demanded. He heard a growl in the back of her throat. Slowly, she scooted one leg and then the other up under her, and Cody's hands went down beside her. "Yes. Now, do you see how you threw me off balance? Reach around my arm and pull it to you and roll out." She followed his instructions, yanked him down to the ground, then rolled over and sat up. Cody did the same.

"See, it's all about throwing the attacker off balance. Once you get your legs up, you have shifted their weight, and they are forced into a different position. Lie down on the floor again." She did what he instructed, and he slowly moved on top of her. "It doesn't matter where I sit, if I am above your hips or below, or even if I have my body lying on you, if you can get your legs under you, you can throw me off balance. Try again."

This time when he straddled her, she moved her legs quickly under her and reached around to find his arm, pulling it in and flipping him over. Jenna stood up quickly and gazed down at him, still lying on the floor.

A smile crossed her face. "How was that?"

"Better. We will continue to work on it and add some other moves later. Do you want to try again, or move to the next step?" Cody shuddered, even before the questions were completely out of his mouth. *Why did I even ask?* He knew what her answer was going to be. He was exhausted from trying to keep his mind cleared of the thoughts of them rolling around. "Or are you tired?" He sat up, and she had disappeared from his view. When she reappeared, she held both of their teas and passed his off to him.

Jenna took a sip of hers. "I'm good with moving on, if you are."

Of course you are. No, I'm not, honestly. Dreading it actually. My body can't take much more of this. Why did I think this was a good idea?

She set her tea on the side table and held her hand out to grasp his glass. "What's the next step?"

Cody felt the warmth of her body as Jenna sat down next to him. He let out a long breath and leveled his eyes with hers. "This is the attack from the front position."

Fear sparked in Jenna's expression and her smile disappeared.

"I know that look. We can wait," he said quickly, hoping she would take the hint.

"No!" Jenna's tone was laced with anger. "I want

to do this. I need to know that I have the ability to fight back if it ever happened again."

Cody's thoughts raced again to the comment from Mitch about the attacker knowing her routine, possibly knowing where she lived, and could strike again with worse consequences. His mind flashed on Brant whispering in her ear at the bar. He knew he needed to help her, but these moves were going to take every ounce of self-control he could muster to not embarrass himself.

"I've got one technique I will teach you tonight. It's a great wrestling move and could do some serious damage to an attacker. Lie down on the floor on your back with your knees propped up." Jenna followed Cody's directions. The mere sight of her lying there made his insides quake. He rubbed his face trying to stay focused. "I will go through every move first, so hopefully that will dispel some of the fear."

"Yeah, I think that will help."

"First, I am going to position myself inside your legs, then bend forward to grasp your neck. You will have two moves you will make with your hands, and three moves with your legs. Once you have done those moves, you should be able to throw me easily. Okay?"

"I'm ready." She let out a long, slow breath. Her lips pursed, and his eyes zeroed in. The rising urge to kiss her was almost unbearable.

Cody spread her knees apart and slowly moved his body into position. Staying focused on her face, he made sure she was doing okay. She fixated on the ceiling with a sober expression. He took a deep breath and leaned forward, putting his hands on either side of her.

The moment Cody got into position he knew he was in trouble. His heart pounded. His mind took off into the far reaches of his fantasies, wanting to pull the band from her hair, fist her mahogany locks, and kiss her like there was no tomorrow. He had lost all control, and his body responded. Closing his eyes, he sat back on his butt and wrapped his arms around his knees. Jenna sat up quickly.

Her brows drew down in confusion. "I'm good, why did you stop?"

Cody shook his head. "I'm not. Give me a minute," he huffed. His dad's words flashed through his head about keeping it professional, but at this point, he knew he was losing the battle. There was no way he was going to be able to continue the training. He averted his eyes trying desperately to regain control when she did the unthinkable. Jenna tugged the hair band from her hair and ran her fingers through her curls again.

Irritation filled him. "Do you have to do that right now?"

"Do what?" She continued to gather her curls into her hands.

He dropped his head to his knees, took a deep breath, and waved his hand not wanting to explain.

After she had reset her hair, Jenna sat next to him. "You ready to go again?"

Cody rolled his eyes and threw his hands up knowing he was beaten. "I guess."

Jenna lay back on the floor with her knees propped up, and Cody scooted in. Her gaze moved up to the ceiling. He slowly lowered himself placing his hands at her shoulders. "You doing okay?"

Her response was quick. "Yeah. Now what?"

"I am going to put my hands around your throat, and you are going to reach across and grip my forearm." Cody slowly moved his hands, and Jenna reacted to his actions. "Great, now take your other hand and go across to my opposite shoulder." She responded as instructed. "Perfect, now put your foot at the bend in my hip and push down while bringing your other leg all the way up under my armpit, moving your body perpendicular to mine." She moved her body into position. "Okay, now bring the other leg all the way around to the other side of my head. Grip my arm with both hands while pushing down with your legs and push me off." Jenna smirked slightly but did as he instructed, and Cody dropped to his back. "See what you have done?" You trapped my arm and have it in a position to where you could snap it in a heartbeat."

"Oh, that's cool. Can we do it again?" Her face lit up with excitement.

He sat up. "Do you think you got it?"

"Yeah." A smile slowly spread across her face. "This is kind of fun."

"For you maybe. It's killing me."

"What's wrong?"

"Never mind." Cody patted the floor and Jenna moved into position. This time he moved a bit quicker, scooting in and placing his hands at her shoulders. Her gaze drifted. As his hands moved to her throat, her hands moved swiftly through the motions. She hit each position perfectly, rendering him immobile quickly. "That was great! Are you sure you haven't wrestled before?"

"Only cows," she said with a giggle. "Once more?"

"I think I'm done." Cody sat back with his knees

again to his chest.

"Please, one more time, and then I promise we can stop."

"You are killing me over here."

She batted her eyes. "Please?"

Cody shook his head. "One more, and that's it."

He patted the floor again and she moved into position. Pulling her knees apart, he scooted in close. His body slowly extended over hers as his hands hit both sides of her shoulders. She let out a sigh, and he immediately searched for fear in her expression. But her eyes weren't filled with fear or staring off emotionless as before. This time they locked on him and were filled with a fire that engulfed him.

Jenna's chest pressed against him as he tried to fight the rising heat. The craving enveloped him like a fog rolling in. A guilty conscience recited his dad's warning, *keep it professional,* but his heart said otherwise. Before he could stop himself, his hand reached up and moved some wayward curls from her face. She wet her lips as his finger traced the edge of her jaw. His mouth hovered inches away from hers. The desire in her eyes made his body shudder. "Oh hell, I give up."

Cody's lips carefully brushed against Jenna's, tenderly nuzzling, before slowly taking it deeper. Soft. Her lips were so soft, exactly like he thought they would be. The touch of her fingers as they wrapped around his neck set off a sizzle of electricity between them. His tongue softly touched her bottom lip and he waited. Hoping. When her lips parted, he got his first taste of her. Sweet and lemony, remnants of the tea. Wrapping his hand behind her neck, he tugged her to him as he sat back while his kisses traveled down her neck. One hand tightened around her waist while the other moved to her hair, releasing the band and letting her long silky strands fall. His fingers dug into the auburn curls. A quiet moan escaped from her as his mouth captured hers, and their tongues brushed against each other. Curls wrapped around his fingers like silk ribbons. Cody backed away just enough for his lips to hover over hers.

"God, I have wanted to do that all night," he said, his voice rumbling from his chest.

Her hands dug into his shirt and she whispered, "I've wanted to do this," pulling him in for another kiss.

Chapter Thirteen

Jenna got out of her truck and quickly turned to make sure Tucker's leash was free so he could hop out. She was curious what Cody was up to since he texted her late last night. He told her to come at six-fifteen instead of five-fifteen and bring Tucker with her to the workout. Not that she could sleep at all, with so much going through her mind.

That kiss left Jenna's soul aching in a wonderful way. The fantasy she had been having continuously for the past month had come true. Her whole body zinged every time she laid eyes on Cody. Last night, in his cream colored, short sleeved, gauze shirt and tan cargo shorts, her body felt like it was about to turn to ash. Every time Cody put his body next to hers, she could feel the ripple of his muscles and smell his chocolatey cologne. More than once, Jenna was mere seconds from pressing her lips to his. But when Cody finally kissed her, it was like he had drained all the energy from her with one touch of his lips. Her body was heavy and limp when he pulled away. He was so gentle and so sweet and so...*why did he stop?* She wanted more, but being the perfect gentleman, he made an exit before things went any further. When he walked out the door, she was surprised, thankful, and disappointed all at the same time. She didn't think she was misreading his feelings. Cody made the first move, but she would give anything to know what he was thinking.

Maybe things would be clearer if they were able to spend more time together this weekend. That's if he didn't have to work. Jenna opened the door to the gym, and her knees nearly buckled. Cody's smiling face peeked up above the computer.

He stepped out from behind the counter and immediately knelt to scratch Tucker's face. Tucker bounced his paws off the cement and put them on his shoulders, then gave him a sloppy wet kiss.

She tugged on Tucker's leash. "All right, Tucker, you have given enough kisses."

Cody stood up. "Good morning." His dimples deepened as a bashful smile slowly captured his face, making his eyes twinkle. His hand glided along her arm sending goosebumps tingling over her skin.

"So, what do you have planned for me and the beast?" she questioned, returning the smile.

"Well, I had a thought. You said you enjoyed running through the park with Tucker, but you didn't feel comfortable doing it yet. The trail is about three miles, and I thought maybe we could run it together. That way you would feel safe, get your cardio in, and Tucker would get his run. He can chill in the office while we go through the rest of your workout."

Her heart soared with the revelation. "That would be perfect."

"So, are you ready?"

"Let me put my stuff in the locker and I will be." Jenna headed off to one side of the gym.

"I will let Joe know," Cody said, while he took off in the other direction. When she got back to the counter, he was already there. "Let's go." He put his hand on her back and guided her and Tucker out the door. They crossed the street and she stopped abruptly. "Are you okay?" Concern filled his tone.

Jenna gazed up at the lofty pines, closed her eyes, and took a deep breath. Instead of making her afraid, the smell of pine tar made her feel home again. She opened her eyes and turned to him. "Yes. I'm good." She grinned and stared directly in his eyes. "Thank you so much for doing this. You have no idea how much I needed it." She was elated to be back in her favorite place, feeling safe, feeling happy.

The sky was barely starting to change from the purple hues to the blues and corals of the sunrise. Pulling a flashlight from his pocket, Cody flipped it on to add light to their path. A twinge shot through her when they jogged through the spot of the attack, but as quickly as it came, it disappeared. Jenna turned and smiled at him wondering if he really understood the magnitude of what he had done. The guilt had plagued her, not being able to take Tucker out to run. It was evident he loved it and needed it. This was huge.

Cody jerked his head. "Come on, I have something I want to show you. It's a little detour." They took off through the woods, off the path. "Have you been out this way before?"

"No." A small flicker of nervousness crept into her chest. *Why is he going this way?* Though there wasn't a designated path, it was obvious this little detour had been traveled many times. Tucker sniffed the leaves and sticks along the way.

"Watch your step," he warned. They headed down a slight hill onto a lower path and switchback. As an opening in the pine trees appeared, there was the sound of rushing water, and it piqued her curiosity. The sky had turned to a beautiful pink and purple, and the sun sent glints of sunlight through the trees.

Cody pointed without saying a word. Straight ahead, amidst a grove of pine trees, was a cave with greenery dangling over the mouth and water spilling down the front and sides. The sight made her stop dead in her tracks and took her breath away. She had lived in Dalton her whole life and never knew about it.

"How, how did you find this?" Jenna held her fingers up to her mouth trying not to let her emotions show. But the shakiness of her voice gave her away, and Cody slid his arm around her.

"Actually, Joe told me about it. He has explored every inch of this park."

"I can't believe this was here and I never knew about it. It's absolutely amazing." Taking in a breath, Jenna pushed up on her toes and kissed Cody's cheek. "Thank you for bringing me here. I have always thought this park was beautiful, but this…this is breathtaking."

Cody snuggled Jenna in close, placing a kiss on her forehead, then brushing his lips against her cheek before bringing his lips to hers. The kiss was chaste at first, and Jenna felt a tingle travel from her toes to the top of her head. But when his tongue teased her lips for more and she surrendered, the tingle turned into a storm, raining sparks of electricity all over her. Pulling away, Cody kissed her forehead once again, and his arm pressed her to his chest.

"I'm glad you liked my surprise."

They stood in silence watching the sun crest the horizon, sending beams of silver light through the white puffy clouds. With her head against his chest, she could hear the thumping of his heart and feel the strength of his arms around her. Somehow, it felt so normal and comfortable. "I don't think 'like' is the appropriate word," Jenna said scanning the surroundings.

Grabbing his hand, she guided him up the trail to a clearing closer to the falls. Tucker found a small pool to sneak a drink before he ventured off with his nose to the ground. Cody pulled her in close again, holding her hand up to his chest.

Jenna lifted her chin. "Close your eyes and listen." When Cody's eyes closed, she breathed deep and closed hers, listening to the sound of the flow of the falls. "It's so calming."

Tears wet her face, but her smile never left. She opened her eyes to see Cody staring at her. He brushed his thumb across her cheek, wiping away the tears. "I am so happy," she whispered. "I can't believe we are the only ones here."

"It's still pretty early. But honestly, I have been out here during the day, and I've never seen anyone else."

Jenna moved down the rocks to examine the cave. "Do you know how far back the cave goes?"

"I've only explored it from the outside. I know it's deep enough to sit down in."

"It would be cool to explore inside."

"Maybe we can pretty soon." Dragging his teeth across his bottom lip, Cody winked, then drew Jenna in close again. A low groan crept from his throat. "I guess we need to get back so you aren't late for work."

"You're probably right." Her eyes peered up at him. "I could stay here like this all day."

"I thought you would like it."

"More than you know." She continued to gaze at the falls as it glittered from the sunlight. "I don't know anything that would be better than this." In one fell swoop, Cody had managed to turn Jenna's place of fear, to a place of wonder.

After several minutes they headed back up the hill at a good pace. Tucker continued to stay at Jenna's side as they turned onto the park trail and jogged through the park.

"So, if I remember correctly, you said you have never ridden a horse."

"Nope, never have. Why?"

"I thought if you weren't doing anything on Saturday, maybe you would like to come out to the ranch and go riding with me."

"That would be great." His body suddenly stiffened and Cody slowed to a stop. A wave of panic crossed his face. "Wait. Would I be meeting your dad and brother?" His breaths were labored, and he set his hands on his hips. "This isn't a setup, is it?"

Jenna laughed. "Well, no. I mean, my dad and brother might be there, but I was just planning to go out there to ride, so I thought maybe you would like to join me."

Cody chuckled. "All right, as long as it's only to ride horses."

Jenna backhanded him in a playful way. His eyes twinkled then he smiled. They jogged back to the gym parking lot and slowed their pace to a walk.

He gave her a high five, then rested his hands on his hips and continued to try to catch his breath. "You have a pretty good pace there, missy."

She turned and gave him a sweaty hug. "This was

completely unexpected and so perfect. Thank you so much."

Chapter Fourteen

Jenna's body filled with electric charge as she waited for Cody to pick her up to head to the ranch. The weight training was going great. The wrestling training was even better. But this would be the first time they had spent free time together, alone. From the amount of coffee she had chugged and the number of butterflies in her stomach, she was feeling a bit nauseous. She went into her bedroom and checked in the mirror for the third time, trying to make sure she didn't look like she tried too hard.

Adjusting her dreamcatcher earrings, she headed up the hallway. Her heart skipped when she heard a knock at the door. Clutching her chest, she let out a deep breath. Tucker snuggled to her side and she gave him a quick rub before answering the door. "Hey," was the only thing she managed to force from her lungs. With sunglasses perched on his head, his curls in full view, and a white button down with the sleeves rolled, one glimpse at him made the butterflies she had in her stomach double in size.

"Y-you look great," Jenna stuttered, then she spied his sneakers. "Do you have boots?"

His eyes darted to his sneakers. "Umm…no, just hiking boots."

Jenna squinted her eyes and twisted her mouth. "What size are you?"

Cody propped his hand against the door frame, picked up his foot and examined the sole, then lifted his eyes to her. "About an eleven?"

"I bet we have some that you can wear. There are always some work boots sitting around."

"Okay, as long as I don't have to do the work." Cody smirked and winked.

"Oh, there is always something needing to be done at the ranch."

"But I'm so pretty," Cody said in a high-pitched voice as he smoothed his shirt, causing her to burst out laughing.

"Yes, sir, you certainly are. Now, pretty man, are you ready to go?"

He smoothed his shirt again and smiled a goofy smile. "Yes, ma'am."

After Jenna got buckled into the Jeep, Cody turned to her with a glint in his eyes. "You're gorgeous, but do you care if your hair gets a little messed up?

She lifted one brow, confused by his question. "No, why?"

Cody moved around quickly, popping the latches on the Jeep until he had the top completely off, then crawled into the driver's seat. She clapped her hands as they headed out on the highway. The wind whipped through their hair, and Jenna put her hands up as if she were on a roller coaster.

A few miles up the road, Jenna instructed Cody to pull down a long gravel path with pine trees on one side and a field of long golden grass on the other. Dust circled behind them as they traveled down the winding trail, finally pulling up to a modest, red brick, two-story house. Cody parked next to a red, Chevy, dually pickup, hooked up to a long, black trailer.

"Whose truck is that?"

She leaned over and took a brief glimpse. "Oh, that's my dad's. He and Ben are getting ready to go to an auction." Her eyes met Cody's again as an uneasiness spread across his face. "What's wrong? I won't let you get hurt riding. I promise."

"Oh, I'm not worried about riding the horse. I'm worried about meeting your dad."

Jenna rolled her eyes. "He's not that bad." Cody squinted his eyes with disbelief. "Plus, he has never met my hero."

They walked through the door and Jenna smoothed her hair working it back into a braid, then called out, "Daddy?" Her voice echoed through the foyer and into the living room. Jenna and Cody heard a commotion coming from the back of the house and headed in that direction. "Dad," she called again, and her dad met them in the kitchen. Her dad's hands were buried in a towel he had slung over his shoulder.

"Hey, Jen. I would hug you, but I've been prepping some steaks for the grill."

His eyes met Cody's. "Dad, this is Cody. Cody, this is my dad, Will," Jenna said with a flourish of her hands.

"Nice to meet you, Mr. Corbett." Keeping his hands shoved in his pockets, Cody nodded intentionally.

A smile filled Mr. Corbett's face. "Nice to meet you too. Jenna told me what you did for her. I sure appreciate it."

"Just glad I was there, sir." Cody pulled his hands from his pockets rubbing them together nervously.

"I am too, son," Mr. Corbett said, glancing at Jenna and smiling. Then he turned back to Cody. "Do you like steak?"

"Oh, yeah," Cody said with a chuckle.

Mr. Corbett turned to walk back to the kitchen. "Well, that's good, because that's what's for dinner."

Jenna followed him. "Okay, we will make sure we are back by then. I am taking Cody out riding for a little bit."

Mr. Corbett picked up the tray of steaks and turned, resting his focus back on Cody. "Ever ridden before?"

"No, I haven't."

Her dad shoved the tray of steaks into the refrigerator, then turned to Jenna who was leaning on the counter. "You might put him on Max. He is pretty easy to control."

"Yep, already thinking the same thing." She reached over to a bowl on the counter and snagged a couple of carrots, then took a couple of bottles of water from the refrigerator. Her gaze returned to Cody whose face had donned a pained appearance. "Are you ready to go?"

"Yes," Cody said a little too abruptly.

She handed him a carrot and a bottle of water.

Cody seemed puzzled but went along. "It was nice to meet you, Mr. Corbett," he said waving with his bottled water.

Across the yard and down a gravel path, a large metal building came into view. The stables. Eight stalls lined the inside, with four filled with horses.

"See the boots over there by the bridles and rope?" Jenna pointed to the tack room in the corner of the stable, littered with bridles and equipment. After no answer she turned to Cody, who was behind her, and realized he was admiring the horses.

Jenna snapped her fingers and pointed.

Cody's head jerked. "Oh, yeah."

"Try those on. I think they will fit."

"All right." Cody walked over, sat down on a small step stool, and removed his shoes. Sliding his foot into one of the boots, he set his foot down and did the same with the other, then stood and stomped each foot a couple of times.

A slight grin crossed Jenna's face. "You did shake those boots first, didn't you?"

He hesitated as one brow shot up. "Umm...no?"

"I don't know when the boots were last worn, they could be filled with spiders or scorpions," she teased. "Do they fit?"

Cody's hands flew to his hips. "You tell me now, after I put the boots on? Now I'm going to die from a spider bite. Great. I had hoped for some grand shoot out for my demise, but no, my obit will read, he died from a spider bite."

Jenna bit her lip trying to hold in a giggle as Cody huffed and sat back down on the stool, gently removing the boot and flipping it over.

"But yeah. They are a bit stiff, but they fit fine." He slipped the boot back on and removed the other, tipping it over and tapping the bottom.

She walked to the first stall and put the bridle on a chestnut-colored horse and walked it out.

"Is that Max?" he called, still sitting on the stool pulling the boot back on.

"No, this is Dusty. She is my horse." She rubbed her in between her ears and down her jaw.

Cody stood and walked over to Jenna, who was adjusting the strap on the bridle. His hands rubbed the horse down its neck. The horse bounced her head up and down as he patted her. "She's beautiful."

Jenna tied the reins off and walked past him, motioning him to follow. Pulling a bridle from the side of the stall, she opened the gate to a large black horse with a white patch of fur in the center of his forehead and speckled socks.

"This is Max."

Cody rubbed Max's neck and mane and scratched him in between the ears. She smiled, watching Cody's face light up when she bridled Max and escorted him out of the stall. His eyes twinkled like a kid on Christmas morning.

"Where is your carrot?"

Cody ran back to the stool where he had laid it. When he returned, he slowly raised the carrot to Max, who fluttered his lips and took the food. Cody stood back while Jenna moved flawlessly around the barn, grabbing the saddle and blanket and throwing them up on the horse. She ran the strap around Max's belly and cinched it up.

"Bring me that saddle and blanket." She gestured to a light brown saddle and plaid blanket sitting on a sawhorse.

Cody jogged over and hoisted it up. "Dang, these things are heavy." He donned a confused expression as he handed off the gear.

Jenna repeated the process as before while he stood with his arms across his chest.

"Well, now I know why you have so much upper body strength. You threw those saddles like they were bags of feathers."

"Been doing this since I was," she stopped, trying to remember, "probably five?" Jenna checked the saddle to get it centered on the blanket. "I was riding before that."

His finger traced the design in the saddle. "This ranch has been in your family for a while?"

"Yes. We inherited it when my dad's dad passed away. It's been in the family for several generations. I have lived here all my life. There are a couple of houses we will pass on our ride. One belonged to my grandparents. My brother, Ben, lives there now. The other is where some of the ranch hands lived way back when. If I had stayed, I would have lived there." She finished saddling Dusty and cinching the strap, then she dusted her hands off and untied her reins. "Get Max's reins and follow me."

They led the horses out of the stable. Sliding her foot into the stirrup, Jenna grasped the saddle horn and in one fluid motion lifted herself into the saddle, while Cody stood and watched. Her eyes lowered as she turned to meet his.

"Bring Max up next to me. Stick your left foot in the stirrup and grip the horn with your left hand, then pull the horn and hop up."

Cody peered up at Jenna, his face filled with doubt, then studied the saddle before awkwardly shoving his foot in the stirrup and reaching for the horn. Each time Cody tried to lift himself into the saddle, Max moved. With his foot still in the stirrup, he tried to move with the horse, hopping on one leg. Jenna struggled to hold back a laugh. He finally got a good grip on the horn and hoisted himself into the saddle.

"That is not as easy as you make it seem," he confessed breathlessly, making himself comfortable. Peeking at him in the saddle from the corner of her eye, she realized the heat radiating throughout her body had nothing to do with the warm August day.

"It just takes practice." Jenna patted Dusty hoping Cody didn't see how flushed her cheeks probably were. "Now, take the reins in your right hand...you're right-handed, right?"

He nodded.

"Okay. Take the reins in your right hand. Keep your left hand on the horn or to your side, whichever makes you feel more comfortable."

Cody gripped the reins and moved his hand into position.

"Let the reins loose if you want the horse to move. Pull back if you want him to stop. If you need him to turn, lean into the side and loosen the reins for the way you want to go." Jenna demonstrated, and Cody nodded. With a little nudge, Dusty moved.

Cody tapped Max with his feet, but he didn't move, and Jenna continued to get farther away. "Uh... Jenna..." he waved, "need some help here." He continued to tap Max while Jenna turned Dusty around and brought her next to him.

"You have to give him a little kick with your heels, so turn your toes out, and give him a good tap. Don't worry. It won't hurt him."

Cody bumped his heels into the horse, and Max and Dusty slowly meandered down the gravel path together.

"Now if you get going a little faster, push your heels down in your stirrups and pull your legs in tight around his belly. If you get scared, pull back slowly on the reins." They walked up the gravel road and Jenna continued to instruct him. "Up the road a little bit, we are going to head off into the pasture and I will let you try your hand at trotting."

"Oh, I don't know if that is necessary, walking is fine." His voice sounded shaky, and the uneasiness that filled his face melted her.

"You will be fine."

For several minutes, the only thing that could be heard was the sound of the horses' hooves against the gravel path. Jenna kept her eyes on him, wondering what he thought about riding and her different way of life.

"So, this is a little glimpse of my life. You've met my dad and will probably meet my brother later at dinner. He's become a bit of a loner, so I never know. But tell me about your life growing up."

Cody patted Max and combed his fingers through his mane. "Typical, I guess. We lived in town, nothing like this. Our house sat in a cul-de-sac, which was great for hanging out and playing basketball. I rode my bike everywhere until I could drive." Cody focused on the open field. "My dad made sure my life revolved around sports from the age of five or six. I didn't have much time to get in trouble.

"Joe and I met in seventh grade. We were in football and wrestling together. He is like a brother. We did everything together." Cody paused to clear his throat. "Wasn't great at school but got by. Didn't get the college scholarship I had hoped for, so I went the military route at the suggestion of my dad. I didn't want to at first, but it helped me grow up. I probably would have stayed in if my mom hadn't disappeared.

"Once I found out my dad bought the gym, I thought it would be best to finish out my commitment and come home to help him out." He shrugged and his eyes landed back on her. "That about catches you up. I'm a pretty boring guy."

Jenna nodded her head and pursed her lips. "Any serious relationships? I mean, you said you were an athlete, so I would have to think you were a catch in school."

Cody chuckled, shook his head, then took a deep breath. "You get right to the point, don't you?"

She shrugged and raised her brows.

"Actually, I was kind of quiet in school." Cody paused. "My dad and I are vastly different in that field. He has all the charisma and confidence with the ladies. Don't get me wrong, I had my moments, but I was never a smooth talker. I did have one serious girlfriend my senior year, Kelly Wolfe. We dated the spring of my senior year, and a few months after I left for the army. It ended when she found someone else. She couldn't handle the distance. It hurt when she broke it off, but I don't blame her. Long distance isn't easy. Since I've been back, I've gone out some, but nothing serious. How about you?"

"Oh, my daddy kept a pretty tight rein on me."

"Really? I wonder why? I would think you would have been such an easy child," he said sarcastically.

Jenna rolled her eyes. "I wasn't terrible. But April and I had our moments. We managed to sneak out occasionally."

Cody's mouth dropped open feigning surprise. "For boys?"

Her lips curled beneath her teeth, hiding her smile. "Sometimes." She paused. "I've had a couple of boyfriends but none really serious. I was dating Ricky Perkins when my mom got diagnosed. As her condition deteriorated, I had to pick up the slack for the household, and I didn't have time to devote to a relationship."

"How old were you when your mom got diagnosed?"

Jenna's eyes drifted. "I had just turned seventeen." Her voice quieted. "A Wednesday. It was one of those strange moments, when you knew that the information you had been given would alter your entire life. It did."

The memories came flooding back. "The doctors started chemo the next week. At first, nothing changed other than more doctor appointments. But within a short time, she started getting sick, then she lost her hair. After the first set of treatments, she got the cancer-free diagnosis. That lasted for quite a while. We thought we had beaten it.

"Then came the news about two years ago that the doctors found more. After that, the chemo got more potent. Mom got weaker. We tried all kinds of different treatments including holistic, but nothing worked. She got a bad report that the cancer had spread and decided she wanted to stop everything entirely because it made her so sick. Mom wanted to feel better during the time she had left. So, we had to come to terms with what that meant."

The pain of the memories left her quiet. Cody was quiet too. After a moment she spoke. "Enough walking, I am going to take off, and Max will follow. Push your heels down in the stirrups and squeeze your knees in.

Try to keep your butt in the saddle. If you feel like you need to slow down, pull back on the reins. Okay?"

"All right," Cody said, releasing a gasp of air. She clicked her tongue, prodded Dusty, and the horse began to trot. Max followed suit, and Cody bounced in the saddle.

Jenna turned and grimaced. "Dig your knees in and pull yourself down in the saddle.

"I'm trying," he said, as his head bobbled.

Jenna slowed her gait and watched as Cody tried to follow her instructions but still appeared to be getting his teeth jarred out of his head.

"Okay, we are going to try a gallop. This will hopefully be a little easier on you, even though you are going a little bit faster."

"Faster?" The shakiness rose in his voice. "Are you kidding me?" He swallowed hard.

"Trust me. The key here is finding the rhythm."

Clicking her tongue again before Cody could say another word, Jenna prodded Dusty and took off. Max followed. Slowing to watch Cody, she saw fear flash across his face, and Cody seemed a bit off balance at first, but after a minute, he fell into a rhythm and his body loosened up.

Strands of golden hay beat against their legs as they rode through the open fields flanked by acres of pine trees. They picked up speed, racing down through a valley filled with wildflowers, only slowing for her to show him the different houses on the land. Following a trail behind the houses, they headed down a steep bank to a creek. Dusty stopped at the edge of the water. Jenna threw her leg over and hopped down.

Cody pulled back on the reins, and Max slowed to

a stop. He threw his leg over but stopped just short of falling on his butt after losing his balance trying to pull his foot out of the stirrup. Jenna watched once he was off and smirked at the way he was walking.

"Holy cow, my legs," Cody whined, and ran his hands down his thighs.

"I guess I should have told you, it takes a little time to get used to riding. You may be a little sore tomorrow."

"A little? I don't know if I will be able to walk."

"I thought you were supposed to be in shape, Mr. Personal Trainer," Jenna taunted.

"I don't know that I have ever used these muscles." He winced, and then gave her a pained smile. Surveying the surroundings, a real smile crossed his face before his eyes made it back to her. "This place is really nice. Very peaceful."

Jenna grinned, then lifted her arms wide. "What you can see from here is all our land. Past the rise of pine trees is primarily forest that butts up to Poppi McIntyre's, and the back of the property backs up to highway fifty-one. We have about eighty acres, fifteen head of cattle, four horses, a bunch of goats, some pigs, chickens, cats, etcetera. Too many to count. This place taught me about life." Jenna could hear the rippling water in the creek and smell the freshness from the open land around her, and it sent a zing through her. "This is my happy place."

Cody pushed his fingers through his hair. The sun reflected in his eyes as his gaze met hers. "But if this makes you happy, what made you leave the ranch?"

Strands of hair blew across her face. "This part of the ranch is what I love. I feel free when I'm out here riding. But if I stayed, I don't think I would ever feel like I had my own life. I would always be under my dad's or my brother's thumb. I need that freedom to explore and create a life of my own."

"It's great that you have that confidence about your life, to step out and take a chance."

Jenna sat down on the rocks next to the stream and yanked her boots off, then her socks. "I don't know so much about that. I have no idea where my life will lead me other than it's not working on the ranch. At least not right now."

Cody remained standing and his eyes drifted to the stream. "I was always raised with the idea that I needed to have my life figured out and tied up by the time I got out of high school. So, being so unsure of what's next scares the hell out of me. I do like the idea of breaking from my dad's legacy and going the paramedic route. I only hope I can handle the classes."

Rolling her pant legs up, she waded into the water. "I think you sell yourself short on a lot of things," she stated, keeping her focus on the stream.

Cody moved closer to the water. "What do you mean?"

Jenna's eyes squinted as she brought her attention back to him. "Well, like Karaoke Night at the bar. You were so scared because you had never gotten up in front of people, but when we convinced you to get up there, you knocked it out of the park. You were a natural."

"It didn't hurt that I had a couple of beers in me."

"Maybe."

"It's just that my dad has always been kind of in control of my life, and he's so good at everything. I wanted to be like that. He has always been so confident, so charismatic, and always knew the right thing to say. There are tons of stories he's told me. Stories of how popular he was. He always had the girls clamoring for him. I never felt comfortable in my skin like that."

"Do you believe everything he tells you?" Cody shrugged. "I don't think you being a little unsure of yourself is a bad thing. You seem very genuine to me, very honest, and maybe a little shy. Sometimes confidence and charisma come at a price."

"True."

"It's fine wanting to make your dad proud. But make him proud by doing things that are uniquely you, things that you have a true passion for, not recreating his life."

"I never thought of it that way." Cody raised a brow. "You are a pretty smart cookie."

Jenna peeked at him from beneath her lashes. "I get by." Tucking her hair behind her ear, she glanced down in the water, then kicked her foot, splashing water all over him.

Cody's eyes narrowed, and for a minute Jenna thought she ticked him off. He dropped down to the rocks, yanked off his boots and socks, then hurriedly rolled his pants up. His body stiffened when he stepped in the water, and his eyes widened. "Oh, geez, this water is freezing.".

"It's a natural spring." She kicked her foot again in his direction.

Cody bent over and chopped his hand at the water, causing a large splash and making a direct hit.

The gauntlet had been thrown. Sheets of water rained down in all directions in an all-out war. After several minutes, with his shirt glued to his skin and water dripping from his hair, Cody found a stick and perched one of his white socks on it, waving it in the air in surrender. They sat on the side of the stream laughing, letting the sun dry them before heading back to the stables.

"I wish I could be more like you," Cody said, shaking his wet hair, then propping himself on his elbows.

"How so?"

"Remembering to enjoy life. Take it as it comes and live in the moment. I always seem to be so hyper-focused on what I need to be doing that I forget to enjoy what is happening in front of me."

"It's something my mom instilled in me. She said you need to appreciate everything around you in order to be happy. Find joy in living life. Even when she was sick, she still managed to do that." Jenna paused. "When I come out here, I feel close to her."

Cody stood after slipping his boots back on. "I love that about you, you know."

Wondering if he meant to say what he did, she stood and faced him. His gaze told her he did.

Jenna wrapped her arms around Cody and ran her hands up and down his damp shirt. "I love how sweet you are." His fingers twirled one of her curls that had escaped her braid and pulled her close. She smiled and wrinkled her nose as their lips met in a soft, sweet moment where everything faded away.

The horses stirred and whinnied, and Jenna's surroundings slowly came back into focus. Pulling away, she cast her gaze to the stream. "I guess we should be getting back." Cody's hand caressed her cheek, pulling her in for one last kiss, before they parted and headed back to the horses. She watched him from the corner of her eye when he shoved his foot in the stirrup and swung himself up in the saddle.

"Yay! You are a quick learner."

He winked. "I have a good teacher." After getting settled in the saddle once again, he pulled the reins to one side, guiding Max, like he had done it all his life.

By the time they were heading back to the stables, Cody had Max in a full run beside Jenna and Dusty and was obviously enjoying himself. When they got to the stable, Jenna showed him how to remove the saddle and bridle. Then she helped him brush down Max and feed him before putting him back in his stall. In the tack room, she was putting the supplies away when she felt Cody's arms quickly curl around her waist. Softly kissing her neck, he whispered in her ear, "Thank you."

Jenna spun around in his arms and dug her fingers in his curls. "I'm glad you had fun." His hand gently caressed the back of her neck, pulling her to him and lifting her mouth to his. Sucking in her bottom lip, he waited for her lips to part, then completely devoured her. Her body felt like shifting sand in his arms.

This kiss was different. This kiss, though still slow and careful, had an intensity behind it that consumed her mind, body, and soul.

Cody backed away, his breath heated and heavy. His lips found her cheek and neck while he pushed her up against an empty stable gate and pressed his body against hers. His hands found the small of her back and traveled south. Short gasps escaped her throat as their lips came together again. Jenna's fingers dug into his back more and more with every hungry kiss. Pulling away, she dropped her head and whispered, "Cody."

His name came out more like a gasp.

"Hmm," he said still planting kisses along her neck.

"I...we..." Jenna couldn't bring herself to say the words, so she moved her hands to his chest. Cody got the hint and backed away. Pressing his forehead against hers, he ran his thumb along her jaw. "I am sure my dad has dinner waiting. We should probably go." The thought sent a wave of disappointment through her.

He placed a tender kiss on her nose and gave her a dimpled smile. "Okay."

Laying a hand against her chest, Jenna tried to still her heart as they headed out of the stable. She snaked her arm around Cody's waist, and he hauled her in close, placing a kiss to her temple.

The slight anxiety Jenna had of Cody sharing dinner with her family eased, watching Cody talk with her dad about the ranch. Ben, her brother, had always been quiet, but seemed genuinely interested when Cody chatted with him about joining the gym.

A smile crossed her face listening to the men talk. Cody's hand found her thigh while they continued with their conversations. His fingers kept flexing, and softly moving over her skin, causing a flood of goosebumps to spread across her body. She pushed her chair out and began collecting dishes around the table, then took them into the kitchen.

Cody appeared in the kitchen a short time later with a few more dishes. Jenna was rinsing plates and setting them in the dishwasher. "Everything okay?" he asked.

Jenna smiled. "Yeah," she paused, "but I kind of would like to head out soon."

Cody tilted his head, still holding a worried expression. "All right, but I was enjoying talking to your dad and Ben. Don't feel like we have to leave because of me. I know I told you I didn't want to meet—"

"Oh, I'm glad you guys are getting along. Honestly, I was surprised at how much Ben opened up to you. He's usually pretty quiet." Her gaze slowly lifted to him. "I thought maybe we could save a little bit of the evening for…us."

A fire sparked in Cody's eyes, and a mischievous grin spread across his face. A pile of dishes still sat on the counter waiting to be loaded. He picked up a hand full and filled the dishwasher.

Chapter Fifteen

A cloud of dust filled the cab of the Jeep as they headed up the gravel road after saying their goodbyes. Thinking about their encounter at the stables made Jenna's core tingle. The way Cody kissed her and touched her set off an explosion within her.

Shifting in her seat, Jenna tried to quell the excitement building within her and wondered if Cody felt the same, until his hand returned to her thigh, and he glanced at her with that irresistible upside-down smile. She was a goner. Goosebumps spread through her entire body.

His lips were full and had the perfect sexy bow in the middle. And boy, could he put those lips to work when he kissed. *My word, how could I have gotten so lucky.*

When they arrived back at the house, a timid smile played on Jenna's lips. Cody's hand caressed the small of her back as they walked up the steps into the house. Tucker met them at the door, and she did her best to get him taken care of quickly. The evening sun glowed through the kitchen window. Cody was lazily reclining against the kitchen counter, holding a glass of tea, when she came into the house and sent Tucker to his bed. Tiny sparks shot through her, taking in his long muscular frame.

"I hope you don't mind, I got us some tea." He

pointed to the glass sitting behind him. Jenna reached to pick it up, and Cody's arm wrapped around her, pressing her to him and sending her heart into overdrive. "I had such a great time today, even if you won the water war," he said with a smirk. "Thanks again for asking me." His genuine smile caused her breath to stall.

Jenna took a drink and then set her glass down. "I'm glad you did. I know you were a little wary of meeting my family, but you seemed to get along well."

"Yeah, I enjoyed talking to them. It was a little unnerving at first, I'm not gonna lie, because I thought you said I wasn't there to meet the family."

"Well, they weren't part of the plan. I didn't know if my dad and brother would be there or not, since they are heading out to an auction tomorrow, but they kind of come with the territory," she said wrinkling her nose.

He snuggled her in closer. "What is this plan that you speak of?" he asked in an exaggerated proper tone, rocking her back and forth.

"Helping you accomplish something you've always wanted to do."

The corners of his mouth curved. "It was fun." His brows arched. "Scary as hell, but fun."

"You did great. I was surprised at how fast you got comfortable with it. You didn't act like you were scared at all." Cody lowered one brow like he didn't believe her. "Well maybe a little at first, but on the way back you looked happy."

"I was." He gazed into her eyes. "And I am." Her fingers gently slid across the small of his back.

"Really?" Thoughts raced through Jenna's head of the way he kissed her in the stable and what would have happened if she hadn't backed away. She wanted nothing more than to let him continue down the path he was on, but fear of someone walking in on them won out.

There was no chance of that happening now. She took a deep breath, wondering if Cody was thinking about that kiss too. "Is there anything else you've wanted to do that maybe I can help with?" she asked in a soft, breathy voice.

Cody's eyes widened, and for a split second she thought he wasn't on the same page, then a slow smile crept across his face.

"Um hum." He pulled the band from her hair. Gently loosening her braids with his fingers, his hand then slowly moved to her cheek lifting her mouth to his.

The minute his kiss deepened, Cody set a flame that turned into an all-consuming, white-hot blaze within her. Jenna knew she was taking a chance that somehow what they were doing might stir up memories from the attack. Things might go south quickly, but she couldn't deny how her body craved him in the stables, and even more now. She wanted him with every ounce of her being.

Cody's fingers tangled in Jenna's long auburn hair, while he brought her lips to his again. Her tongue gently brushed his bottom lip, tasting the sugar of the sweet tea.

Stubble scraped against her skin as his kisses became more forceful, then slowly he backed away.

Moisture glistened on his lips. His hot breath stoked the fire as he yanked at the collar of her shirt and moved her strap, allowing his lips to brush kisses down her neck and shoulder.

A moan curled up the back of her throat. She was paralyzed.

Cody's hands slid down Jenna's body and pressed her hips to his, holding her firmly against him. The rich scent of his chocolatey cologne caused the heat to pour through her veins.

Tugging at his shirt, she ran her hands up his bare back when it released.

A deep groan rumbled in his chest as his body responded to her touch.

His kisses were heated, passionate, but still tender as his fingers threaded through her hair.

The pounding of her heart increased with every move his hands made, but not from fear. Cody kept the darkness at bay. It was like he instinctively knew what she needed. Jenna had longed to be touched the right way, and his touch made her come undone.

Breaking the kiss, Jenna backed away and Cody quickly lowered his eyes to hers. "If you want me to stop, tell me. I will." She could see in his eyes that he was worried. But she wasn't afraid. There was nothing about him, or what he was doing, that made her want him to stop.

Dragging her teeth over her lip, Jenna peered up at him and shook her head. His eyes twinkled as her fingers interlaced with his and she led him into the bedroom.

The dim light of the lamp on the nightstand gave the room a warm glow. Jenna turned back to face Cody, wrapping her arms around his neck, she let her fingers dance in his thick curls.

A playful smile formed on his lips as Cody pressed his body against hers, and his fingers gently brushed against her cheek. She could feel the thump of his heartbeat.

Lowering his mouth to hers, Cody's lips touched softly, teasing hers open, then he took what he wanted.

Desire built with every second his lips touched hers.

His hands slid up her T-shirt unlatching her bra, and in one continuous move, he slid them both over her head. With a wolfish grin, he tossed them over his shoulder.

The palms of her hands gently traced down his shirt to his buttons, pulling them open one by one. With each, she pressed a soft kiss against his chest.

She lifted her eyes to his, wondering if he needed her as much as she did him. Beneath his thick, dark lashes she saw a hunger waiting to be unleashed.

Slowly, Jenna slid her hands up his stomach onto his shoulders and pushed his shirt down his back, then lightly kissed his bare chest again, feeling his muscles constrict beneath her lips. His grip grew tighter on her, and his breath grew shaky the lower she went.

Lifting her mouth to his, the hunger and desire was released, and his kisses consumed, possessed, and claimed her.

A whimper escaped her when he pulled away, pecking her cheek and nipping at her neck and shoulder.

Eyes closed, she relaxed in his arms, leaning her head back, letting him have his way. He pressed his body to hers and pushed her back against the bed.

Jenna lay back. Feeling the warmth of his body leave, she ached to have him against her again. The bed gave, and he moved over her. Her eyes widened as a devious grin crossed her face.

"Well, this position is familiar," she taunted.

"Don't try anything," he shot back with a breathless growl, but without heat.

Jenna stuck her lip out, and Cody captured it with his teeth, then tenderly brushed his tongue against hers in long languid strokes.

Her hands moved slowly up his arms and coaxed his body to hers, wanting to feel his warmth against her.

Gently sucking in her bottom lip, Cody moved from her lips to her chin, planting kisses down her neck to her chest and then breast, leaving a trail of electricity that might have caused her heart to completely stop for a moment.

His hands worked the button on her pants while he continued to dust her stomach with feather-light kisses, then slid her pants to the floor.

Barely breathing, Jenna reached for the covers from the bed and wrapped them around her, then sat up and slowly unfastened his jeans.

Cody's thumbs tugged at his waistband and everything fell to the floor. Jenna's eyes widened at the sight of him standing before her. A perfectly cut body. Evidence of the work he put in at the gym. With his brow raised, his eyes questioned her gaze.

Jenna's teeth bit her lip, and he chuckled as he leaned over her, using his body to push her back down on the bed.

Sliding under the covers, Cody ran his fingers through her hair, grabbing her neck and pulling her to him.

His lips softly touched hers. Gliding his fingers over her body, he gently cupped her breast as his mouth moved down her neck and explored every inch of her.

Tender kisses, and the gentleness of his touch, made her feel like a delicate piece of glass.

The intensity of her need grew, and Jenna's body trembled in anticipation when he slowly lowered his body on top of hers. She let out a soft whimper. Cody braced himself on his elbows and moved her hair away from her face so they could be eye to eye. "You okay?"

Her tongue pressed against her teeth in a lustful smile and she nodded. He lowered his mouth to hers then threw the covers over them both.

Their fingers interlaced as their bodies connected and moved together in a slow perfect dance. Cody's hair brushed Jenna's cheek as he peppered kisses along her shoulder to her neck, and she turned toward him. With his lips slightly parted she felt his warm breath, and she brushed her lips against his cheek.

A vulnerability crossed his face when his eyes opened. He was so beautiful.

Cody kissed her softly, and his hand skimmed her cheek, then slowly made its way down her body, grasping onto her hip.

Desire bloomed and took over with every movement.

Jenna's breaths came in short staccato bursts.

Her fingers clenched in his hair.

Cody's lips pressed against hers, the kisses more frenzied with every caress. Each move took her to the brink of ecstasy.

The vibration of his chest when he released a deep moan plummeted her over the edge, taking him with her. Cody held her tight as her back arched and body quaked with strikes of lightning pulsating through her.

Jenna's fingers dug into his sweat-soaked skin as her body writhed beneath him, and she let out a breathless cry.

Dusting her with light kisses, Cody's body slowly relaxed and he moved off her, pulling her to him.

Curled up in his arms, Jenna teetered between sleep and awake, her body completely sated. Cody's fingers slowly grazed her skin leaving a trail of goosebumps. He rolled toward her and groaned.

"I guess I need to head out," he rasped, his fingers pushing her hair out of her eyes.

Jenna blinked slowly a couple of times before focusing on the sadness on Cody's face. "Why? Do you have to work tomorrow?" she asked, rubbing her hand across the muscles in his abdomen.

"No, I actually don't, but—"

"Then stay."

****

Cody was suddenly awakened by wet, sloppy kisses covering his face. Blindly, he reached his hand up and rubbed Tucker's head. A fuzzy face stared back at him when he peeled open his eyes before they became heavy and he closed them again.

The smell of coffee teased his senses along with something else. Bacon. Rolling to his back, Cody threw his arm across his face while he continued to pet Tucker. His mind drifted to the day before.

Warmth filled his body. The intense connection he felt with Jenna was like nothing he had ever felt before. Thinking about their night together sent aftershocks through him. Once he had her, he couldn't get enough. And it wasn't only physically.

The honest conversation they had had while

horseback riding stirred up something deep inside him; courage to be himself; to go after what he wanted; and what he wanted was Jenna. It all became so clear, and when it did, he could barely control himself in the stables. She felt so good in his arms.

It would probably cause trouble between him and his dad, but at this point, he didn't care. Jenna was right, he needed to do what he was passionate about, live the life that was his and his alone, not his and his dad's.

"Tucker?" Jenna's loud whisper came from up the hall, and then he heard the floor creak as she tiptoed toward the bedroom. Cody turned his head and opened one eye. His body shuddered hearing her voice, and it took everything within him not to smile.

"Tucker," she whispered again, "get out of there, he's asleep."

"No, I'm not." Cody opened both eyes, and the smile emerged as she entered the room in a lace camisole and satin shorts. Every muscle constricted as Jenna walked up to the bed and brushed her hand through his hair, then leaned over and gave him a quick kiss.

"Are you hungry?" she asked in a sweet voice.

"Oh yeah," Cody flirted, wiggling his eyebrows and his smile turning into a full grin.

"Oh geez, I mean food."

Wrapping his arms around Jenna, Cody threw her on the bed and rolled on top of her. She squeaked, and her hair fell into a halo around her when her head hit the pillow.

"Was last night not enough for you?"

"Never," he growled, his lips brushing her neck.

Jenna moaned and combed her fingers through his messy locks.

All Cody wanted to do at that moment was keep her nestled in his arms.

Grabbing his face with both hands, she stared into his eyes. "Maybe later, the food is hot now."

"But so am I," he whined, and sent kisses down her neck.

"I made pancakes," she sang sweetly.

He stopped and sighed, his face buried in her neck. "With blueberries?"

"Um-hum."

With his face still buried, Cody surrendered. "Okay." Rolling over, he allowed his captive to be free. His hands wiped his eyes and he sat up. "I'll be there in a minute."

Jenna turned and strolled up the hall. A small chuckle escaped as he watched.

Within a few minutes, he stumbled up the hallway in his jeans, no shirt, with Tucker close at his heels.

"Tucker, leave Cody alone."

Finding a mug sitting on the counter, Cody wondered if Jenna had reconsidered their earlier conversation when her fingers reached up and softly followed the lines of his bare chest. One brow raised in question, and her cheeks flushed but her hand dropped and she backed away. *Later couldn't come soon enough.*

"Can I use this cup?" he asked, holding it up.

"Yes, that's the one I set out for you." She turned and opened the refrigerator. "Do you need cream or sugar or anything?"

"Do you have cream, like real cream, not the

flavored stuff?"

"Yep." She reached in the door of the refrigerator and retrieved a glass container.

"I know I don't want the answer to this, but I have to ask. Is this cream from your cows?"

She twitched her head. "Maybe."

Sniffing the container, Cody made the same twitch with his head, poured some in his coffee, and took a sip. His lips smacked together. "Oh, that's good."

She walked in front of him and he pinned her against the counter and gave her a peck on her lips, then his lips traveled south.

Jenna's body shuddered. Cody loved how his kisses could make her come undone. She blew out a long breath and put her hands against his bare chest. "Okay, okay." Lifting her hands to his cheeks, she gazed at him through her lashes. "Eat now, play later."

With her hands still on his cheeks, she turned his head. "Scrambled eggs are on the stove. Bacon and pancakes are on the counter." Moving her hand, she pointed. "And over there is fresh blueberries, syrup, and butter," bouncing her finger from one item to the next.

"Looks delicious, just like you." Cody kissed her forehead and picked up a plate. Shoving a chunk of bacon in his mouth, he loaded on some pancakes with the blueberries, bacon, and eggs and headed to the table.

Just as he set his coffee cup down, he heard her call out, "Nope, not the table."

Turning around to the island, he lowered his plate, but she spoke up again. "Nope, not there either."

Cody rolled his eyes and sighed. "You gotta eat now, it's hot," he said in a sing song voice mocking her.

"I have a surprise."

Jenna picked up a fork and waved it at him to follow. Tucker slid in between the two of them as she opened the door to the back yard.

The sky off in the distance, over the valley, was beginning to brighten with a glow of yellows and pinks against a spray of fluffy silver and gray clouds. But up above, the sky still held its shades of purple and indigo and was filled with stars.

Two rocking chairs with a square wooden table in between sat on a cement porch, situated perfectly to take in the sunrise over the valley. The light shining through the window from inside the house gave them enough of a glow to make the setting perfect.

"See, isn't this amazing?"

"Yes, I would have to say this is a much better setting." He eyed Jenna, who sat mesmerized.

"To me, there is nothing more beautiful. The colors are so fantastic, the pinks and yellows and purples…and then you still have the stars. It's perfect." Jenna took a deep breath and turned to him. "I know, you think I'm crazy."

"No, not at all. I agree. This *is* perfect sitting here with the sun breaking over the horizon. But you left out one crucial ingredient." Cody rocked a couple of times staring out over the valley, then turned his gaze to her. "It's perfect because I get to do it with you."

Jenna rolled her eyes, but then smiled. "Well, aren't you the charmer."

The way the light reflected in Jenna's eyes and glinted off her skin made Cody's insides fill with heat. Even though she still appeared a bit sleepy, she was absolutely stunning. She glimpsed him from the corner of her eye, and he quickly diverted his eyes, but she smirked, and he knew he had been caught. He cleared his throat and leaned on the arm of the chair. "So, what do you have going on today?"

"I am going to be hanging out with your buddy, Sergeant Gallagher, at ten, then I guess coming home and studying for the biology test."

Cody grew confused. "You're going to the police station?"

"Yep."

"What for?" He filled his fork with some eggs. "Does he have information on the case?"

Jenna shook her head. "No. I am meeting with the rest of the women who were attacked, to see if our stories can trigger any memories and provide some new information."

"Are you nervous?" Cody asked, as an uneasiness filled him.

Dredging some pancake through her syrup Jenna shrugged her shoulders. "Maybe a little. I am kind of hoping something comes of it."

"It would be great if information were revealed that cracked the case."

"So, what do you have going on?" Jenna rested on her elbow and put her hand on her cheek.

Breaking off a bite of bacon, Cody shoved it in his mouth and dusted his fingers. "Not much. I guess I will go to the gym if you are going to be busy. But you gotta let me know what you find out."

"I will give you a call when we get done." Jenna popped the last of her bacon in her mouth, picked up her plate, then motioned to him, but he waved her off.

"You don't have to do that, I can help." He picked

up his plate and followed her into the kitchen. Setting her dish in the sink, she turned on the water and he slid his on top while she rinsed another dish. "Why don't you go ahead and get your shower. I will get this cleaned up."

Her face softened. "Are you sure?" She continued to rinse the dishes.

"If I can handle a bachelor pad with two bachelors, I can handle this." He took the dish from her hand and gave her a quick kiss. "Go."

****

Jenna smiled and trotted down the hall. Shedding her clothes, she turned on the shower and stepped in. The steam filled her lungs from the water covering her. Filling her hair with soap, Jenna closed her eyes and let the rich bubbles drizzle down her face. Her fingers combed through her hair, and her hands were suddenly met with another pair.

Turning around, Jenna felt Cody's hands wiping away the soap from her face. Her eyes opened, and he pulled her in for a heated kiss. His lips moved to her neck and he whispered, "I'm. Still. Hungry."

Chapter Sixteen

Jenna entered the police station, and after speaking with the woman behind the glass, she was buzzed through where Sergeant Gallagher met her and ushered her back to a conference room.

Three of the other victims had already arrived, and she was introduced. Her gaze was met by each of the other victims and she wondered why they were all chosen. They were all attractive, in their twenties and thirties possibly, but so different. What made them targets? Was there some kind of connection?

The conference table was surrounded by several large black desk chairs. She sat down, trying to steady her nerves.

Although she told Cody she was fine, she knew coming here meant she would have to call upon the memories she tried so hard to store away. The counseling had helped, but sitting in the room with others who were having to do the same didn't make it easier. Her heart ticked up with memories of the attack flashing in her thoughts. She would do anything to have Cody there with her.

Glimpsing the victim's faces, it was apparent, by the looks in their eyes, they were feeling the same apprehension she was, and none of them chose to speak after their introduction.

She thought about her encounter with Cody this

morning to try to keep her mind off the memories of the attack, but even picturing him covered in soap bubbles only worked for a momentary smile.

The final victim arrived and Sergeant Gallagher, along with three officers from the other towns the crimes happened in, came in and shut the door. Introductions were made, and the officers produced their files and yellow legal pads, then sat down.

Sergeant Gallagher took a position at the head of the conference table and remained standing.

"We are here to listen to your stories and hopefully get some new information for this case that will lead to an arrest. We know this isn't easy for any of you, but please try to recall as much as possible of the incident. What did you see around you? Think about his appearance. What was he wearing? What did he smell like? What did he feel like? What did you hear? You all have introduced yourselves, so we will start with the first victim and work our way to the last. Any questions?"

With no questions, Sergeant Gallagher took his seat.

As each victim told their stories, Jenna listened intently, trying to see what rang true. A couple of the girls were attacked during daylight, so they were able to give a better description of his clothing, but it was still the same, black pants, black hoodie, a black mask covering his face, and black gloves, although a couple of the victims gave different descriptions of his shoes. They all were attacked from behind and rendered immobile. All were attacked in a concealed area so that they wouldn't be seen.

All said the attacker never made a sound. Then

Jenna remembered, he did. When it came time for her to tell her story, she carefully relayed the information about how he popped his neck and then moaned.

Sergeant Gallagher sat up. "I don't see that in your account of the incident. What do you remember about that?"

"When Tucker knocked him off balance the first time, I got my hands free and hit him. We struggled for a second, but he was able to pin me again. After he did, he let out a laugh, then popped his neck and made this kind of wheezy groan."

From the other end of the table a pretty woman with dark skin and long braided hair lifted her head. Pain filled her face. "He did that with me too." Jenna perked up, as did the other officers in the room. They asked the other victim to recount what she remembered, and each one scribbled on their legal pad.

When the meeting ended, Sergeant Gallagher escorted Jenna out of the conference room and up the hallway.

"So, do you think that our information might help the case?" Jenna asked, as they walked out to the lobby.

"It's another piece to the puzzle, and since it happened to two of you, it's a pretty good piece." Sergeant Gallagher walked with her to the door and pushed it open. "If there is anything else you remember, or anything you want to talk about, let me know."

"I will." She slid her sunglasses on and dug out her phone to text Cody.

Jenna: *Meeting over, where are you?*

Cody: *At the gym. Get your bathing suit and come by. I had an idea.*

Waves of heat crashed into her like a hot summer

189

wind as thoughts of the night before flashed through her mind. The expression on his face when they were making love about broke her. It was like he was seeing a beautiful delicate flower for the first time when he looked at her.

She hopped in her truck wondering what Cody had planned. The other young woman who had spoken up with a similar story walked to her car as Jenna drove away from the station, and her thoughts drifted to the stories each of the victims told.

She could still feel her heart pounding from having to relive the incident, but she was somehow comforted by knowing others understood. Her only real saving grace from the whole thing was meeting Cody.

After stopping by the house for her swimsuit, Jenna pulled into the gym parking lot. A tall, muscular man was getting out of his car wearing a Captain America tank top and black wind pants. His well-groomed ash blond hair and striking chiseled features gave him the appearance of a runway model, but there was something vaguely familiar about him that she couldn't put her finger on, and she noticed him staring at her. They landed at the front door together, and he held it open.

"I didn't know you were a member here," he said, and gave her half a smile. "Hey, sorry I spilled my drink on you the other night." She was confused by his comment, but then figured he might have mistaken her for someone else, so she politely smiled.

Cody was on the phone but peeked up from over the computer. He smiled, but it quickly disappeared, which caught Jenna's attention. She glimpsed at Joe and said, "Hi," as he greeted the man she came in with, but the guy didn't respond so Joe turned to Jenna and smiled. Todd walked up to the counter and nodded to her.

Cody lowered the phone and glanced at Jenna. "Give me one minute." Holding his finger up and hopping up from the stool, he walked off with his phone to his ear.

Joe slid up on the stool Cody vacated. "So, Miss Jenna. How's life treating you?"

"Not too bad actually. Cody is taking me somewhere, but he wouldn't tell me where. Do you have any idea?"

"Nope. Sorry, he didn't share."

"All I know is, it involves water. He told me I needed my swimsuit."

Jenna noticed Todd was still standing at the counter, but his cheery expression had turn to one of annoyance. Her smile was met with a glare as he picked up some papers and walked off toward the office.

"So how is April doing?" Joe continued, not realizing what had taken place.

Jenna, confused by Todd's sudden obvious icy attitude, turned her attention back to Joe.

"I'm sorry, what?"

"April. You know, blue eyes, short dark hair?"

"Oh, she's fi—" Her response was cut off when she heard Cody's voice coming from the office.

"I am well aware of what you told me, Dad. I am choosing to do things my way."

Joe's eyes grew big. He sat back on the stool and turned his head toward the office.

"It's my decision who I choose to date," Cody bit out.

"Not if it affects the gym," Todd bellowed. "This is our livelihood. She could ruin us."

Heat crept up Jenna's neck, and her eyes darted to Joe. Shame engulfed her at his expression as his eyes stayed riveted on the office. Everyone had stopped what they were doing in the gym and listened to the fight between Cody and his dad. It broke Jenna's heart that she was the issue. Tears burned and spilled down her cheeks.

"I'm done with this conversation." Cody's voice was tight with anger.

Jenna's eyes returned to Joe's. He grimaced and let out a heavy sigh.

Cody stepped around the corner, fury in his eyes.

Jenna swallowed. "Cody, maybe we should—"

Gripping her arm without saying a word, Cody hauled her out into the parking lot. When he got to the Jeep, he pushed her up against the hot metal, wrapped his hands around her chin, and crushed his mouth against hers. The ferocity of his kiss caught her by surprise, but within seconds she was melting into him, wrapping her arms around his neck, and letting her fingers dive into his hair.

Cody backed away and wiped Jenna's wet cheeks with his thumbs before opening the door to the Jeep.

Jenna crawled in. Her eyes locked on Todd, standing in the office window witnessing everything.

Cody glared at his dad after getting in.

The pounding of his heart against her, and the pain in his eyes when he kissed her, nearly wrecked her. She had never seen him so upset.

She glanced at Cody, then back to Todd who hadn't taken his eyes off her. "You want to talk—"

"Nope. I'm done. We are going to go have some fun."

He slid his sunglasses on, put the Jeep in reverse, and peeled out of the parking lot.

"Where are we going?"

"We have to make a quick stop to get some lunch. Is the Collective okay?" He still had a bit of a scowl on his face, but damn, his sunglasses absolutely made her shudder.

"I love the Collective. I've only eaten there a couple of times, but everything was delicious."

After retrieving their sandwiches, Cody placed them in a cooler in the back of the Jeep and they headed back up the road.

Curiosity was getting the better of her, but Cody still wasn't doing much talking, so she finally asked, "Are you going to tell me where we are going?"

"You will figure it out soon enough."

Within minutes they pulled back into the gym parking lot and her stomach clenched.

****

Cody was relieved to see that his dad's car was no longer in the lot when they arrived. He could imagine him blowing through the front doors of the gym, trying to finish the fight they had, and Cody didn't want to have any part of it.

It surprised him when his dad burst into the office while he was on the phone, demanding to know why he didn't heed his warning. Cody knew the risks and knew the possible outcome, but decided Jenna was a risk worth taking. His dad would have to deal with it.

Handing a large plastic bag to Jenna, he lifted the small cooler out of the back of the Jeep. With his fingers laced in hers, they strolled across the street to the back entrance of the park, heading down the trail through the pine trees. They hadn't been back to the waterfall since he showed it to her.

The trees opened to the rocky ledge around the creek and the falls.

"Ok, before we go any farther, we need to strip down to our suits and put our clothes in the plastic bag."

Jenna pushed her sunglasses back onto her head and crossed her arms. "What are we doing?"

Cody lifted his brows and gave her a crooked smile. "Quit asking questions. Trust me…and strip."

Once their clothes were safely zipped in the bag, he grasped Jenna's hand and helped her up to the ledge by the falls.

"Follow me but be careful. It could get slick." Stepping out onto the ledge, they slowly climbed up to the mouth of the cave and disappeared behind the falls. Cody shook the moisture from his hair like a wet dog, while Jenna twisted the excess water out of her hair, then piled it on her head in a messy bun.

The view was muddled as Cody gazed out through the waterfall, then turned and surveyed the area behind him.

"Oh my gosh, this place is amazing." Sunlight lit the front of the cave, but it extended into a deep, mysterious darkness. "I can't believe it's so big." Pulling his phone from the bag, he flipped on the flashlight. "Let's go explore." Jenna laced her fingers in his, and they headed off into the darkness.

Sounds of water dripping echoed through the chambers that were carved out, heading both right and left. Cody decided to head right. Ducking through a narrower passage, a room opened in front of them with a large flat slab of limestone covering a portion of the floor.

Tilting the flashlight up revealed thousands of delicate formations

"Wow. This place is cool. Look at the ceiling," Jenna said in a gasp.

"The ones that kind of resemble fingers are stalactites, and the long tubes are called soda straws. If you break one of those off, it's hollow in the middle. You can actually use it as a straw," Cody said.

"How do you know that stuff?"

He chuckled. "Been to a few caverns in my time."

Jenna stood with her mouth gaped open, pointing. "They're iridescent."

Cody continued to hold the light up to see the rest of the room and spied the slab on the floor. "This is the perfect spot for a picnic."

A smile spread across Jenna's face. They unpacked the cooler and retrieved a couple of beach towels from the bag to sit on. Cody stuck his phone in the middle of the slab to give them a nice glow of light that reflected off the formations on the ceiling, making them glitter.

After a few minutes of silence, Jenna broke in. "So, at some point you are going to have to tell me what is going on with you and your dad."

"Not right now. I don't want to spoil our picnic."

Jenna turned to him with her brows raised. "Why doesn't he want you to date me? What did I do wrong?"

Realizing Jenna needed an answer even though he didn't want to get into it, Cody let out a long breath. "You didn't do anything wrong. Dad's just pissed. The police are investigating some of our members and employees. It includes him and Joe.

"What? Why?"

"Because they both work the early shift, and that was when you were attacked."

"But you were working the day I was attacked."

"Yes, but they are the normal crew, and the sergeant said it could be someone who watched you and knew your routine. You ran past the gym every day, and it's one of the only places open in the area that early in the morning, so it's on their radar."

"Oh my gosh. I had no idea."

"Don't worry about it, it's not your fault. You were the one who was attacked." Cody took a bite of his sandwich. "He also thinks it could be possible that we are simply infatuated with each other because of the trauma we experienced together. I guess it happens to people in service fields like the police, EMS, and fire department sometimes, where the victim falls for the rescuer."

Jenna took a bite of her pickle spear and bobbed her head. "Well, I guess that could be true, but I would have figured the attraction would have worn off by now, not gotten stronger."

Cody pressed his lips together, hiding a smile at her confession.

"Dad thinks if we get into a relationship and something happens and we break up, it would be bad for the gym."

"Why? Does he think I would spread rumors or something?"

"I don't know, I guess."

"I wouldn't do that...not unless you become a

gigantic jackass."

Cody peered up at the ceiling with a smirk. "I guess you are going to have to find that out."

"Hmmm...you do have that assault charge against you. Maybe I should have been a little more cautious before—"

Cody's chest tightened. "Speaking of which, what did Brant say to you?"

Jenna's face filled with confusion. "Who? When?"

"When he came into the gym with you. I saw him talking to you."

"Oh, that was Brant? Okay, it all makes sense to me now. I guess I didn't get a good look at him the other night. He apologized for spilling his drink on me."

"Spilling his drink?"

"Yeah, remember at TopHops? Remember he spoke to me? He must have spilled his drink, and that was what he was telling me. That's why my shirt was all wet."

"Ah, got it. Probably so. Did he say anything else?"

"No."

Silence took over once more.

Jenna's voice softened. "So, your father doesn't want us to see each other?" Cody could tell it was hurting her. "I mean I understand. I am sorry for all the trouble I've put you through."

The sadness in her voice was destroying him. Cody's body stiffened. His dad's words had obviously made Jenna feel guilty. He scooted into her and dragged her into his arms.

"Stop it. You were the victim. How many times do

I have to tell you that? It was not your fault. It was the jackass who attacked you, and nothing my dad says matters."

"But I don't want to come between you and your dad, Cody."

"You aren't the problem. He's doing what he does best, looking out for himself."

"But I—"

His mouth enveloped hers. Talking was getting them nowhere. He was done. Done with the discussion and done with letting his dad control his life.

The pain in her voice was killing him, and the thought of her ending things just as they were finding each other sent a wave of fear through him.

From the first day they met and Jenna grabbed his hand, he knew there was something about her. Even though he tried to fight his feelings, something told him there was a connection, and now he would do anything to make sure he didn't lose her.

His lips brushed kisses against her neck, lightly sweeping them up to her jaw.

"You're trying to distract me, aren't you?"

Tucking away tendrils of hair in his way, he continued to suck at the base of her neck.

"Is it working?" he said with his mouth pressed against her neck.

Her eyelids lowered. "Um hum."

Cupping Jenna's face in his hands, Cody brought her lips to his and traced her bottom lip with his tongue, slowly closing his mouth over hers. Their tongues brushed against each other, sending flames shooting to his core. Her lips were so perfect. He couldn't get enough of her.

Thoughts of the night before raced back to his mind. Every minute he was with her was better than the last.

"I want you in my life, Jenna," he whispered. "You are the one sure thing I know I want. Don't let my dad's words scare you away." Cody kissed her lightly on the forehead then gazed into her blue-green eyes. "There is something about you. You have this vulnerability, but you are so feisty and fearless. I have never met anyone like you, and I can't get enough of you." Cody paused. "When I'm around you, it's like you wake me up. You give me the confidence to be who I really want to be."

A rosy hue filled Jenna's face as she gazed at Cody through her lashes. The intensity in her glistening eyes caused the hunger within him to stir. Their mouths collided, tongues danced, bodies heated. She backed away breathless, her mouth brushing his lips.

"Cody?" Her soft whisper broke the drunken lustful state.

"Hmm?"

"I want you in my life, too."

The words made Cody's heart flutter, and a smile slowly formed on his lips as he captured Jenna's mouth again. She trusted him and it made him want to be there for her. Protect her.

His fingers trailed lightly up and down her shoulder with his lips following. His body was craving to connect with her.

Not saying a word, Cody scooted back and cleared the rock slab of their lunch while Jenna watched. Grabbing one of the beach towels, he covered the rock, then laid another on top of it.

Moving back to her, Cody tucked some loose strands of hair behind Jenna's ear, then tugged her to him.

Her plump lips sent electricity through Cody as he softly pecked them over and over. Then, barely sucking in each, he waited. A low moan rumbled from his throat as she joined him, and their kiss deepened.

His hands skimmed her sides, and he began to explore, while he brought her lips to his and kissed her tenderly. When he backed away, he softly brushed his lips against her nose, then glimpsed at the slab, and they both moved together to the pallet he had made.

Brushing his hand against her cheek, Cody pressed another kiss to her lips, then let his hands roam. His kisses trailed down Jenna's neck, nipping at the soft skin of her earlobe. Reaching behind her head, he released her hair, then moved down to untie her top, letting it fall away. Her hair slowly cascaded down her bare back, the light bouncing off her damp curls ignited a need to taste her again.

Curling his fingers into a fist in her hair, his lips pressed to hers as he dragged her down, but Jenna stopped him, resting on her elbow.

Leaning forward, she dusted soft kisses across his chest and down the hard-packed muscles of his stomach, trailing lightning strikes the lower she moved. Her hair fell into her face and she brushed it to one side.

Closing his eyes, Cody dragged his teeth across his lip, letting her kisses drive him crazy. When it was all he could take, he wrapped his arm around her and rolled her to her back again. Brushing her nose and mouth to his cheek, Jenna continued down his neck, softly pressing her lips to his shoulder.

Cody's muscles tensed with the feel of her soft bare skin against his. Jenna fit so perfectly in his arms. His hands traveled over her silky skin and down her back, resting above the top of her bikini bottoms before slowly pushing them down.

A soft whimper escaped her throat, her breath was hot against his neck as she peppered him with kisses while her hand slipped his suit down. Her light touch and the brush of her lips sent his mouth crashing against hers as his hunger took over.

Every inch of Jenna's body was bathed in the glow of the light from his phone. "You are so beautiful." Her hooded gaze met his, and every ounce of restraint Cody had unraveled. He couldn't wait any longer.

With a low growl, Cody rolled over and brought Jenna under him. Her lips parted with an escaping breath as his hand gripped her thigh and he sank into her. He lowered his head and smiled before lightly kissing her lips. The warm glow of the light caused her eyes to sparkle as he stared into them and began moving against her.

Tingles flooded his body from her fingers gently massaging his back, down his hips, and back up, making circles in his hair with her thumbs. Another groan escaped. She made him feel wanted, loved. This was what it felt like.

His lips pressed against her neck and down her chest, and his fingers quickly covered her lips when she suddenly moaned.

"Shhhh." Cody chuckled. "I don't know how far the sound carries. Don't want to freak anyone out that may be close by."

"Speak for yourself. They probably think there is a

bear in here."

"Can't help it. You feel so good."

His hand moved pieces of hair from her face, and her arms tightened around his neck. This little feisty redheaded woman was everything.

Sweat glistened. With his restraint crumbling, Cody ran his hand down her side to her hip, letting his hand glide over her silk skin while his lips traveled down her neck to her chest.

Their breaths and their movements quickened. Each of her raspy breaths, each of her whimpers from those soft plump lips, every grasp of her fingers drove his body closer to the point of no return.

A cry of surrender echoed through him as her body became undone with pleasure. Electricity shot down his spine and his body shook with his release.

Cody held her tight, kissing her neck as he continued to try to catch his breath with his face buried in her damp curls. He slowly rolled to his side and Jenna snuggled up to him, and they lay quietly in the glow of his phone.

"I can't believe we did that." Jenna giggled.

Cody leaned down planting light kisses on her mouth. "Not everyone can say they had sex in a cave."

"Was that your plan all along?"

Cody's mouth dropped open. "How could you think that of me?"

"Easy. You're a guy. That's what guys do."

He plucked at the threads on the towel. "Do you want the truth?"

"Sure. Lay it on me."

"I can't say it hadn't crossed my mind, but I seriously only planned on exploring and having a picnic. I thought it would be a fun distraction since you had that meeting. This…" his finger pointed up and down their naked bodies, "this was…a delicious surprise dessert."

"Uh-huh."

"Seriously."

"Well, I am thinking this is now my favorite dessert." Jenna's fingers traveled over his stomach causing goosebumps to rise.

Cody kissed the top of her head. "I agree."

"But we really need to get going though, I need to do some studying for the biology test."

"You would rather do that than hang out with me?"

"Well, I was going to invite you to come study with me at the house actually. We could maybe call out for pizza."

"That sounds like a great idea. I will need to get my book and folder from the gym though before we head over there."

After playing in the falls for a while, they toweled off and threw their clothes on over their suits and headed back through the trees to the trail. Cody's mood changed when he saw his dad's car parked in the parking lot.

"Great. He's back."

"Do you want me to wait outside? I don't want to cause you any trouble."

Cody's gut tightened at her words, but he was done letting his dad intimidate him. "No. Come on in. It shouldn't take me long."

They entered the gym and were met with Joe, Brant, and Todd, standing around the counter talking. Cody's eyes met his dad's. Not wanting Jenna to possibly get caught in the middle in case his dad decided to follow him into the office again, Cody turned to Jenna and said, "Stay here. I'll be right back."

Chapter Seventeen

Jenna sat in one of the plastic chairs just inside the door. Joe stood behind the computer staring at the screen, while Todd, Cody's dad, and Brant talked about a piece of equipment.

Turning away so she didn't appear to be eavesdropping, Jenna pretended to be interested in something outside. All three men began to laugh at something one of them said, but the sound of one laugh sent chills down her spine and caused her to turn.

From the corner of her eye, she saw him. He moved a certain way, popped his neck, and then wheezed a moan. Her eyes connected with his for a split second before she turned away.

Flashes of the assault raced through Jenna's mind, taking her back to that day. Back to the attack. The feel of his hands on her. The cold glare in his eyes. It felt like it was happening all over again.

Terror overwhelmed Jenna. She froze. A cold sweat broke out all over her body, and she began to shake. She couldn't breathe. Acid filled her stomach and crept up her throat. Was he staring at her? Did he know? How would she get away? Willing herself to turn, Jenna noticed he had looked away. She slowly stood and clutched her chest. *Now. Run!* Her body banged against the door just as Cody came back around the corner.

****

Cody turned to his dad. "Where is Jenna going?" He ran out the door to catch her, but she had already jumped in her truck and was speeding out of the parking lot. When he came back in, Brant turned to him. "I don't know what happened, I was talking to your dad and suddenly she stormed out.

Cody walked up to Brant and got into his face and growled, "What did you say to her?"

Brant put his hands up. "I didn't say anything."

Dragging his phone from his pocket, Cody quickly called Jenna. It went to voicemail. "I've got to see what is wrong," he said to the group, pushing his back against the door.

Tires scattered dust and rocks as Cody raced out of the parking lot and sped up the road. When he got to Jenna's house, he took the stairs by two and peered through the window, then banged on the door.

"Jenna?" A knot caught in his throat. Cody could see her curled up in a blanket on her sofa, rocking and crying. His hand banged against the door again. "Open the door." There was no way for him to bust in the door with all the locks she had added. "Please, baby, please open the door."

The creak of the old house had Cody peering through the window once more. Jenna was making her way to the door with Tucker at her side. Tears stung Cody's eyes when he got a clear look at her. The minute she opened the door, he rushed in, took her in his arms, slammed the door, and locked it.

Tears covered Jenna's face. She was choking with every gasp of air, and Cody could feel her body quaking and heart racing against his chest. It felt like it was happening all over again, just like the day of the attack. But this time he knew her, and it was taking every ounce of courage within him not to break down with her. He couldn't though. He needed Jenna to know he was there for her.

Pressing her body against his, Cody massaged Jenna's head with his fingers and softly shushed her, hoping to calm her down. His lips pecked at the top of her head as he stood and swayed with her. He didn't move until her breaths settled into a more normal rhythm. Then, picking her up in his arms, he carried her to the sofa, settling her in his lap and draping the blanket over them both.

Jenna's head leaned against his chest, and she continued to cry. Cody rubbed her shoulder and kissed her forehead as thoughts raced through his head of what might have happened. He needed to find out, so he could fix it.

Finally, the sobs subsided to the point where Cody felt safe to broach the question. Lowering his voice to a soothing quiet tone, he asked, "What happened? Did Brant say something to you?" She shook her head but didn't speak. "Did he touch you?"

"It's not Brant," Jenna said softly, in short broken breaths.

Surprised by her response, Cody questioned again. "It's not?" She shook her head emphatically.

He took a deep breath and continued. "Then what happened?"

Pain filled Jenna's face. Tears spilled down her cheeks.

The ache in Cody's chest continued to grow, wishing he could do more. Wrapping his arms tightly around her, he rubbed his thumb up and down her arm, soothing her, wondering exactly what could make her this upset. "Baby, I hate to see you like this, and I want to help you, but I can't unless you talk to me."

"I can't." Sobs shook Jenna's body as Cody held her against him.

"Do you want me to take you to the station to talk to Sergeant Gallagher?"

"No."

"Do you want me to call him?" She shook her head. Cody's hand moved to her back, letting it slide up and down, hoping it would calm her down enough to talk to him again.

"I don't know what to do," Jenna finally said, hiccupping through her words.

"Please Jenna, tell me what is going on."

Tears streamed down her cheeks. "I can't."

Cody's head hit the back of the sofa. He let out a heavy sigh of frustration. *There has got to be some way to get through this.* He sat silently for a few minutes letting Jenna regain her composure again.

"All right, so let's take this slow. Does this have to do with the meeting this morning?" Cody continued to rub her back, but she didn't respond. "Something happened at the gym?" Her eyes darted to the ceiling, and her chest began to heave.

"Okay, okay. And it wasn't something Brant did." She shook her head.

"Was it one of the gym members?" Cody asked.

"No."

Joe, Brant, and his dad were standing at the counter when they arrived. Brant was the obvious suspect, but he was ruled out.

Although he trusted Joe and could never believe he would do anything so horrible, his mind suddenly played through the evidence against him, he had the clothes, the scratch, and he had been in the park. It tore at his gut even to ask, but he had to be sure. "Did Joe do something?"

Jenna's "are you kidding me" expression almost made him chuckle, and she shook her head again.

Gathering his thoughts, Cody played through the series of events after they walked into the gym.

"So, we came in, and you stopped at the counter. The only other person at the counter was my..." He stopped, and his gut clenched.

Jenna turned away, and a flood of tears spilled down her face.

Rage rose inside of Cody at the thought of his dad saying something to Jenna regarding the earlier fight. He tried to pull Jenna's attention back to him, but she wouldn't. He barely could speak. "Jenna, what did my dad say to you?" His voice shook with emotion. "You have to tell me. He has no say so on what I do with—"

"It's not about the fight," she blurted out.

Cody closed his eyes trying to fight his way through his confusion and keep his tone gentle. "But it is about my dad?" Her barely visible nod told him he was on the right track. "Then what is this about?"

His fingers played in her hair and he waited.

A whisper broke the silence. "I remembered something about the attack."

"The attack?"

Jenna stared at the blanket, nodded, and began to cry again. Cody finally put the pieces together. His hand flew to his mouth. "Shit! You think my dad...?"

Unable to hide the indignation in his voice. He slid Jenna from his lap and stood, his mouth tight, eyes searching. *She can't seriously think my dad did this to her, can she?* The pain in her eyes gutted him and he softened his tone. "But why?"

"Please, Cody." She gazed up at him. Her tear-filled eyes begged.

"No, Jenna." he rasped. "You need to tell me now why you think my dad might have done something to you. I am sure it is a misunderstanding, but I need to know what happened, right now." The muscles in Cody's jaw clenched as he paced. His heart pounded so hard he could barely catch his breath.

The blanket fluffed as Jenna brought her legs up under the covers. Her hand wiped across her cheeks and she took a deep breath, letting it slowly out.

"When I met with Sergeant Gallagher, I remembered something that the attacker did." Cody glimpsed at her when she went silent, hoping she would continue. Her eyes lifted to his and then she quickly turned away. "When Tucker jumped at him the first time, he knocked the attacker off balance long enough for me to get my hands free. I tried to fight him off, but he managed to get me pinned again. Once he did though, he laughed, then jerked his head, and popped his neck." Jenna's voice softened to a whisper. "When I was at the gym earlier, your dad did the same thing."

Cody's gaze drifted off, and he nodded, relieved in what he thought she was saying. "So, the attacker popped his neck, and when my dad did, it reminded you of the attacker?"

She shook her head and closed her eyes. "No."

A rush of anger penetrated his chest from her

accusation. *She can't be serious. He wouldn't do something like this. Geez, he was a cop.*

"There are tons of people who do that. I do it. It's a common issue after years of wrestling," Cody said trying his best to defend his dad and dispel her suspicions. But the fear remaining in Jenna's eyes tore at his heart. The corner of his mouth turned up, giving her a half-hearted smile, hoping it would calm her, but her eyes continued to be haunted. The girl who was more courageous than anyone he had ever met, the girl who always seemed to find the goodness in everything, was obviously petrified. Nothing about her would make him think she wasn't being honest. And she would never make these accusations if she weren't certain.

"What is so specific about how my dad popped his neck that makes you believe he attacked you?"

"The way he did it. He laughed, then popped his neck and let out this wheezy moan afterward."

Cody felt like a bomb had detonated in his gut. It was true. He had heard his dad make the noise a thousand times and knew exactly what she was talking about. Cody's body went numb. *She's wrong. She has to be. It's just a coincidence.* His sober eyes met hers.

"Do you remember anything else the other victims revealed during the meeting with Mitch?"

"One of them said something about the sneakers, but I can't remember what she said."

"Think, Jenna," he grumbled and instantly regretted it. Kneeling, he calmed his tone. "Baby, this is really important."

Studying Cody, she put her fingers to her lips. "I can't remember, I'm sorry. I think it had to do with the color, but I'm not sure." Tears streamed down her cheeks again.

The churning in his stomach felt like a volcano about to erupt. Standing, Cody cupped his hand to his mouth and paced, worrying his lip. Did he want to get Mitch involved? *Maybe Mitch could help me find something that could clear Dad. But what if there isn't anything? Do I really want to lay all the cards on the table and open that can of worms? Shit! Dad would be so pissed. He couldn't have done anything this heinous.*

Tears continued to stream down Jenna's face as Cody knelt in front of her again. Brushing her tears away with his thumb, he bent over and kissed her temple. "It's okay, baby. It's okay. We are going to get through this." The shakiness of his voice surprised him. "Do you trust me?"

She closed her eyes and nodded.

Managing a smile, he ran his thumb over Jenna's cheeks again and stood. "Give me today to do some investigating on my own. Deal?"

"Okay."

"Do you want me to stay with you tonight?"

"Would you?"

"Absolutely. I kind of enjoyed the last couple of days." Cody leaned down and kissed Jenna gently. "But I will have to leave you alone for a little while. Are you going to be okay here by yourself? I mean, I could take you to April's if you want me to."

Bringing her feet to the floor, Cody held out his hand to help Jenna stand with the blanket still wrapped around her. "I think I will be okay, as long as you are coming back."

Putting his arms around her, Cody snuggled her in tight. "I will. Do you need me to get you anything before I go?" His hand stroked her back through the blanket.

"No, I'm good," she said, brushing away more tears.

"Where is your phone? I want you to keep it beside you."

She pointed to it on the table.

"If you need me for anything, I want you to call me." Cody's lips grazed her forehead. "We will get this figured out."

Tapping his phone, he opened the door and headed down the steps.

"Yeah?"

"Hey, Mitch, can I come talk to you?"

"Sure. Can we meet at the station?"

"I will be there in five minutes."

It all seemed surreal. Climbing in his Jeep, Cody sat staring at the steering wheel, trying to organize his thoughts. He knew many people had a habit of popping their necks, so because his dad did it didn't make him the attacker.

The Jeep roared when he started it and headed down the road. Thoughts still clouding his mind. On the other hand, Jenna was specific about the noise his dad made. That needed to be checked out. Still, he didn't relish the fact of his dad being investigated...again.

Pulling onto the main road heading into town, Cody thought about the fact that nothing was ever found when the police investigated his dad early on about the incident.

But something still gnawed at him. That question that always stayed in the back of his mind. *What about Mom? What happened?* The case was never closed, just shelved. *What if...?* Cody's chest tightened. The parking lot was empty when he pulled in, and his tires chirped to a stop.

Mitch stood at the lobby door with a confused look, in a pair of faded denim jeans, black graphic T-shirt, and black and red sneakers. Cody met him, and they walked to the back offices with barely a word spoken.

"I'm sorry for bothering you on your day off, but thanks for meeting me," Cody said.

"It's not like I wasn't up here earlier working. You were keeping me from doing some yard work, so it's all good."

As they entered Mitch's office, Mitch flipped the light on, and Cody shut the door.

Mitch's face went cold, and his eyes darted back at Cody. "There is no one else here. What the hell is going on?" He stepped behind his desk. "And if it has to do with Brant Ellington, don't bother. I did some investigating, and he has an interesting past. He doesn't have an alibi so I could be wrong, but I doubt very seriously he has anything to do with the attacks."

Cody shook his head. "It's not about him, but now you got me curious." Pushing the chair away from Mitch's desk, he sat down and crossed one ankle over the other.

"Do you know who Brant Ellington is?" Mitch asked, leaning forward on his desk.

"No. Other than an angry son of a—"

"He's the son of Sandra Gerrard and George Ellington." Cody's mouth dropped open.

"Oh, you gotta be kidding me. Sandra Gerrard, the actress?"

"Yep. And her husband is some hotshot cinematographer who has won an Academy Award. She is from Dalton, and her mom still lives here."

Astonished from Mitch's news, Cody adjusted in his chair.

"That's not all. Brant is a decorated Airforce medic. He was medically discharged after taking a bullet to the leg last year. He moved to the area a while back after his wife was killed in a car accident. Probably why Brant has been drinking himself into oblivion."

"Damn, I had no idea."

"With that information and the fact that he hasn't lived here that long, I doubt seriously Brant had anything to do with the attacks."

Cody froze as his thoughts returned to the issue. Staring straight ahead, he sat up with his hands clasped in front of him trying to gather his thoughts. His nose stung, and his eyes darted away. A knot formed in his throat when he tried to speak, and he pressed his lips together trying to clear it. "Brant's not why I'm here." Standing, and leveling his focus at Mitch, Cody said, "I need your help."

"Okay?" Mitch's tone remained calm and steady.

"I need to know what happened today with the victims. Any new information that was revealed." Mitch listened and then sat back in his chair and propped his feet on his desk.

"May I ask why?" Mitch's hand brushed against his short silver hair.

Cody's mind flashed on the conversation with Jenna. Remembering the terror that filled her eyes sent a cold chill through him. "Something happened with

Jenna today. I need to know what all the evidence is."

"You know I may not be able to share that with you. What happened exactly?" Mitch yanked his feet down and clasped his hands on his desk.

"Jenna saw someone do something that made her believe she found her attacker."

"Did it have to do with someone popping their neck?"

"Yeah." He scratched his neck, still wondering if he had made the right decision to confide in Mitch.

"You know one of the other victims said he did the same thing with her."

"Really?" Cody sighed and rubbed his hands together trying to keep his composure, even though his heart felt like it was about to leap out of his chest.

"Cody, you're obviously tormented by something, so why don't you let me in on it."

Gazing at the floor, again fighting against the tears trying to fill his eyes, Cody ran his tongue over his teeth then spoke. "I need to know what the other evidence is."

Mitch sighed. "I don't know what else I can give you that I haven't already."

"Any other information revealed when the victims got together?" Mitch thinned his lips in obvious frustration. He sat for a moment before scanning his folders, pulling one out, and opening it. Examining the yellow legal pad's scribblings, his pencil went line to line, flipping one page to the next.

"There really isn't anything," he said, exasperated. "Black pants, hoodie, black mask, and gloves." Continuing to skim the information, he flipped to another page and tapped his pencil. "One victim described a pair of sneakers as purple with a white emblem that resembled a bird. I thought that was pretty interesting."

Cody's gaze locked on Mitch, although he didn't look up. It was a gut punch that took his breath away. Though Mitch went on, evidently not noticing Cody's reaction, Cody's thoughts went back to the sneakers his dad had on the day Jenna got attacked. They were so odd, and so off from the normal way his dad dressed.

This visit with Mitch was to prove his dad's innocence. Prove he didn't attack Jenna. Write it off as a coincidence. Not prove his guilt. But he knew too many pieces fit. His chest tightened, unable to inhale enough air. Mitch needed to know but...

Cody's body shook like the temperature dropped below freezing in a matter of seconds with the realization of what he was going to have to do. Pacing, he brought his hand up to rub his temple as tears welled in his eyes. He heaved, trying to fight back tears, and turned to see Mitch staring at him.

"Cody?" Mitch leaned in, closing the folder. "You need to tell me what's going on."

Tears rolled down his cheeks as he tried to swallow, but his mouth had gone dry. Feeling his knees about to give out, he took his seat and ran his hands down his face. *How could this be possible? Why?* He couldn't even fathom his dad being a part of this. Pursing his lips, Cody let out a long breath. "It's my dad, Mitch." It was hard to comprehend that the words even left his mouth. The tightness of his throat rendered his voice a raspy whisper. He focused on the ceiling as his body began to shake uncontrollably. His arms folded around his stomach and he leaned forward, breathing hard.

Mitch frowned. "Let me get this straight. Miss Corbett thinks your dad attacked her?"

Cody clenched his jaw, his chin quivered, he closed his eyes, and nodded. He sniffed and opened his eyes. "Dammit."

"Do you want to elaborate?" Mitch's tone continued low and even.

"My dad was at the gym when Jenna and I were there. I left to go to the office, and when I came back, Jenna was freaking out and running out of the gym. I went to her house, and she said she remembered something from the attack. The attacker popped his neck.

"My dad does have a habit of popping his neck. It's from an old wrestling injury. I figured it was a coincidence, and honestly it pissed me off that Jenna would think it was him. But she described the sound he made as a wheezy moan, and Dad does that every time. I just couldn't get that out of my head.

"You have always been straight with me, so I wanted to talk to you about it. I thought maybe there would be something that might clear him."

"Well, it could be a coincidence." Mitch tapped the folder on his desk. "It is compelling and does need to be investigated, but beyond that, was there anything else that made you concerned it was him?"

His fingers pinched his nose, and he nodded his head slowly. Blinking, he took a deep breath trying to will away the tears. "Gah." Mitch pushed a box of tissues to him, and he grabbed one.

"When he came in the day of Jenna's attack, I noticed Dad had on a wild pair of sneakers. They caught my eye because they were so out of the norm for him, and I had never seen them before. They were purple with this weird design on the back, that kind of resembled a bird."

Mitch's eyes narrowed. Cody could tell by the sudden sober expression Mitch was convinced.

"We don't have enough to arrest him until we find the evidence. We will need to get warrants." He stood from his chair and rubbed his hand over his mouth. "Where is Jenna?"

"She is at her house." Cody's heart ticked up.

Mitch leveled his gaze. "Your dad saw Jenna leave the gym?"

Cody nodded. "And she was upset."

"Call her. Get her out of there, now." Mitch thumbed through papers on his desk.

Cody tapped his phone praying that she would pick up.

"Hello?" Her voice rang through the phone. Cody's heart skipped. Standing, he dragged his fingers through his hair.

"Jenna, listen to me. You need to leave right now. Grab Tucker and get out of there."

Silence remained on the other end so long that Cody began to worry the line had gone dead. "Where do you want me to go?" The sounds of her movements distracted him, and he couldn't think. "Should I go to April's?"

April? No, she has been to the gym, it would be too easy for him to get her address. She could come to the station, but she would have to be taken somewhere, no good. Then it dawned on him. "Go out to the bunkhouse at the ranch. I think you'll be safe there. Let your dad and brother know so they can keep an eye out."

"They left for an auction this morning. They are in Fayetteville all week."

"Shit." He rolled his eyes and wiped his mouth. "Doesn't matter, head out there now. Let me know when you get there."

"I'm scared, Cody."

"I know you are, baby, but I'm not going to let anything happen to you."

"Okay, I'm getting in the truck now."

The sound of her truck starting gave him some reassurance she would be safe, and he lowered the phone. But his gut still churned.

He leveled his eyes with Mitch. "What now? How long will it take to get the warrants?"

"It depends, it might be a couple of hours, it could be longer." Mitch put his hand to his mouth. "Your dad knows all the tricks of the trade being an ex-cop, so we are going to have to move fast, be smart, and be careful. We don't know if your dad is aware of what is going on yet. If he saw Jenna leave the gym upset, he may already be thinking she knows. But we need to get to the evidence, we need to find the mask and shoes."

"Dad knows I went after Jenna, so maybe that will buy us a little time. I think she will be safe if she can get to her family's ranch. They have a couple of houses out on their land, past the stables. So even if Dad went to her dad's house, he would have to know the other houses are back there to find Jenna."

"Okay, that might work. I've got to get warrants started to search the house, the gym, and his car."

"What if I do it? I have a key to the house and

access to the gym. We can start there while we wait for the warrant for the car."

"Good idea. I don't think he would keep anything in his car anyway. It would be too easy to find if he got pulled over. So, my first thought is the house. These crimes date back to before you guys had the gym, and chances are, he would not change the routine."

They walked to the front of the building. "He should still be at the gym. I can drive by on my way to the house to see if his car is still there."

"What does he drive?"

"A blue Chevy Camaro."

"All right, I'm going to put some officers on your dad, so we can keep an eye out. Do you own a gun?" The words spilled out of Mitch's mouth effortlessly, but they made Cody stop dead in his tracks. A gun? Yes, he owned a gun, and he knew how to shoot it. He spent countless hours at the gun range with his dad, but the thought of using it against his dad was unfathomable.

How could Cody ever live with himself if he had to shoot his own dad? But this monster could not be the man he knew. *What the hell happened?* Could it be something snapped when his mom disappeared? Or is it why she did? "Mitch, when did you say the first girl was attacked?" The answer, he really didn't want to know.

"Five years ago."

What if Mom figured out what Dad had done, or found something, confronted him, and he killed her? What if Hillary was right?

"Cody, you still haven't answered me. Do you own a gun?" Cody was tugged from his thoughts.

Jerking his head, he said, "Yes, I own a gun. It's in

my glove box."

"Keep it on you."

Mitch's words chilled him. His mind kept drifting. *Things were so perfect twenty-four hours ago.* Somehow, he had fallen into a nightmare with no good way out.

"I'm going to make some calls, set up some surveillance, and figure out how to put a tail on your dad without him catching on. Text me the address of Jenna's dad and give me some information on where she is at, and I will have some officers keep an eye on the area."

Cody sat stunned, continuing to play through the last twenty-four hours.

"Cody?"

Mitch brought him back to reality. "Yeah. Okay."

Walking around his desk, Mitch put his hand on Cody's shoulder. "You can do this."

He managed to nod but couldn't stay focused. Everything blurred as he tried to pull together a plan. Get the gun, text the address, check the gym, go to the house, check on Jenna. Why hadn't she called? She should have made it there by now.

"As soon as I get everything tied down here, I will call you, or if you find something, let me know."

"Got it." His finger was already tapping on his phone as he walked out of the station.

"Hello?" There was that sweet voice.

"I wanted to make sure you made it."

"I'm leaving now. I had to get Tucker's food and something for me to eat."

"Call me when you get there."

"I will."

Chapter Eighteen

Cody stopped in front of the gray stucco house and sat, still trying to come to terms with what was happening. Every nerve in his body was shot. Digging his phone from his pocket, he texted Mitch the directions to the bunkhouse, and then scanned the area to see if anyone was watching.

Somehow, it felt wrong to be sneaking around his dad's house, even though he was used to being there every couple of weeks. But wrong didn't even begin to describe what his dad might have done. The question that lingered in his brain was, why? *What possessed Dad to do this?*

As he fumbled for the keys to unlock the door, his phone chimed. Dad. His mouth went dry, and he contemplated answering it. The minute he heard his voice he would know something was wrong. But maybe he could make sure he wasn't on to Jenna.

Trying to calm his nerves, he answered. "Hello?"

"Hey, son, I wanted to check in with you. Is Jenna okay? I hadn't heard from you since you left. Did you figure out what happened?"

Cody froze. The last time he spoke to his dad, they were screaming at each other about Jenna. Why was he acting concerned about her now? Did he know? What would be a good lie his dad would buy? He glanced at his phone. Almost two. Sam would be up at the gym at three, and his dad would be leaving.

"Jenna was upset from the argument you and I had earlier. She doesn't want to come between us. I think it got to her. I am out getting us some stuff for dinner right now. I think, if it's good with you, I will keep Jenna company for the rest of the day. I don't think I will be back up at the gym."

"That's fine. I didn't mean for Jenna to hear that. I'm sorry. Hope she feels better." The timbre of his voice almost made Cody believe he might be clueless about everything. Could it really be a coincidence? His beliefs swayed like the branches of a tree, shifting with the wind.

The last thing Cody wanted was to be right about this whole thing, and maybe his suspicions were in overdrive, but something about the call didn't sit right either.

The door creaked when Cody pushed it open. The small house was nicely decorated with rich leather furniture and brushed nickel accessories. Not much hung on the wall except a few store-bought paintings left from their old house.

Other than a couple of weeks after his military discharge, Cody had never actually lived in his dad's house, so he wasn't sure where everything was. Scanning for places things could be stashed, he tried to picture where his dad could have hidden the items that the police might not have checked. Everything seemed neat and tidy.

Cabinets, drawers, behind furniture in closets, Cody checked everything. In the kitchen, he opened all the cabinets, drawers, and pantry, and then went into the utility room. But nothing appeared suspicious. The extra bedroom closet contained boxes, but all of them seemed to be old photos and Christmas decorations. Nothing seemed to be out of the ordinary. He searched under the bed and the mattress, and his hand skimmed the walls and bookcases in the office for hidden panels.

The master bedroom seemed to be a bust too, but when he turned to walk out, Cody spotted something. An electrical cord ran from behind the bed to a nightstand that had no lamp. The drawers seemed to be empty except a few papers and old remotes. After removing all the papers, he checked the bottom drawer again. When he pushed down on the bottom of the drawer, it unlatched. Underneath lay a small laptop. He unplugged it, lifted it from the drawer, and opened it up to see what might be on it, but the screen was locked. Unplugging the cord, he wrapped it around the computer and continued to wander around. This still wasn't what he needed.

As Cody made his way through the house, he remembered his dad saying something about the shoes being in the garage when he threw them on. Could he have been that careless, to say exactly where the shoes came from? He flipped on the light to the garage and surveyed the area. Nothing was left out in the open. Boxes and tubs were neatly stacked on racks up against the wall. The result of moving from a much larger house.

Studying the area, he tried to get into his dad's head. It would need to be a place that had easy access, so nothing up high, nothing with other items stacked on it. Tub after tub that Cody dug through had nothing but photos and stuff his mom had collected, from when he and Hillary were in school. His mind pondered the idea again that maybe his dad was a victim of circumstantial evidence. Nothing was out of place.

Maybe Dad didn't have anything to do with this. But why did he hide the computer? After rifling through a fishing bucket and toolbox, and coming up empty, he hit the garage door button and walked out to the driveway. The computer he had tucked under his arm landed in the seat of his Jeep before he continued to wander around.

Standing on the sidewalk, staring at the exterior of the house, Cody searched for anything that might be hiding something. With his arms crossed, he scanned the front of the garage, and his eyes were drawn to a garden box that sat off to one side. It was barely noticeable, blending in with the landscape and the color of the house.

Dread filled him. Something told him he would not like what he would find. Could he do this? Walking through the fresh cut grass to the box, his legs felt like dead weight. He let out a long, relieved breath when all he saw when he lifted the lid was a large green water hose coiled on a spool. Nothing out of the ordinary at first glance, and he started to lower the lid. Then a piece of shiny black fabric beneath the spool caught his eye.

Pulling on the material, he withdrew a black vinyl bag. His hands shook as he placed the bag on the ground. Thoughts filled his head of what was inside, but he wanted to believe this was anything other than what he knew it was. Everything inside him told him to leave it and walk away. But he couldn't. Not with Jenna in danger. His hand gripped the zipper.

The realization of the moment consumed him, and he stood, backing away in disbelief, his breaths coming in jagged gasps. Jerking his head, his eyes scanned the neighborhood again to see if anyone was watching.

Bile rose in his throat, and he coughed, feeling like he was going to vomit. Memories raced through his mind of his childhood. Now, staring at the bag, he couldn't believe what he stood on the edge of setting into motion. Slowly walking back to the bag, he knelt.

With each item he hauled out, the acid crawled farther up his throat. Black hoodie, black gloves. Tears pooled in the corners of his eyes as he gagged. Swallowing hard, he tried to force the bile back down. Black athletic pants. Mask. Breathing hard, he pinched his lips together and reached into the bag once more. Grabbing something firm, he pulled it out. A sneaker. Purple with gold stitching and a white emblem on the heel. It dropped from his hand like it had caught fire, and he stumbled back. This was really happening. Cody's heart stopped.

Tears streamed down his cheeks. Chunking the bag in the seat with the computer, he dug out his phone and walked back into the garage, shutting the door, then headed through the house and out the front door, locking it behind him. An unsettling calm washed over him. Mitch finally picked up. His fist pushed against his lips as he tried to clear his throat.

"I found it," he said, his voice trembling. Swallowing hard, trying to keep the tears at bay, he added, "It's him. I'm bringing the stuff by." That was all he had the strength to say. Numbness crept over him as he hung the phone up. In a matter of hours, his life had become completely foreign to him. *How could he do that to Jenna?*

Jenna. She was supposed to call. Why hasn't she?

His gut clenched. Tapping the screen on the phone, his mind raced with visions of his dad finding her. How long had it been since he talked to his dad? *Shit. I told him she was alone. What if he got to her? Dammit, why isn't she picking up?* "Pick up the phone, Jenna," he growled through gritted teeth.

He shoved his Jeep in reverse and peeled out of the driveway, leaving dust and rocks flying behind him, and raced up the street dialing again. "Pick up the freaking phone," he roared, and hit the end button when it went to voicemail.

Speeding up Spruce, he made a right turn and ran through two stop signs. He pulled up to her house. The truck was gone. *Could she just be away from her phone? God, please, let her be okay.*

Dust sprayed from beneath his tires. He sped out of her driveway and headed up the road. Scanning the parking lot at the gym, no Camaro. His heart pounded as he tapped the screen of his phone.

"Yeah?"

"Mitch, Jenna's not answering her phone, and dad's Camaro isn't in the gym parking lot. I'm worried he got to her. Meet me at the farm." The phone dropped in the seat as he turned onto the highway. Thoughts flashed of yesterday's drive down this same road with Jenna sitting next to him in her sunglasses and her hair blowing across her face. He pounded the steering wheel, willing the Jeep to go faster. Turning up the country road, he flinched, seeing his dad's blue Camaro sitting in the grass, in front of the entrance to the house. *Please, God, don't let Dad find her.*

The roar of his tires against the gravel set his teeth on edge. Heading out past the stables onto the dirt path, he pulled up next to her truck and slammed his Jeep in park.

The metal of the gun against his sweaty hand felt awkward as he retrieved it from the glove box. After checking for bullets, he pushed off the safety and jumped out. Tucker's bark echoed in the distance. Something was wrong.

A scream came from inside the house. Jenna. Bounding up the steps, the front door stood open, and he stepped inside. "Dad!" His voice boomed. Todd had Jenna pinned beneath him, and at the sound of Cody's voice, their eyes locked. In that instant, before Cody could make a move, Jenna gripped Todd's arm, and in one fluid motion, flipped him over, pinning his arm. Todd froze momentarily, then reached with his other hand, snatched his gun, and pointed it at her. Terror shot through her face, and she let go. Cody lunged forward, but Todd dragged her to him and jammed his gun in her ribs.

Cody jerked his gun from his waistband, planted his feet, and took aim, like his dad taught him, but this time his aim lay squarely at Todd. "Don't do it, Dad!" His voice thundered.

Todd gritted his teeth. "She knows."

The gun dug into Jenna's side, and she winced in pain.

Cody's eyes narrowed. "Knows what, Dad? That you attacked her? The police know. I went to your house and found everything. It's not going to do you any good to kill Jenna. Everyone knows, so let her go!"

Jenna's tormented eyes met Cody's, and his blood boiled when he saw new marks on her from his dad's attack. Cody steadied his aim as his focus returned to his dad.

"Why did you have to get mixed up in this?" Todd growled.

"I didn't have a choice; I was there when it happened."

"You weren't supposed to be. You weren't supposed to be a part of any of this." Todd squeezed Jenna in tighter.

"I'm sorry I screwed up your plan," Cody seethed, clenching his teeth, trying to fight back the tears. "Why? Why did you do it, Dad?" Angry tears spilled down his face.

"Cody I, I can explain," Todd stumbled, and softened his tone.

"Really? Explain? How do you explain hurting an innocent woman? How do you explain five women? How do you explain this?" His voice caught in his throat.

"I told you to stay away from her. She is nothing but trouble. She's going to ruin us, Cody. We're going to lose the gym."

"Jenna didn't do anything. You attacked her. Don't lie, Dad. You're the reason this is happening. You couldn't care less about the gym. You didn't want us together because you were scared I would learn the truth. And I did." Cody glared at Todd. "The past five years have been nothing but lies, Dad.

"What else have you lied about? What other secrets are you hiding?" He paused. "Where is Mom?" Todd's eyes widened. Cody knew he hit a nerve. "What happened to her? Because I am sure you lied about that too. Tell the truth for once." Lifting his chin defiantly, he asked, "Did Mom find out about your dirty little secret? She did. Didn't she?" He let the questions hang in the air for a moment. Waiting. "What happened?" His eyes narrowed, remaining laser focused on Todd while silence filled the room. "Did you kill her, Dad?" he asked calmly, his voice filled with pain. Silence returned, and fury ignited within him. "Answer me, dammit," he raged, tears streaming down his face. "Did you kill her?"

"It was an accident," Todd barked back.

The confession hit Cody so hard all the air escaped his lungs, and he stumbled back, but quickly regained his stance. He sucked in a jagged breath and glared at Todd. "I don't even know who you are."

Bright flashing lights broke through the window, filling the darkened house with strobes of color. Todd's eyes darted at the distraction. Jenna stomped on his foot and elbowed him in the gut, knocking the wind out of him. She turned and punched him in the throat, and he stumbled. His grip loosened. She broke free, just as a bright burst of light flashed, and a loud pop echoed through the room...and then another. Cody fell to the floor, and then Todd.

****

Mitch appeared with his gun raised, followed by several other officers.

Blood poured from Cody's body. Jenna ran to him and knelt beside him. His head turned slowly, and he blinked at her. Tears streamed out of the corners of his eyes.

"He shot me," he wheezed and lifted a bloody hand.

Jenna blinked back tears as she pressed on the bloody area, trying to stop it.

231

"Everything is going to be all right." Tears flowed down her cheeks.

Mitch walked over to Todd and slid the gun away with his foot.

Cody tried to laugh and dragged Jenna's attention back to him. "I changed my mind. I think a spider bite is a better way to go out." He coughed and his body writhed. "This. Hurts. Too much."

Jenna's breaths quickened. "Don't talk like that. You are going to be fine." She searched for something to put on the wound. A stack of towels sat in a basket on the counter. She jumped up, grabbed one, and placed the towel over the wound. It immediately turned crimson.

"God please, don't let him die," She whispered as her hand caressed his forehead. He coughed again. She stared into his eyes, watching as he tried to focus, then they closed.

"Cody." She screamed. His eyes fluttered open. "Don't go to sleep. Stay with me."

"I didn't...mean to...shoot him." Jenna turned when she heard Todd's voice. Mitch was standing over him. "My hand flinched...when Jenna hit me."

Jenna swallowed hard. *No, no, no.* She replayed the incident in her mind. The flashing lights, her chance to escape...he stumbled, then the shot. *Oh, my God. I got Cody shot.*

The scene around her vanished. All she saw was Cody lying before her in a pool of blood, gasping for breath, and she was to blame. His dad was right.

Paramedics surrounded Cody and brought Jenna back to reality. She backed away and caught Mitch still standing over Todd out of the corner of her eye.

"Never point a gun at someone you don't intend to shoot," Mitch scolded.

Jenna stared at Todd, trying to remember what he had done, but she couldn't help blaming herself.

The gurney carrying Cody clicked. An oxygen mask now covered his face, and they hurriedly wheeled him to the ambulance. She followed them out and stood next to Mitch.

He put his hand on her back. "I'm going to take you up to the hospital to get checked out."

"I'm fine. I can drive myself." Jenna's words were broken by sobs.

"I don't think you are in any condition to drive, and I am going to need to get a statement from you anyway, so let me drive you."

The conversation was cut short when a commotion in the ambulance caught her attention.

"Stay with us, Cody."

Beeping noises sounded above the groan of the engine. Red lights blinked on one of the machines Cody was hooked up to. Cody lay still on the gurney. One paramedic ripped open a bag as another bent over Cody and started chest compressions. Jenna fell to her knees. The doors slammed shut and the lights and sirens blared as they disappeared in a cloud of dust up the road.

****

The dimly lit waiting area was quiet. Mitch, Jenna, Joe, and April sat in silence, waiting for word from the surgical staff. The putrid smell of burnt coffee hung in the air. Doctors and nurses wandered the hallways. Jenna leaned up against April, who had arrived with Joe within an hour of her frantic call. Her mind played the horrible nightmare over and over. It was early morning, a little past two. Nearly seven hours since they got there.

Three hours were spent in the emergency room, only for them to tell Jenna she was fine. Not true. The new cuts and bruises would heal, but she was empty, completely drained of any life. Jenna had spent the better part of the day frightened for her life, only for that fear to come true when Todd grabbed her as she let Tucker out at the bunkhouse. Jenna knew she should have left when Cody told her. But she went back to get food for her and Tucker, and Todd must have followed her.

The memory of Cody getting shot played over and over in slow motion and ripped her heart out, but realizing it was her fault was almost too much.

There was so much blood. He was in so much pain, and his eyes were dark, and lost. Then, seeing the paramedics doing chest compressions in the back of the ambulance, all of it kept filling her eyes with tears. She couldn't live with herself if he didn't make it.

There had been no word on Cody's condition when they arrived, other than he had to have emergency surgery.

Jenna's dad and brother had come and gone after she refused to leave with them. They had left the auction after she called to tell them what happened. When she told them she hadn't seen Tucker since Todd found her and took a shot at him, they headed back to Dalton to hunt for him.

Mitch stood and walked out to the hallway when two other officers arrived. They stood talking, directly outside the waiting room door, still in her line of sight. The heavy metal doors to the surgical area opened periodically with doctors, nurses, and staff strolling in and out, paying no attention to them. The murmur of the officers' conversation lulled her into a daze. Her trance was disrupted by the buzz of the doors. The doctor, dressed in green scrubs, scanned the waiting area, then turned his attention to Mitch. Jenna hopped up and ran to the hallway.

All she heard was, "we did all we could," come from the surgeon.

The words pierced her heart. Her body quaked. "Nooooooo." Her shrill cry echoed in the hallway. April and Joe jumped from their seats.

Mitch gripped her arm before she hit the floor and stared into her eyes. "It's Todd. Not Cody. Cody is still in surgery."

April held her, and she draped her arms around her neck. "He has to make it."

"Don't worry, he will." April stroked her head a couple of times before escorting her back to the chair.

Joe quietly sat down beside them and put his head in his hands.

Mitch continued talking to the doctor and officers, going over paperwork, when the buzz of the door caused Jenna to jump up again, followed closely by April and Joe. A young female surgeon appeared. Her mask still shielded her face, and she lowered it to her neck. They all converged on Mitch at the same time.

"Mr. Spencer made it through surgery. The gunshot was a through and through. He lost a lot of blood, and we had to repair his spleen, but barring any setbacks, he should make a full recovery. He will be in recovery for a few hours and then the surgical ICU on the sixth floor."

Jenna turned to April and wrapped her arms around her, allowing herself to finally breathe and feel something other than dread. She caught Joe, leaning up against the wall outside the waiting room, out of the corner of her eye. He had barely spoken since he and April arrived. "He's like a brother. We did everything together," she remembered Cody saying. This beast of a man appeared completely broken.

She stepped up to him and pulled him into a hug. "He's going to be fine. Don't worry," she whispered. Joe nodded but remained silent.

After the surgeon left, Mitch turned to her. "Since it will be a while before he gets into a room, I am going to head out and get some sleep. I suggest you do the same. I'm guessing you have a way home?" Shoving his hands in his pockets, his eyes bounced between Joe and April.

"Yeah, I'm good. Thanks for everything."

His shoes squeaked against the freshly polished tile floor as he turned to walk away. "You have my number, right?"

"Yes."

"Call me if you hear anything, and I will do the same," he called out without turning around.

"Absolutely."

Mitch disappeared up the hallway. Jenna glanced at April and Joe, who headed back to the room and gathered their stuff.

"I'm staying."

April's eyes darted to hers. Confusion stretched across her face. "They won't have him in a room for a few hours. You heard the doctor. Where would you stay? This is not a hotel. It's not like they have a room you can rent."

"They have a waiting room in the ICU with some sofas. I slept there when my mom was in the hospital. I'll stay there. It will be fine."

"I don't think it's a good idea. You shouldn't be alone, Jenna."

"I can't leave him."

"I'll stay with her," Joe offered. "I don't think I would be able to sleep if I went home anyway, so might as well not sleep here."

"Well, if you guys are staying, I guess I am too." April plopped on a chair and rolled her eyes. "Joe's truck is a manual transmission, and I can't drive it."

Joe turned to April. "You don't know how to drive a stick?"

"Nope. Never thought I needed to learn."

"Well, I guess I will need to teach you," Joe said, with a chuckle. Jenna smiled at the thought of April trying to drive a stick and seeing Joe smile, finally. They walked up the hallway and boarded the elevator.

The surgical ICU waiting room was smaller than the room they had been in, but black vinyl chairs and sofas wrapped the walls, giving them plenty of room to sleep. Jenna disappeared up the hallway. When she returned, she carried pillows and blankets.

"I let the nurses know we were staying here for Cody, so they will come and get us if they have updates." Tossing a pillow and blanket on one of the sofas, she pointed. "I will take this one, and you guys can take the long one. When we were here with mom, we slept with someone at each end, and it seemed pretty comfortable."

Joe snagged a pillow and blanket. "Geez, Jenna,

you sound like you own the place."

"Trust me, I've done this plenty of times."

"I'm sorry, I didn't mean—"

"Oh, no, don't feel bad, I wasn't here only for my mom. I was here when Ben got stepped on by his horse and had to have his leg put back together, and then when he fell out of the back of the trailer loading some cattle and had to have surgery on his shoulder. He was a little bit accident prone when he was a kid...well he still kind of is. Anyway, the waiting room isn't only for the ICU. It's kind of a surgical catch-all." She snuggled up on her sofa and got a glimpse of Joe and April, who had gotten settled and seemed happy, and she slowly drifted off to sleep.

Chapter Nineteen

The smell of fresh coffee stirred Jenna from her drowsy state. Her eyes fluttered open and she jerked, trying to remember where she was. The stark surroundings made her come face to face with the previous day's events once again. It wasn't merely a nightmare.

The large clock on the wall read seven forty. Twenty minutes before visiting hours started. Long enough for her to get some coffee and run to the bathroom to wash her face.

No one had disturbed them through the night, so she took that as a good sign. Although it wasn't like she got more than an hour of sleep anyway, between trying to get comfortable and dealing with the sickening feeling of getting Cody shot. The moment had played over and over in her head.

Wrapping herself in the blanket to fend off the chill in the air, Jenna's gaze landed on April and Joe who appeared completely content and sound asleep. Sometime in the night, April moved and was now snuggled up against Joe.

Jenna sat up, fluffed her hair, and ran her fingers under her eyes, trying to wipe away the smudged mascara that might have collected.

The hallway was already becoming busy with hospital workers flowing in and out of the metal doors.

Planting her feet on the cold tile, she looked around for her flip flops and slipped them on before standing and quickly realizing the toll that sleeping on a hard sofa could take on a body.

After twisting from side to side, trying to relieve the pain in her back, she poured herself some coffee, adding two containers of the powdered cream from the caddy on the counter. The steaming drink burned her lips but didn't taste half bad for hospital coffee.

The blanket that kept her warm during the night sat wadded in the middle of the sofa and made her wish she had something other than a T-shirt and shorts on. She pushed it to the end and sat back down.

Picking up her purse from the floor, she retrieved her phone from the side pocket and tapped the screen. A photo of her in her scrubs with Tucker the day she adopted him appeared. *Oh crap, I am supposed to be at work at nine. April too.* Quickly dialing the number, she hoped someone was at the hospital early.

"Bruin's Veterinary, this is Tracy."

"Tracy, this is Jenna." Noticing the two still sleeping, she stepped out in the hallway to avoid waking them.

"Hey, Jenna, what's up?"

Her fingers combed through her hair as she propped herself against the wall. "Long story, but I'm at the hospital. Cody got shot." The words soured in her mouth and a pain shot through her chest. The terrifying ordeal took over her thoughts again. She clamped her eyes shut, trying to ward off the tears already stinging her eyes, and continued. "April is here with me. I can't come in today, and I don't think April will make it in either. What do I do?"

"Holy cow, Jenna, what happened? Are you okay?"

The heavy metal doors buzzed. Jenna's eyes followed two men in green scrubs as they passed by.

"Again, long story that I can't get into right now, but yeah, I'm just shaken up," she responded. "But Cody had to have emergency surgery last night, and he's in ICU right now."

Pacing the corridor, she spoke quietly as she watched a steady stream of doctors and nurses pass by.

"I'll take care of everything," Tracy said. "Please keep me posted on his condition."

"Thank you so much. I will let you know."

As she ended the call, a nurse came through the doors and zeroed in on her. "Are you Jenna Corbett?" the middle-aged woman asked.

"Yes ma'am." She tucked her phone in her back pocket, then folded her arms across her body, trying to keep from shivering.

"Mr. Spencer is awake. He's in room fifteen. You will need to hit the button by the door and give them your name before you are allowed to come in."

Jenna's insides instantly felt like they were being squeezed in a vise. She rubbed her hands on her arms while a thin smile crossed her face. Her mouth went dry, but she managed to quietly answer, "Okay, thank you."

The nurse left, and Jenna walked back into the room, tapping April and Joe, letting them know before she ran to the bathroom to freshen up.

When she returned, April had folded the blankets and set the pillows beside them. Breathing deep, trying to stave off the tears that were threatening to pour out at any minute, she picked up her purse, slung it across her body, and walked over to hit the button. A voice came over the intercom.

"Name?"

"Jenna Corbett to see Cody Spencer." The door buzzed and slowly opened.

The ICU had glass cubicles around the perimeter of the area, with a private nurse's station outside. A center station was manned by several people clad in scrubs. The area was teeming with doctors, gathered from room to room.

They walked around the center station to the glass front cubicle. A curtain was draped halfway across the closed sliding door. Jenna caught the attention of the nurse sitting outside the room, tapping on his computer.

"There should be only two visitors at a time, so don't stay too long. Hit the button over there." The nurse pointed to a metal button on the wall.

The hiss of the oxygen machine and beep of the monitor echoed in the room, along with the intermittent hum of the blood pressure cuff. Bags of solutions hung from I.V. trees, encircling the head of the bed that was raised slightly.

The sight of Cody's helpless state had Jenna shaking uncontrollably. His eyes were closed. The dark brown five o'clock shadow accentuated his pale skin. He had pillows under his head and the hand that held the I.V. An oxygen cannula and feeding tube were in his nose, and a blood pressure cuff on his upper arm. A tear escaped as she approached the side of his bed and carefully touched him.

****

Cody felt something brush across his forehead, and then the warmth of a hand in his. Slowly, he was dragged back into consciousness. A heaviness had filled his body. It took everything within him to turn his head, to see who was touching him. At first, everything was out of focus. His mind felt scattered, trying to figure out what was happening. Nothing made sense. Had he gotten drunk? The noises around him sounded like he was underwater. Trying to clear his head, Cody slowly blinked, and the room started to come into focus. *Oh, yeah. Hospital. Jenna?* He took in a breath, coughed, and immediately winced when pain shot through his core. *Ow. Damn, that hurts. But it's kind of funny. Why do I feel so weird?* Blinking again, he peeled his eyes open. It *was* Jenna. The corner of his mouth tipped up.

"Hey, this seems strangely familiar," he blinked several more times trying to keep everything in focus, "but a little backward." The words came out slurred.

Tilting his head, Cody squinted, trying to make out who else was in the room. "What are you guys doing here?" Finally recognizing Joe and April. "What time is it?"

Joe put his hands in his pockets. "A little after eight, but we've been here since last night." He nodded to Jenna. "She didn't want to leave you."

Cody winced again, and chuckled, then slowly turned to Jenna. Tears filled her eyes. His brows creased together. "Hey." His thumb rubbed the back of her hand. "Don't be sad. It's over. I'm going to be fine, the doctors said so."

She opened her mouth to speak, but words didn't come. Cody waited, but she waved a hand in front of her face and turned away.

He snorted a laugh, "Man, I must look really bad," trying to make a joke. Pushing his hand into the mattress, he tried to scoot up in the bed, but failed.

Joe nodded and motioned with his finger. "You are a little pale, and you got tubes coming out of everywhere."

"Oh, trust me, they are coming out of places you do not want to know." Jenna giggled at the comment. Cody turned to her and gave her a drunk smile.

"That's what I wanted to see."

A rap on the glass made everyone jump. Mitch entered. "How are you doing this morning?"

"I'm doing good, thanks to these high-powered pain meds," Cody managed to say almost clearly, while he continued to try to scoot up in the bed but still couldn't quite get comfortable.

Mitch chuckled, "Please leave them here when you go home. We don't need any more of them on the streets."

Cody slowly raised his hand to his chin. "Wonder what the going rate is?"

"Not worth the jail time."

"True."

Mitch took in all the equipment surrounding the bed. "Seems like they got you hooked up to almost everything. How long did they say you would be in here?"

"The doctor came by earlier. I think she said if all goes well, I will be in ICU probably another day or so, then a regular room where I will start rehab. I should be home in a couple of weeks."

"Good to hear." Mitch tapped the folder in his hand against the edge of Cody's bed, and his expression turned serious. Cody knew what the folder meant. "So, are you up for a little chat?" Mitch's eyes darted from

Cody to Jenna.

"Sure. But I don't know how much I will remember, I'm on some high-powered pain meds."

"Yes, you told me," Mitch said with a chuckle.

"You already got my statement. Do you still need me here?" Jenna asked.

"I think it would be a good idea." Mitch nodded to Cody. "Just in case his story goes off the rail. He's on some high-powered pain meds."

Jenna tucked her lips between her teeth. "I heard."

Mitch chuckled again. "I bet drunk Cody would be fun at parties."

Joe nodded knowingly.

April caught Jenna's eye. "We'll go get some coffee and be back in a little while."

They exited the room and Mitch tossed the folder on the rolling table, causing Cody to jump and then wince.

"Are you sure you are up for this? I thought I would stop by and get this done before I headed to the office. That way you don't have to deal with it later. But if you need some time, I can wait."

"I'm good." Cody locked eyes with Mitch. "Let's get this party started."

Mitch reached in his pocket and dug out a small recorder. Placing it on the table next to the notepad, he hit the button. "What do you remember from last night?"

Cody inhaled, coughed, and winced. "Where do you want me to start?"

"Start when you left the house."

The pillow crushed beneath his head as he allowed the memories to wash over him. The bag, the clothes,

Jenna didn't answer, the darkness in his dad's eyes. The memories flooded in, and he blinked several times trying to clear his head. His face was sober, and his eyes focused. "I was headed to the station when I realized Jenna hadn't checked in to let me know she made it to the house. I drove to her house and she wasn't there. I then drove past the gym and noticed my dad's car was gone, and that's when I contacted you and headed to the bunkhouse.

"When I got to the turn off, Dad's Camaro sat halfway off the road. I pulled up to the bunkhouse. Jenna's truck was there. I took my gun from the glovebox and shoved it in my waistband.

"The door to the house was open. I heard Jenna scream as I entered. Dad was on top of her. I yelled, and she flipped him off her. I lunged at him, but he grabbed his gun and had it pointed at her, so I drew mine and pointed it at him."

Cody looked up, pausing to make sure he didn't forget anything. Mitch scribbled on the yellow legal pad. He waited until Mitch made eye contact. "I tried talking to him, to get him to let her go, and bide some time. I figured you guys weren't far away. When I saw the lights flash through the window, I saw Dad turn. That's when Jenna broke his hold on her and escaped, and then he shot me."

Mitch continued writing. "Do you remember anything else?"

"Things got a little fuzzy after that. I remember hearing the bang and feeling like I got punched in the gut. When I hit the floor, it felt like I got the air knocked out of me, but then the burning pain hit. Then I remember grabbing my stomach and seeing blood on my hands. That's when I realized he had shot me. Next thing I know, the paramedics are loading me on the gurney. I think I passed out after that."

"You coded," Jenna said quietly.

"I did what?" Cody questioned.

"Your heart stopped. They had to do chest compressions."

"I died?" She nodded, her mouth quivering. Cody's face filled with surprise. "Would that be why I have this?" He yanked the covers up and lifted his gown on his side to show a large red circle next to the surgical dressings.

"Yeah, they must have had to use the AED," Mitch confirmed. "That is from where they connected electrodes to shock you."

I have one in the middle of my chest too." Cody tugged the collar of his gown down.

Mitch leaned on the table. "Do you know what happened to your dad?"

"No, all I remember is Jenna hitting him, and him shooting me." She turned away, but Cody noticed the tears streaming down her cheeks. "You did arrest him, didn't you?"

Mitch's lips thinned. "No, actually, he was shot."

Cody's brows knitted together. "I shot him?" He let out a long sigh. "Mitch, I swear, I don't remember pulling the trigger."

Mitch shook his head and put his hands in the air. "You didn't. I did." Cody's eyes widened. "I came around the corner when he shot you."

Cody scrunched his face not wanting to ask the next question. "So, what happened to him?"

Mitch set his pen down and leveled his eyes at

Cody. "He didn't make it."

Cody's gaze drifted, then he nodded his head. He peered over at Jenna then back up to Mitch. "Thanks for protecting us, Mitch."

"I wanted to be the one to tell you." Mitch's tone softened. "I sure didn't want it to end that way."

"He chose how to end it."

Mitch nodded then paused. "We got everything out of your Jeep and have search warrants for the house, the car, and the gym, so we will be conducting those this week. I've also talked to the sheriff in Montclair and he's pulling your mom's case. It was never officially closed, but there's been no movement on it in a while, so I will be starting my own investigation into that case." Cody thought about the conversation between him and his dad, and he suddenly remembered his dad's confession.

"She's dead, Mitch," he said, and let out a sigh. "Dad told me last night. Said it was an accident, whatever that means."

"I can't say I am surprised." Mitch rubbed the back of his neck. "So, this information changes things a little."

"In what way?"

Mitch took a deep breath. "I don't know how to put this, but if you think of a location he might have taken her, let me know."

"Like, where she might be buried?"

"Basically," he said and paused. "Since we have no real clues for what he might have done with her, it's up to you to search your brain for locations where your dad has taken you throughout your life. It might be a long shot, but it's the only shot we got for finding her."

"Yeah, that's not going to happen right now. I'm having a hard time searching my brain for what happened ten minutes ago. I'm on some high-powered pain killers."

Mitch's eyes met Jenna's and he shook his head. "Do you have anything to add?"

Jenna responded, "I think he did pretty well, considering he's—"

Mitch chuckled. "Drunk?"

"I'm not drunk," Cody whined.

A soft knock interrupted the conversation. A tall blonde woman poked her head into the room. "Cody?"

Jenna looked at him from the corner of her eye then back at the blonde. Mitch watched Cody's face as he studied her.

"Hillary?" His expression filled with confusion.

The woman's face softened, and she entered the room. "You were all over the news this morning."

He turned to Jenna and Mitch, "This is my sister Hillary," then turned back to her. "This is Jenna Corbett and Sergeant Gallagher."

Hillary stepped back with her eyes darting between Cody and Mitch. "Oh, did I come at a bad time?"

Cody glanced back at Mitch. "No, I think we were pretty well done." He paused. "How'd you find me?"

"I figured they brought you to Fayetteville, so I called the hospitals until I found you."

His gut tightened, letting her words about him being on the news sink in. He let his eyes drift to something out the window and took a deep breath. "So, the story was on the news?"

Hillary's voice was barely audible. "Yes."

"I guess you know then...he's gone." Planting his

fists into the bed, he tried to adjust himself again, and a deep pain shot down his spine. His eyes slammed shut, and he let out a pained groan through clenched teeth.

Jenna stood quickly. "Do I need to call the nurse?" Hillary moved to the side of the bed.

Cody grimaced and nodded. Jenna hurried across the room and poked her head out the door, summoning the nurse stationed outside his room. A tall muscular man in blue scrubs appeared at the door and stepped up to the bed.

"What's going on?" the dark-haired bespectacled guy asked in a cool tone.

"I need to move. My legs are going numb." Cody groaned.

"Do you want to sit up more or lay down?"

"Sit up."

"Gotcha." Hillary stepped aside as the nurse moved the bedrail.

"Do we need to leave?" Jenna asked, worry filling her voice.

"It's not necessary. It will only take a minute," the nurse said as he laid the bed down. He gripped the sheet and then turned to Cody. "This might not feel so good, but just bear with me, I will get you situated." The nurse pulled the sheet, and Cody gritted his teeth and groaned, then cried out in pain.

Jenna stood at the end of the bed with her hand to her mouth. Tears streamed down her face. The nurse continued to adjust pillows around Cody, causing him to grimace again, and then raised the head of the bed back up. "How's that?"

Cody let out a breath. "Better." His eyes peeked up at Jenna, who had her hand covering her mouth and tears streaming down her face. He hated seeing how upset she was.

The nurse checked the bags hanging from the IV tree, and then the other bags attached to his bed. "Where is your pain level right now?" His eyes connecting with Cody again.

Cody moved his arms and let out a jagged breath. "I'm good now." He peeked at Jenna again trying to reassure her.

"If you need anything, my name is Jordan." Punching the silver button, he stepped out of the room. Cody slowly reached for his water. Hillary quickly retrieved it and handed it to him.

Mitch tapped the file on the table. "I have all I need so I am going to get out of your hair. I will be in contact as we get things processed. I've been put on administrative leave while they investigate, but they've given me permission to finish the paperwork."

Cody's eyes darted to him. "Why did they put you on leave? You saved our lives."

Mitch walked to the side of the bed. "Strictly a formality. Any shooting is an automatic leave. Don't worry about me, you need to focus on getting better, and call me if you need anything."

Cody nodded, and slowly lifted his hand to shake Mitch's hand.

Jenna gave Mitch a quick hug before he turned to leave. "Thank You," she said as she backed away.

He patted her. "Take care of him."

Jenna turned to Cody, wiping the tears from her cheeks and pasting on a smile. "I'm going to see if I can find Joe and April and give you guys some time to catch up."

Cody's heart ached for Jenna. He could tell the smile was only for show and hated that she was clearly hurting. He knew she was still dealing with everything that happened, but something about the sadness in her eyes had him wondering if there was something else going on. Her face sobered when he grasped her hand as she was leaving, and she pulled away. His brows drew together, confused, but he nodded and wiggled his fingers.

Chapter Twenty

Cody tugged at his covers trying to get them adjusted. "Hillary, I gotta admit, I am kind of surprised to see you, I mean, it's been a while."

Guilt filled her face. "It had nothing to do with you. It was Dad." She sat in the green vinyl chair next to his bed. "I'm so glad that you are going to be okay. The news said you were in critical condition."

"Yeah. I guess I coded in the ambulance. I have these wicked marks from where they shocked me." He lifted the sheet slightly but dropped it when Hillary's face lost all its color. "They said the bullet went through me and nicked my spleen."

"You are so lucky, Cody." Relief saturated her voice, and she gave him a crooked smile. "It sounds like you are quite the hero."

He rolled his eyes and chuckled but then became sullen. "Why did it have to be him?"

"I know. You don't know how much I wish it weren't. Dad and I never saw eye to eye. We were constantly butting heads, and Mom always had to intervene, but I honestly never saw this coming. I hoped we would someday have a closer relationship, but it never happened."

"I should have tried to make it up there, but he kept me busy morning, noon, and night," Cody explained. "I just recently was able to set my own hours."

He moved his hand slowly and raised his bed. "So, I guess I should tell you since you brought up Mom, she is gone too." Hillary shook her head and sighed. Her hand lightly touched her lips and tears glistened in her eyes. "When I confronted Dad about it, he said it was an accident. Mitch is taking the case."

"I kind of had a feeling," Hillary said, her words thick with emotion. "I mean we haven't heard from her in three years. She and I used to talk quite a bit, so you would think if she were still alive, we would have heard from her by now."

Cody played with his hospital band on his wrist. "Can I ask you a question?"

"Sure."

"Why did you tell the police you thought Dad could have done something to her when they talked to you?"

Cody stared at Hillary as she peered out the window. "I don't know. Dad always made me uneasy. I couldn't put my finger on it, but I always felt like he was hiding something or putting on an act, especially when his temper would kick up. Comments he would make bothered me."

"Well, we will never know what happened. What flipped the switch. But something sent him way off-kilter." Hillary pushed his table toward him when he reached for his water. "Mitch wants me to come up with some places to search. Places where Dad might have taken us as kids."

"I don't think we went anywhere other than the amusement parks, and I had already left by the time you and Dad went and did stuff."

"True." He raised his arm slowly and checked the

I.V. attached to his hand before running his hands through his hair. "How long are you here?"

"It depends on what you need." She sat on the edge of the bed. "I can rent a hotel room if you want me to stay, but there isn't much I can do while you are in the hospital. I was thinking though, once you are out, it might be a good idea for you to come and stay with us while you recover. We have plenty of room.

"I know your life revolves around the gym, but it might not be the best atmosphere to walk back into right now. Kind of a lot to deal with. It probably would be good to get away from all the ghosts."

Cody hadn't had time to think about the fallout that would occur. "There's no need for you to stay. Your kids need you, and you're right, there is not much you can do here. I may take you up on the offer though, about after I get out. I never thought about what might happen in the aftermath. Anyway, I would like to meet my niece and nephew."

Hillary's words played in his head. Cody didn't relish having to deal with whatever people now thought about his family and all the legal issues that might arise. "I don't know what we are going to have to deal with on the legal end."

"I'm not talking about that, as much as memories, and how people respond. But, on the legal end, I don't think anything can be processed legally until we find mom. If she is not found, we will have to wait for the remainder of, what I think is, seven years from the time she disappeared to do anything with the estate. Plus, we may wind up with some lawsuits before this is all over."

Cody rolled his eyes. "I have no idea how all of

that stuff works. Right now, my only hope is my insurance is still good, because I figure this little stay at this lovely establishment is going to be pretty expensive."

"Don't worry about it right now. Concentrate on getting better." Patting his arm gently, Hillary stood. "I'm going to go for now, so you can get some sleep, but I'll be back later. I'm not heading home until this evening. Think about my offer."

The door closed behind her and he buried his head deep into his pillow. Hillary's words raced around in his mind. Everything in his life, his entire livelihood right now, was deeply entangled with his dad…the serial attacker and murderer. What would happen to the gym? Would the members even want to come anymore? Even though he was gone, the stigma would still be there. What if the victims decided to sue?

Dalton was such a small town. Cody was sure everyone had already learned of the incident. It was all over the news.

The reality was suddenly overwhelming. He wished he could wake up from this nightmare. He tried to picture what life might be like once he was out of the hospital.

The more Cody thought about it, the more he wanted to leave for at least a little bit, to get away from the craziness. It would take time to wrap his brain around what he was going to have to live with, and how to move forward. Maybe Dalton wasn't where he needed to be. Maybe it would be better to move and get a fresh start.

But what about his friends? What about Jenna? His body suddenly ached for her. She was the best thing that had ever happened to him, but every time he thought about her, he now relived last night, with his dad pointing a gun at her and the terror in her eyes.

Then it hit him. What if she was doing the same thing? He wondered what she saw when she looked at him. That light that sparkled in her blue-green eyes had dimmed this morning when he saw her. Every time their eyes connected he could see her fighting to keep the tears at bay.

The comment his sister made about "getting away from the ghost" made his gut tighten. His dad was her ghost. What if all she saw in him now was an incarnation of the monster who made her life a living hell? Could that be why she was so upset?

He would never want to be a constant reminder of the worst time of her life, but the more he thought about it he knew, if he stayed, he would.

The thought of not having her in his life suddenly made him feel like he had been shot all over again. His dad may not have killed her last night, but he still managed to take her away from him.

Jenna, April, and Joe piled back in his room, and Cody could barely breathe. Wiping his face, he took one look at Jenna and shame engulfed him. He cleared his throat trying to feign a better mood.

"Guys, this party has been great, but I'm fading fast. I appreciate you guys staying last night, but I know you have lives you need to get back to. I will be fine."

Jenna reached for Cody's hand. "I'll stay. You need someone to stay with you. You don't need to be alone."

"Jenna, you don't have a car," April reminded, "and you have barely slept in the past twenty-four hours."

Cody removed his hand. "You need to go home."

Her eyes glistened with tears. She moved her hand slowly and crossed her arms.

"Oh, all right," she said as she stepped back from his bed.

"I will be fine. They are taking good care of me. I am just exhausted."

"We'll head out, too," Joe said, tapping the end of the bed. "Get some sleep, man. We'll come back and check on you later."

They headed for the door. "Thanks again." Cody waved as the door shut behind them, and a tear escaped from the corner of his eye.

In a matter of hours, his life had been turned upside down. Things had been going so well. He finally had a grasp on his future, but his dad completely obliterated all semblance of happiness he had hoped for.

****

The drone of the truck tires was all Jenna had to listen to. She didn't even feel like turning on the radio. Peeking over at Tucker propped up in the passenger seat, she couldn't even manage a smile at the big fluff ball that had become her confidant. But she was so glad to have him next to her.

Cody wasn't the only one in her life hurt that night. Jenna's dad had found Tucker in the field by the bunkhouse, with his back leg bloodied. Although it was only a flesh wound, she knew it was the reason he hadn't come after Todd.

Life the past couple of weeks had been rough. Trying to find her new norm proved to be harder than she thought. Guilt overwhelmed her. During the day she visited Cody at the hospital. Even though he kept telling her she didn't need to, she felt she had to do everything she could to help him get better.

In the evenings she continued her classes and got Cody set up to do his online until he could return.

She had hoped things would quiet down, but she wasn't prepared for the onslaught of phone calls from reporters. If they weren't calling, they were banging on her door. Even though she refused to say anything, it didn't stop them from putting her on display. Every night, it seemed, her face was sprawled across the screen. It would be great, she thought, if she could move on with her life.

After Cody was moved to a regular room for rehab, it was evident his feelings had cooled for her. She couldn't blame him. It was her fault he was even there.

Blaming it on the rigors of physical therapy, he finally told her he didn't want her visiting anymore. It was probably better anyway. Every time she was there, it broke her heart to see him fighting through the pain. Even walking was hard for him.

But it bothered her that she couldn't be there to help in some way. She wanted to make it up to him for the pain she had caused him.

Not long after she stopped visiting, her calls and texts went unanswered. It might be better for him if she said goodbye, but she couldn't let him go. Something about him had a grip on her soul that she couldn't shake.

When she told him she wanted him in her life, she meant it. Once he was home and feeling better, she planned to sit down with him and ask for his forgiveness.

Stashing her purse behind the desk at the vet, she turned on her computer. Tucker snuggled up against her. The tip of his tail was the only part moving. April came around the corner with two large dogs.

"Wanna grab Tucker on your way?" Jenna sassed, knowing it was taking every ounce of muscle for her to handle the two she had. April scowled at her.

"Hey, don't go anywhere. When I get back, I need to tell you something," April yelled while the dogs yanked her down the hall. Jenna went through the mail and threw away a handful of junk. Turning, she picked up the phone and hit a button, then found a pen to take messages that had been left.

April reappeared and chirped her lips, calling Tucker, then rubbing his face and neck when he sat down in front of her. The hair on his back leg had already started growing back. He gave her a couple of licks as she peered up at Jenna, and stood. "So, I got a call from Joe this morning." She dusted her shirt and pants, causing white fur to scatter like a blown dandelion. "He informed me that he is picking up a certain someone when he gets off work this evening."

Jenna's eyes widened and a grin filled her face. "Really?" she squealed. Her eyes darted as she thought. "We need to do something." Tapping her finger to her lips, her eyes widened. "We need to do a welcome home party."

April's mouth formed a thin line of uncertainty and she tilted her head. "I don't know that we could pull something together that fast," she challenged. "Plus, he might not be up to it."

"He wouldn't have to do anything except let people fawn over him." Jenna ran her fingers through her hair, and within a minute her face lit up. "We can do it at TopHops. I can run by Party Supply and get a banner, and then take a poster to the gym, letting them know that he will be home this evening and to show up at the club. Then we don't have to do anything but show up."

Regardless of how the past couple of weeks had gone, Jenna held out hope things would work out between them, and this might be the first step. She sat down in front of the computer and began typing. "I might buy some cupcakes, but other than that, it should be easy." April tugged on Tucker's leash and headed to the back. "What time do you think we should tell everyone to get there?"

"Joe said he is meeting him at five. I figure once they get all the paperwork signed and they eat something, it will be seven before they get back here."

"Okay, I will put, be at TopHops by seven. Stay in contact with Joe so we know if the plans need to change."

"All right. But I honestly don't know if it is such a good idea, with Cody just getting out."

"We won't keep him out too late, plus the place is not going to be that crowded on a Wednesday night."

"All right, I'll let Joe know what's up." April disappeared around the corner.

Jenna rubbed her hands together and started to create the poster she would later take up to the gym. Staring at the computer screen, she deemed her creation done and sent it to the printer. Her thoughts turned to Cody as she studied the finished product, imagining how surprised he would be. She smiled and tucked the small poster behind her purse so she wouldn't forget it at lunch.

The minutes clicked by so slowly, she thought lunch would never come so she could put her plan in motion. After calling Mitch to let him know, she left for lunch and ran by the gym. When she got there, Joe told her he also had reservations about her little surprise. Cody had not been himself, and Joe didn't know how he would take it, but she wasn't going to let him come home without a celebration.

At five, she processed the last of the patients and headed out, picking up some takeout before running home to change clothes. After getting Tucker taken care of, she headed to the party supply store for the banner and balloons, and then to the bakery for the gourmet cupcakes. Her whole body tingled with the thought of seeing him. It had been a while.

TopHops was practically empty when she arrived. The banner was hung, and the balloons were tied to the back of a couple of chairs. Bite-sized cupcakes were set out. Stepping back, she examined her handywork and smiled. Now, it was time to wait.

People began streaming in around six thirty, and April let her know Joe had called. He had Cody, and they were on their way. Jenna's heart pounded in her chest. The place was filling up fast, much more than a usual Wednesday night. The closer it got to seven the more crowded it got. She was ecstatic that so many had come out for him. He was a hero after all, and her banner, with a colorful confetti background, said as much. Welcome Home Hero!

Music wafted through the room. April watched the door to signal when they got there. Minutes went by and finally April gave the signal. Jenna ran up to the front and watched as Joe and Cody made their way through the door.

"Welcome home, Cody!" rang through the air. Cody was obviously startled at first, and then confused. Then his pale cheeks filled with color and he smiled. His dimples, that had been hidden for so long, tucked deep into his cheeks. Jenna's body filled with heat watching him. Even though he seemed a little worse for the wear, he still managed to send sparks scattering through her when his eyes locked on her.

She could tell he was genuinely surprised.

Cody slowly made his way to her. "Did you do this?" She nodded reluctantly, hoping the warmth in his tone conveyed his true feelings. He sat down in a chair with balloons, and one of the waitresses came by the table with a plate of hot wings and loaded nachos, compliments of the house. Everyone around the table grabbed a bite to eat, and people streamed by to shake his hand and welcome him home personally.

Jenna was so excited that everything went off without a hitch. Cody seemed to be enjoying himself, and that was all she cared about. Maybe, just maybe, he could see past her mistakes and let her back into his life. But that was later, right now she wanted him to see how much he was loved.

She bent down close to him so he could hear her over the music. "Are you having fun?"

"I'm having a great time. I can't believe you made this happen in such a short time. I was completely surprised." He smiled. "Joe said we were stopping by because he left his credit card here accidentally. I wasn't even going to get out of the truck, but he talked me into coming in."

A familiar song intro filled the air and his smile

grew even bigger. Jenna had asked them to play his song. Suddenly the crowd broke out singing "It's My Life" from Bon Jovi. Cody began to sing along. Jenna couldn't have been happier. Mitch approached the table. He put his arm around her and gave her a squeeze. Cody stood up gingerly and shook his hand.

"Glad to see you home," Mitch commented cheerfully.

"Glad to be home. Everything good at work?"

"Oh yeah. They didn't give me much time off."

With the evening ending, people stopped by Cody's table before heading home for the night. Surprise filled Cody's face when he commented to her that he didn't recognize some of the folks.

The light in his eyes had returned along with his infectious laugh. Jenna could barely keep herself from running up and kissing him when she heard him laugh at something Joe said. Cody was back. He picked up a second cupcake and filled his cheeks like a chipmunk.

Mitch snagged a chip and walked up to him. He stood as Mitch wrapped him in a hug. Jenna watched as he leaned in to say something to Cody, and just like that, the light went out. After Mitch said his goodbyes, Cody leaned over to Joe and told him he was ready to go. Gone was the smile and the laughter and more importantly, gone was the warmth.

Jenna glanced at Cody and he immediately turned away. She put her hand on his arm. "Is everything okay?"

He gave a lifeless smile. "Yeah, just tired." He stepped closer so she could hear him. "I really appreciate you going to all the trouble to do this. It was so sweet."

It was like someone flipped a switch. Joe picked up Cody's jacket and helped him put it on. He reached over, grabbed one last cupcake, held it up, and gave Jenna a half smile and walked out.

What did Mitch say to him to make his whole demeanor change on a dime? She sat down on one of the chairs and took in the surroundings. It was the perfect night, until it wasn't.

Chapter Twenty-One

Cody sat on the edge of his bed, glad to be home but dreading the day ahead. Last night was such a huge surprise, especially seeing all the people that came out to the party.

But reality kicked in when Mitch informed him he had an update on his case, whenever he was ready to come by. He really wasn't ready but would rather get it over with. Joe had agreed to take him over to the station since he still hadn't retrieved Rubi from Jenna's ranch yet.

Jenna. Another thing he needed to take care of today. Another thing he dreaded. She had confused the hell out of him by coming to the hospital, and then planning the welcome home party, but nothing she did surprised him. That was Jenna, always willing to help, always smiling, always wanting to make others happy even if it was at the expense of her own happiness.

When he was with her, everything slowed down. She helped him enjoy life so completely. There wasn't one thing he didn't love about her. Why did his dad have to take away the one thing that brought pure joy to his life? He wanted to be with her so bad, but he couldn't get the nagging thought out of his head that he would be a constant reminder to her of the horror she went through. The sadness on her face at the hospital told him all he needed to know.

A deep ache pierced Cody's chest, and he tried desperately to brush the thoughts away. Running his hand around the back of his neck, he stood up and grimaced. He pressed his hand to his stomach hoping it would stop the sharp pain. Anger simmered in his veins. Yet another way his dad managed to control his life, even from the grave.

Grabbing his T-shirt, he slid it over his head, tucked it into his shorts, and shuffled out to the kitchen. With a cup of coffee in one hand, Cody sat down on the sofa, set the cup on the coffee table, and put on his shoes. Joe came out of the bathroom, dragging his hand through his hair, and locked eyes with him.

He reached for the coffee pot and poured him a cup. "Are you about ready?"

Cody sat up. "Yeah, as I'll ever be." He let out an exasperated breath and slowly stood.

They slid into Joe's late-model black Tacoma. Sprinkles of rain dotted the windows. The wipers quickly streaked across the windshield, brushing away the water when the sprinkles became a heavy downpour as they eased onto the highway.

"Do you want me to stay there at the station or would you rather handle this yourself?" Joe asked keeping his focus on the road.

Cody shifted in his seat. "I think I would rather do this alone. I don't want to drag anyone else into my problems."

"That's fine. But you do get the fact that you have family here. You don't have to do this alone."

Cody nodded. Joe would always be more like a brother to him than a friend. Truth be told, he didn't want to have to deal with this on his own. But he would rather hear the gruesome information by himself and then choose what to let everyone in on.

"Trust me, you guys have gone far above the call of duty, but I would rather be alone on this."

"All right, man. I get it. Call me when you get done. I am scheduled to work at one, so I should be able to pick you up and drop you back at the apartment before I head in."

The ache in his chest was a constant reminder of what he was leaving behind. He focused on the falling rain. "Sounds good."

Joe had always been there for him, and he knew he could rely on him for anything at any time, and Cody appreciated it. Joe's life hadn't been easy by any means, but he never let that defeat him. Even with working two jobs, he always managed to show up to the hospital to check on him at least once a day.

They pulled up to the station and Cody took a deep breath before stepping out of the truck. The hospital had actually been a nice reprieve from the nightmare. Even though he was dealing with the gunshot wound, it somehow took his mind off the incident surrounding it. But today was his day of reckoning.

Entering the station, he was buzzed through by Sheri, who he now considered his friend. She smiled when he came in and let him know she had been praying for him, which he knew, coming from her, she had.

Mitch's door was cracked open, and Mitch opened it the rest of the way and gave Cody a hearty handshake. His chair awaited him. There was a pinch in his stomach but not from the injury. The memories of the last time he sat in the chair, and what was revealed, caused him to take a deep breath.

"You look good, man," Mitch commented. He walked around his desk and sat down. "How are you feeling?"

"Pretty good. Still weak, but hey, I'm upright and walking around, so that's saying something."

"Yep. And the weakness will go away. It will take some time though." Pulling a folder from the tray next to his desk, a concerned expression appeared on Mitch's face. "Are you sure you are up for this? I didn't expect to hear from you so soon. I thought maybe you would take some time to relax before delving into it, but I guess I should be used to your timing by now." He tapped his pen on the file in front of him.

"I figured the sooner I get this taken care of, the sooner I can put it behind me, or at least try." Cody scooted his chair up next to the desk so he could have eyes on the papers Mitch might pull from the file. "First, I wanted to say something."

Mitch folded his hands over the folder.

Cody's eyes narrowed as he leveled them with Mitch. "I can't thank you enough for what you did. I don't know if Jenna or I would be here if it weren't for you."

"It's my job, Cody." Mitch paused. "And by the way, I take back *all* I said about the boring life of a small-town cop. When I said that, I didn't think you would take it upon yourself to single handedly prove me wrong." They both laughed remembering their conversation. "Anyway, there's quite a bit to go over in here." He picked the folder up and then set it back down. Cody could see the uneasiness in Mitch's face. "I contacted your sister. She said that you agreed to handle everything on her behalf, is that correct?"

"Yes. I will be going up there tomorrow to stay for a while, so any paperwork she needs to sign, I can take to her."

"Oh. So, you're leaving us? How long?" Mitch's surprised expression didn't faze him.

"I'm not sure. Will that be a problem?"

Mitch shook his head and paged through the papers. "I don't think so, but we will go over everything so you have all the information in front of you. First things first, we have talked to all the victims. All but two have signed off on pursuing any legal action, and those two are just asking for compensation of out of pocket. Luckily, none of the victims were seriously hurt. Ms. Corbett had the most serious injuries."

Cody took a deep breath and flexed his hands trying to dispel the build-up of frustration. *Of course, out of all of them, Jenna got hurt the worst.* His thoughts flashed on her face the day he rescued her. The blood, the pain, the fear, it was all inflicted by his dad.

Mitch continued, "So, you shouldn't be out that much from the estate, once everything gets settled."

"Well, it's good to know my dad didn't manage to leave us destitute."

Mitch thinned his lips. "Unfortunately, that is the good news. Are you ready to move on?" Mitch pulled out a paper and pushed it to Cody, who leaned forward.

"Yep, bring it on," he said with an exasperated huff.

"First, we found clothing fibers and skin tissues on the clothing you found that were consistent with the victims, and skin tissue consistent with your dad on the mask. We matched shoe prints with two of the four pair of the sneakers and got a confirmation from one of the victims to the purple pair you found. So, with all that, we have confirmed he was the assailant in all of the attacks."

Cody tightened his jaw and took a deep breath. He stood up and rubbed his hands down his face.

Mitch flipped another sheet in Cody's pile. "You tell me if you need to stop or you need to take a breather."

Cody circled his finger, indicating for Mitch to continue.

"As far as the motive, we were able to unlock the computer you found, and we found quite a few salacious sites, so we feel fairly certain this was an addiction your dad had developed over the years." Mitch paused. Setting his pen down, he laced his fingers. "Let me stop for a moment and say something.

"For what it's worth, I want you to hear this. What you did, coming to me when Jenna accused your dad, had to have been the hardest thing you did in your life. I honestly can't imagine what you were going through. You knew what coming in here meant, you knew the magnitude, or maybe you didn't, but I know it had to have been extremely hard for you." Mitch's attention stayed squarely on Cody.

"I want you to know, typically, with people who have lost control of an addiction like this, things go south pretty quickly. The crimes escalate. It didn't so much with your dad, he pretty much had the same M.O. with each victim over a five-year period, although did become more violent with Ms. Corbett. It could have had something to do with his police training and not wanting to leave behind evidence. But typically, the incidents become more violent, more insidious, with each victim. So, your suspicions quite possibly saved victims from rape, or worse."

Cody nodded. "Thanks, Mitch." A lump filled his throat. "I just wish I could have helped my mom."

Mitch pushed another paper toward him, finally making eye contact again, and Cody let out another desperate sigh, trying again to push the frustration away.

"You doing okay?" Mitch said clearing his throat.

Cody nodded.

"We have finished processing the house, the car, and the gym for items pertaining to the case, but basically you found all we needed to close it. We didn't find anything else during the search that added to the case. So, after the paperwork runs through the system, the case will be closed, shut down, locked up, as far as that side of the case is concerned."

Cody eyed Mitch, who quickly examined the paper and then pushed it forward. "We have processed the house at Corbett Ranch, and your vehicle, since you had the evidence, and have found Ms. Corbett's statement to be consistent with what happened in the incident, as well as your statement.

"We have recovered both guns, and bullets, and found that the bullet that hit you was consistent with the markings from the gun your dad possessed. The markings of the bullet found that hit your dad was consistent with my service pistol, not your gun. He died from a single gunshot wound to the chest." Mitch set the paper down. Cody locked eyes with him. "I'm sorry, Cody."

"Why are you apologizing, Mitch? You did what you had to do. He shot me and probably would have killed Jenna, or you, or someone else." His focus drifted.

"He was your dad, Cody."

"Yes, he was my dad, but he had hurt so many, and I honestly don't think he was planning on coming out of that situation alive."

"You might be right."

Another paper appeared in front of him.

"Now we come to your mom's case. As you know, I requested her file from Montclair and I thoroughly went through it. From what I have read, everything was done by the book. I didn't see any inconsistencies or missed steps. It appears the case was handled well by the department.

"When we did the search of the house, we didn't find anything that would raise a red flag. We didn't find anything at all of your mom's. I am thinking your dad got rid of her stuff when he moved." Mitch sat back in his chair.

"So, as I said, we need some locations to search. Also, it might be helpful to have something of hers that would have her scent. Since your dad got rid of her stuff, we are at a standstill."

"But if he killed her three years ago would the scent be a factor?" Cody picked up the paper and examined it.

"I have a buddy with a bloodhound. He is a trained rescue and recovery dog. You wouldn't believe what this dog can do. If we had something with her scent, it might aid in the search. He may not need it, I mean, I don't know that much about the tracking dogs, but it's worth having it in case we need it."

Cody sat up, thinking about what he might have of his mom's, and then leveled his eyes at Mitch. "I have something that might work."

"Great! That would help. The other thing is narrowing down possible locations."

"I've been thinking, trust me. I have been wracking my brain. I want this to be over so bad." He rubbed his hands against his face. "So where are we at right now?"

"Right now, we are done until you give us a location to begin the search. We have a few locations we can rule out, but other than that, we are wide open. I would suggest you start writing down the trips you have been on with your dad. Once we hit upon something, we will start the search." Mitch sat back. "The house, the car, and the gym, are yours and your sister's responsibilities until we can confirm your mom's whereabouts."

He rolled his hand. "And that means?"

"That means, you and your sister need to talk to the banks and creditors. We can give you the information on the accounts we have found that your dad held, as well as the insurance. Also, you and your sister need to decide what to do with your dad's remains, since his body has been released for burial.

"Okay." Cody felt ill-equipped for any of it, so it was a good thing he was going to his sister's. Maybe she had some idea of what needed to be done. Mitch pushed the last paper to him.

"Most of the stuff can be handled through the mail, over the internet or the phone. You will need to send or take death certificates to the creditors and the banks and any insurance. You can request those through the

County Clerk. Your dad's remains are at the hospital. Once you know what funeral home you will use, let them know where his body is and they can pick it up."

Cody picked up the papers and skimmed them.

Mitch handed him a folder then leaned his elbows on his desk. "Can I ask you something?"

Cody tilted his head. "Yeah?" He leveled the pages on the desk and then shoved them into the folder.

"Are you leaving because you need time to heal, or are you running from the demons? If it's the latter, good luck." Mitch's tone softened. "I'm not judging you. I know from experience, it's better to face your demons head-on or they will haunt you wherever you are."

Cody glimpsed out the window and scratched his neck. "I think it's a little of both, to be honest. I'm feeling overwhelmed. This is a lot to handle." He picked up the folder and laid it on the floor next to him.

"I know it is, Cody. I hate that you have to go through this. Trust me. But running isn't the answer. I know you think this small town can't handle it, won't accept you, think you are cursed, whatever, but what you saw last night should clue you in that you are not your dad, and the community doesn't see you in that light."

"That may be true for some, but not all, Mitch, including me. What my dad did was despicable, and for my entire life I followed in his footsteps."

"From what you have told me and what I have seen, you were pushed to follow in his footsteps and accomplishments, but that doesn't make you like him."

"Regardless, I don't want to be a constant reminder of evil."

"I think who you see yourself as, and who others see you as, are two entirely different things." Mitch tipped back in his chair. "Cody, there are those who aspire to become heroes and there are those who just are. Some wear badges and guns hoping to one day get the opportunity. Then there are those who step into it naturally. I'm not trying to tell you what to do, I just hope you give the town a chance to show you who we think you are."

****

Jenna studied herself in the mirror. Pressing her lips together, she rubbed the excess lipstick off with her finger then fluffed her hair. The phone call from Cody earlier in the day had her whole body wafting from panic to euphoria.

Her mind went in a million different directions, and even though he said he simply needed her to take him to get Rubi, it still meant time alone with him, and that was what she needed to tell him how she felt.

Pulling at the legs of her cut off shorts and smoothing her shirt, Jenna took a deep breath, picked up her purse, threw it over her shoulder, and scrubbed Tucker's fuzzy face.

A mist of rain spread across her windshield as she passed by the gym and the park. She played through the memory of Cody taking her to the secret waterfall the first time. His sweet gesture gave her the confidence to take Tucker jogging again, visiting the waterfall several times since. Then she flashed on the picnic. So many things he did were so thoughtful and made her fall so hard for him, she only hoped he would give her the opportunity to tell him that she still wanted him in her life.

The rain had been intermittent throughout the day, and now it was turning into a heavy downpour. After pulling into the complex, she took a deep breath, stepped out of the truck, and ran to the door while large drops pelted her. *So much for trying to be cute*. With her hair matted to her head and mascara streaming down her face, she figured she more likely resembled a horror movie victim.

Her pulse sent her head spinning as she stared at the door, then knocked. A queasiness had plagued her since the day before, and this had heightened the issue.

The door opened. Cody's forehead creased, and his face filled with a "what happened to you" expression. Without saying a word, he motioned her inside with the phone pressed to his ear and disappeared through a doorway while she stood in the foyer. After a short time, he returned with a towel and handed it to her.

Cody wandered through the apartment with his brows furrowed, obviously worried. All Jenna heard was uh hum, uh hum, yes, no, uh hum. Finally, after a couple of minutes, Cody said goodbye and walked out of one of the other rooms.

"I'm sorry, I was talking to my sister." With his hands on his hips, he stood in the middle of the room, his eyes darting from place to place.

"What are you hunting for?" she asked, still standing right inside the door, continuing to blot the water from her hair.

"My keys. It's not going to do me any good to have you drive me out to get the Jeep if I have no keys." His lips pursed, which made her insides feel like churning lava, but she tried to restrain herself.

"When was the last time you had them?"

"Um...oh, they should be in the hospital bag. I wonder where Joe put it. I remember him bringing it in." He wandered off into another room.

Stepping onto the carpet from the entry, Jenna began to search also and noticed a white plastic bag sitting next to the sofa.

"Is this it?" she asked loudly, snagging the bag and hurrying off in the direction he went.

Finding him, she stood in the doorway. The room was painted in a smoky gray. There was a dark wood chest in one corner and a brushed metal and glass side table with a small lamp next to the bed. She knew it was his room from the clothes she saw strewn on the floor. Clothes she had seen him wear before. His favorite cap sat on the chest, and the smell of the chocolate cologne hung in the air. Jenna could picture herself wrapped up in the covers that currently were wadded on his bed.

"Yes, where did you find it?" His hand brushed against hers as he took the bag, which brought her back to reality. Walking back into the living room, Cody dug through the bag, then set it on the sofa and dug his keys out, and then his wallet.

"It was sitting right there." She pointed to the side of the sofa.

"Thank you, I was starting to panic." He shoved his wallet in his pocket and tapped his back pocket to make sure he had his phone. "All right, I'm ready."

Jenna finished with the towel and handed it to him. "Do you have an umbrella? You might need it." Opening the door, her eyes opened wide when she realized the rain had stopped. "Or maybe not."

The mid-September evening, along with the rain,

had left a slight chill to the air and had goosebumps peppering Jenna's skin.

They drove out of the complex and she cleared her throat trying to come up with something to say. "Have you eaten dinner?" Cody's gaze turned to her, and it was the first chance she had gotten to really look at him. He seemed tired and conflicted, which set her on edge. "It…it's nearly six."

"No, I haven't, but I had a late lunch, so I'm not that hungry. But I don't mind stopping if you are." His tone was flat, and his eyes were lifeless.

"If you don't mind, I haven't eaten much today, and I need to eat something. It will be my treat." Trying to cheer him up, she bounced her shoulders and gave him an enthusiastic smile. "We can stop at Grillerz and sit in the car and eat, if you want?"

"You don't have to do that. I should be treating you since you threw me the party last night."

The words were sweet, but the awkwardness was evident. Jenna hated how fragile their conversations had gotten. She remembered how easy it was to talk to him before. Now it was like walking on glass. She didn't know what was off-limits and what wasn't.

"Trust me, it was nothing. You've been through a lot, and I enjoyed brightening your day."

"I really did enjoy it, but let me get this. It's the least I can do." She shrugged her shoulders but then nodded. When the food arrived, she sat back against the door and set the bag between them to sort it out. Peeking over at him, she watched as Cody shoved the burger in his mouth. It was obvious he was hungrier than he let on. Heat flooded her and a smirk played on her lips. He tilted his head when his eyes met hers.

"What?" Slowly sitting back in the seat, he wiped his mouth with his fingers. "Do I have something on my face? I do, don't I?" The sight of his fingers wrapped around his mouth, was not helping the butterflies in her belly in the least bit.

"No." Seeing the confusion on his face, Jenna decided to change the subject. She pointed and smiled. "It's a good burger, isn't it?" then took a bite. He chuckled, but then fell quiet.

She couldn't stand the awkwardness any longer. It was time to clear the air. "Cody, I know what we have been through has been hard," she said in a tender tone, "and I wanted to tell you I'm—"

Taking a deep breath, he interrupted, "Jenna stop," he said gruffly, then softened it. "Just...stop." His eyes instantly went cold, then closed, like he was fighting with himself. He put down the remainder of his burger and wiped his mouth and hands with his napkin. "I. Can't. Handle this right now. Okay? I know what you are going to say, and I get it. I'm leaving tomorrow." His voice was solemn.

Her throat tightened. "You're what?"

He let out a breath. "I'm leaving." Wadding his burger in the paper, he shoved it into the paper sack. "I'm going to my sister's for a while," he mumbled.

"But why? What about the gym? What about the case?" Jenna tried to fight the tears, but one escaped down her cheek.

"Why? Of all people, I figured you would know. It's too hard, and I'm overwhelmed. We can't do anything with the estate until it is determined that my mom is dead. As for the gym, I have turned the management over to Sam since he's been there the longest. He will be hiring some new employees. The assault case is closed. He did it. It's done. Everything else, Mitch said, can be handled through e-mail or over the phone." She sat and gaped at him in disbelief. Cody turned and gazed out the window.

"But you are coming back, right?" She sniffed back the sting of tears, and hope filled her voice.

"I don't know. Maybe not. I kind of would like to spend more time with my sister and get to know my niece and nephew. They are all the family I have now. It would be really hard for me to stay here, so I'm going to try to find something up there and try to start over."

Cody's words ripped through Jenna's soul like a dull knife. "So, that's it? You hit a little bit of a rough spot, and you want to give up and run away...leave everything you love...all of your friends...and me?" Her words were sharp, and she could tell she hit a nerve by the pain building on his face.

He turned and glared at her. A storm brewed in his eyes. "A rough spot? That's all you think this is? Shit, Jen, this is killing me. And yes. Maybe you think I'm a coward. Hell, maybe I am running, but there is much more behind it than you realize, and right now it's a little hard to live here."

"You don't think it isn't for me?" She bit back unable to contain her pain. *Leaving?* That was the last thing she thought he would do.

"That's exactly why I'm leaving." He threw the bag in the floorboard of the truck. "Can we go...please?"

All air escaped in the cab of the truck. Her chest felt like it was caving in. Tears streamed down her cheeks. Out of everything she had gone through, this hurt the most, by far. It was an accident. She didn't mean for him to get shot. Didn't Cody realize that?

"Fine. Let's get you to your precious Jeep, so you aren't here any longer than you have to be." Jenna's hand slammed on the shifter throwing the truck into reverse. Gripping the steering wheel with both hands, her foot hit the accelerator. The tires squealed as she stomped on the brake and threw the truck into drive. Hitting the accelerator again she peeled out of the lot, jumping the curb before making it onto the highway.

"Geez, Jenna, slow down." Cody's hand reached for the door grip.

"Oh, no, I need to get you to your precious Rubi, so you can get the hell out of town and leave us all behind. Man, did I have you wrong. Our time together meant a whole lot more to me than it obviously did to you." Tears streamed down her face.

Cody sat silently staring out the window. Jenna raced up the farm road and fishtailed onto the gravel path by her dad's house. Dirt spewed behind her. Pulling past the stables, she hit the curve in the path, and slammed on the brakes at the front of the house.

He opened the door and slowly climbed out, then turned around and gazed back at her. "Jenna, I'm sorry." His tone was soft. She caught a shimmer in his eyes when she turned and glared at him.

Her brows dipped. "No, Cody, I'm sorry. That's what I was trying to tell you earlier. I'm so sorry. I know I screwed up, and you got hurt, and I hate myself for it. But dumb me, I thought you were the forgiving type. Boy, was I wrong." Jenna turned her head and stared out her window, tears burning her cheeks.

"You...wait...wha..." Turning back to him, she

noticed confusion filled his face. But she was tired of his games. He had made up his mind.

"Bye, Cody." She leaned over and shut the door and backed out.

Chapter Twenty-Two

Rain pounded on the roof of Cody's Jeep a few miles outside of Bonner Springs. The entire trip took him less than three hours but felt like days. Leaving Dalton seemed like the best thing to do under the circumstances. He was the last piece of the Spencer family horror, at least for now. The town could get back to its quaint way of life and not have to worry about having the black cloud of his family there. Everyone seemed happy to see him at the party, but once the niceties wore off, he figured his presence would be unwanted.

Leaving Joe was hard. He said he understood when Cody told him his plan, but that was Joe. Nothing ever seemed to bother him too much, and he knew he would see him again. But still, he felt bad since he had moved there on Cody's request, to be his roommate and work at the gym. Now, Joe would have to search for a new roommate, and working the construction job, plus working more hours at the gym, would make it difficult.

The conversations he had with Mitch and Jenna could have gone better. They both said he was running, and they both were probably right to some extent. But it would be better for everyone, or at least Jenna, wouldn't it? There was no way Cody could believe Jenna didn't think of the attack when she saw him, and yet, the way she cried when he told her about leaving confused the hell out of him. How could she want him to stay? Was he wrong? And why did she feel like she needed to apologize? What did she mean? The conversation kept playing over and over in his head, to the point where he was fighting a headache. Every time he thought of Jenna, it made him hurt all over, and that's all he seemed to be doing, was thinking about her.

The map on his phone led him to a small red brick house in a nice subdivision. Cody rolled up to the curb and grabbed his bag. When he got to the door and knocked, he could hear tiny voices on the other side.

Jack, a tall thin guy with wavy black hair, black retro glasses, and a striped button-down shirt, opened the door. Next to him was a sandy blond-headed little boy, who hid behind Jack's leg, and a happy, blue-eyed, blonde-headed little girl who seemed to have mastered the art of squealing.

"Hey, Jack. Looks like you got your hands full." Cody leaned in for a one-armed hug, then pushed past the pint-sized minions. "Nice place you got."

Jack rubbed his hand over the little girl's head, who was now firmly attached to his leg. "I hope Hillary prepared you for the life of a stay at home dad with toddlers." He ushered Cody to a living room strewn with building blocks, blankets, action figures, and dolls. The television had some cartoon with farm animals playing.

Setting his duffle bag beside the sofa, Cody made eye contact with Joel and smiled before peering back up at Jack. "She did say it could get a little loud at times."

"Oh, yes, especially when the crying starts at

bedtime." Jack motioned for him to have a seat on the charcoal sectional, then retrieved his laptop off the coffee table. "I have to finish up this one section if you don't mind. If I don't, I will forget."

"Oh, no, go right ahead with what you need to do." Cody sat down and took in the surroundings.

Jack studied the computer screen. "Being able to work from home a few days a week is great, but sometimes it takes a great deal of concentration."

"Well, let me know if there is anything I can help out with."

Cody watched the kids play in the floor for a little bit and remembered scenes from his childhood of his dad getting on the floor with him, playing with his action figures. He recalled it fondly, but it also left him depressed.

"No, you're fine," Jack said staring intently at the screen.

Joel walked over to the sectional, holding a couple of action figures. He bounced his arms on the cushion and Cody stared at him.

"What's your name?" the little boy asked shyly, in a husky voice.

Cody lowered is eyes to him. "My name is Cody. What about you?"

"Joel." He danced around with his feet, keeping his elbows resting on the cushion.

"And how old are you, Joel?"

His hand shot up proudly. "I'm four."

"And who is that?" Cody pointed to the blonde-haired little girl sitting on the floor putting shapes into the sorter.

"That's my sister Hallie." Joel turned away from

the sectional and bounced his back against it.

"And how old is she?" Joel gazed at Jack, who was still staring at his computer, then scampered over and patted him on the leg.

Jack peeked up momentarily. "Daddy, how old is Hallie?" Joel asked in a loud whisper, tucking his hand next to his face.

"She is seventeen months."

Joel strolled back over to Cody, grinning, evidently thinking that Cody didn't hear Jack, and wouldn't be able to hear him otherwise. "She is sebnteen months." His head bobbed with each syllable. "She doesn't talk a lot."

Cody's eyes grew big and he nodded with the information he'd been given. "Really?"

Joel danced his action figures on the cushion and continued sharing information, keeping his attention on his toys. "But she can scream really loud."

Cody's eyes met Jack's, and they both busted out laughing. Joel's eyes bounced between Cody and Jack, and he walked over to Hallie. Cody knew a demonstration was about to ensue, but with his eyes still locked on his computer screen, Jack responded, "Don't do it, Joel. You know you will get in trouble."

Joel's eyes darted to his dad, then back at Cody, who tried to stifle a snicker, and managed to shake his head.

The cushion behind Cody suddenly moved. He noticed a black and white ball of fur slink across the back of the sectional.

Joel pointed. "That's Booger."

Cody smirked at the name of the cat, and he had to ask. "Why is your cat named Booger?"

Joel ran up and snatched the cat from the cushion and shoved it in Cody's face. "Because it looks like he has boogers in his nose."

Cody examined the poor cat that squirmed trying to free itself from the vise grip of the four-year-old. "Well, he sure does. Can I hold him?"

Joel released the cat to Cody's lap, and Cody stroked his back once before the cat returned to his perch on the cushion.

Jack shut the laptop, pushed it aside, and sat on the edge of the cushion on the other leg of the sectional.

Cody sat back into the cushion and crossed his ankle over his knee. "So how long have you guys lived here?" He scanned the place from his seat. The house was nicely decorated with several paintings and framed family photos. The big-screen TV sat on the wall across from the sectional, and a brick fireplace sat in the corner. A large island separated the kitchen and dining room, that fed out to the living room.

"We moved out here when Hillary got her job about three years ago. We were in a two-bedroom before. It was an easy commute for me to Fayetteville, but since I didn't need to go into the office as often, we decided to move where Hillary had an easier commute."

Cody stood up and walked to the sliding glass door that opened to the backyard. A large playhouse with a slide and swings stood front and center in the yard, and a fluffy white dog stood on the porch. His heart squeezed. Tucker. "It's nice. Do the kids ride the Shetland pony much?"

Jack chuckled at Cody's comment. "Oh, that's Lulu. I put her outside so she wouldn't pester you. She loves to love on people but has a problem with invading people's personal space."

"Oh, no, she's fine. Let her in. My girlf…" He stopped himself and a pain pierced his chest thinking about Jenna and Tucker. He wanted that life.

"Your what?"

"A friend of mine has a dog like Lulu named Tucker. He's a great dog." Cody peered off into the yard again and imagined what his life would be like with kids and a dog…and a wife. Jenna. Her face flashed in his head, of the first night they kissed. His body instantly warmed. He heard the door pull open and the jingles of Lulu's collar. She rubbed up against the back of his knees and he reached around and dug his fingers in her fur.

"Again, watch out, she loves to get in your space."

Cody watched as Lulu licked Joel in the face a couple of times, then moved on to Hallie who giggled and squealed and pulled up on Lulu's fur. Hallie tried to hang on, while Lulu trotted through the living room into the kitchen but let go when she spotted a doll she wanted to pick up.

Cody continued to take in the surroundings. "So, what time does Hillary get off?"

Joel came up and latched on to Cody's leg. "Are you going to stay wiff us?"

He met Joel's gaze and ran his hand over his soft honey-colored hair.

"Yep, for a little while at least."

Joel's eyes grew wide, along with his smile. "Do you want to sleep in my bunk bed? You can have da top. Mommy and Daddy won't let me sleep up der yet."

Cody laughed. "I think I might be a little big."

Jack turned to him. "She should be home in about twenty minutes. They have been making her work late recently because they had to fire some people. Hopefully, she won't have to tonight."

Jack pointed to Cody's duffle bag. "I'm so sorry. Let me show you where your room is." He strolled over to the sectional and picked up Cody's bag and walked him down the hallway. "Your room is here on the left, and the bathroom is right there." He flipped on the light of the small guest room and then pointed to the bathroom. "And don't worry, our room and the kids' rooms are down the other hallway, so the screams should be fairly quiet in your neck of the woods." Cody laughed at Jack's candor. "That doesn't mean that you may not have a night visitor at some point, either being the fuzzy variety or the toddler variety."

Cody chuckled. "Duly noted. I will try not to scream too loud if that happens."

Jack laughed and dropped his duffle on the bed, and then turned to walk out of the room.

"Kind of comes with the territory," Jack tossed back as he strolled to the kitchen. "I'm going to start some dinner. Is spaghetti good with you?" Cody followed behind him. "We don't do fancy around here. We are kind of limited to what the kids will eat."

"Spaghetti sounds great to me." Jack bent down and Cody could hear him rummaging through the pots and pans.

"Would you like something to drink?" He popped up above the counter and placed a large pot in the sink. "We have water, juice…beer?"

"Water would be great."

Jack filled the pot with water and set it on the

stove, then reached in the refrigerator, took out a bottle, and handed it to him.

After a few minutes, Cody wandered back into the living room and sat down on the sectional. As Joel began placing action figures in his hand, he heard the front door open.

Joel dropped all his action figures in Cody's lap and ran. "Mommy."

He watched as Hallie stood up and toddled to the front door to greet Hillary.

"Hi, babies."

Cody slowly stood, realizing the long ride had caused the pain from his injuries to spike. He smiled and waved at his sister.

"How was your trip?" Hillary leaned in for the hug with the kids at her knees.

"Fine, boring."

Joel tipped his head up to his mom. "Daddy is making baghettis." He jumped up and down as Hillary tried to make it into the kitchen. With Hallie on her hip, she kissed Jack, who was struggling to open a jar of spaghetti sauce.

Finally hearing the desired pop of the lid, he dumped the contents of the jar on top of the browned meat. "So how was work?"

"I'm really glad I have hair left." She moved around the island to the other side to give Jack more room to work. "I have done everything I can to organize the office, but it's not going to get any better unless they utilize the tools I provided, which they aren't. I'm about ready to chuck it and say goodbye, good riddance."

She took a deep breath and waved her hand.

"Anyway, how did it go here today?" She bounced Hallie to move her up higher on her hip.

"Oh, the usual madhouse."

Cody sat on one of the black bar stools and watched their banter. His chest ached. He knew Hillary was dealing with the same thing he was, but she had someone to lean on who loved her. He wanted what they had. The two beautiful kids, a nice home, obvious love for each other, even the sharing of the monotonous day. He wanted it all. Why was it so wrong for him to have those things, and why was it that now, every time he thought of it, only one person came to mind? Jenna. He took a deep heavy breath.

Throughout dinner, the two kids managed to wear more of their spaghetti than they ate. Cody nearly choked on his spaghetti laughing so hard. Jack finally ran them to the bathroom while Hillary cleaned up the mess in the dining room.

"This visit might scare you away from ever wanting kids." Hillary giggled, wiping the strands of spaghetti from the table.

"It seemed pretty fun. I thought about joining in." Cody stood slowly, let out a groan, and rubbed his hand across his stomach. Hillary's eyes held concern watching him.

She walked into the kitchen. "You hurting?"

He lifted his arm slowly, trying to stretch out the cramp that had formed in his side. "A little bit. Sitting that long on the drive in, I guess aggravated it." He walked to the end of the island. "Is there anything I can do to help?

Hillary shook her head and rinsed some dishes before popping them into the dishwasher.

After a moment she peered at him through her blonde bangs. "Are you still taking your pain meds?"

"Nah, just over the counter."

She pointed to a cabinet above the oven. "I have some in the cabinet if you need some."

Cody nodded. "I will get some here in a little bit."

Hillary wrung the rag out and walked to the dining room table and wiped it off. "You said something about paperwork you wanted to go over with me?"

"Yeah, I'll go get it."

When he returned with the folder, Hillary was already seated at the table. Cody opened it and handed her the first sheet Mitch had shared with him. He gave her each page as Mitch did for him, and she read them one by one, signing where she needed to. They discussed what to do with their dad's remains, deciding to cremate the body and scatter the ashes. Cody talked to her about their mother's case and told her he would be touching base with Mitch when he had possible locations for them to search.

Hillary hopped up and walked into the kitchen. "So, have you come up with any locations?"

Cody played with the folder, spinning it on the table. His mind went back to Mitch's comments. "I haven't really thought about it. Everything has happened so fast. I'm feeling a bit overwhelmed." Leaning back in the chair, he lifted his hands above his head, trying to stretch out a little to alleviate the pain growing in his stomach.

Hillary came around the island with two bowls of ice cream. "I know you need some time to decompress and relax, but remember, the longer you put it off, the longer the nightmare will continue. Plus, and I know this sounds like I'm all about the money, but because mom was still the benefactor of Dad's estate, all his assets will be frozen, and that might cause you some issues with the gym."

"I've thought about that." Cody picked up his spoon and slowly slid some of the cold cream into his mouth. "My next issue is, what will happen if her body is found? What exactly happens then?"

"Well, if she is found, then everything goes to the benefactors. So, that is basically a matter of processing it. If not, we wait out the allotted time to declare someone legally dead. Since Dad confessed to you that he did something to her, I don't know if that affects it or not."

"I don't even know where to start the search. I mean we went a bunch of places together."

"Well, what kind of trips did you and Dad take?" Hillary dipped her spoon in her ice cream and slowly licked it off.

"We did some fishing trips at the lake on the Missouri border. We went to some races in Oklahoma at the speedway and went camping and hiking along the border."

"Anywhere closer in? Closer to home?"

Cody leaned back and scrunched his mouth, thinking about the football games and baseball games that he and his dad went to, and the bike rides and fishing trips. None of which he would consider as possible locations.

He sat in silence, recalling more memories, then his eyes widened and he sat up. "We went hunting with Mr. Hamilton. He had a bunch of acreage with deer stands outside of town. I don't know where it is because

I only went a few times, but I know it isn't that far away."

"I would start with that. I am sure it wouldn't be hard to figure out where that land is." Hillary dipped up the last of her ice cream and stood up. She motioned to him and he handed his bowl off.

"I'll give Mitch a call in the morning and see what he thinks." He pushed out his chair and stood as Joel and Hallie came around the corner. Their jammies clung to their still wet bodies, and their hair was combed and slick. Moving to the sectional, Joel bounced up next to Cody and crawled up close.

"Will you come play cars with me?" Cody held his arm out so he didn't accidentally bump his injuries.

Hillary gently grasped Joel's arm. "Joel, be careful, Uncle Cody is hurt."

Cody smiled hearing the moniker. He was finally, officially, Uncle Cody. He liked the title and liked the feeling of being part of the family. "I would love to play cars with you, but it would have to be up here on the sectional because I can't get down on the floor."

Joel ran and grabbed a handful of cars and lined them up along the arm of the sectional. One by one they launched them off the end. After that, Joel sat at the opposite end of the set of cushions from him, and they launched the cars at each other, making them crash. Hallie took her turn and brought her doll for Cody to love on. By the time the kids were sent to bed, he had made best friends with both his niece and nephew and Cody felt a little bit of the dull ache in his chest dissipate.

****

Cody woke before sunrise the next morning and

walked out to the living room to find his sister sitting at the dining room table, drinking coffee and staring at her laptop. When she saw him, she stepped into the kitchen and got him a cup.

"Do you take cream?" she questioned, barely above a whisper.

Cody peeked out the sliding glass door. He remembered Jenna asking the same question. "Do you have real cream?" No one has real cream except Jenna.

"No."

"I'll take it black."

Returning his gaze through the door, his eyes rested on the sea of rooftops. The streetlights silhouetted the outlines of the houses. Nothing like Jenna's view. That sunrise was spectacular. It was the best two days of his entire life...followed by the continuous nightmare he was now living.

"Cody!" Hillary snapped her fingers and brought him back to reality. "Where did you go?".

His eyes drifted to her and he took the coffee she had been trying to hand him, then returned his gaze outside. "The same place I go every time my mind wanders." His chest heaved, and he shifted his focus back to her. "I feel like I am in a freaking nightmare."

"I am so sorry. I know all of this has been so hard for you."

Clearing his throat, trying to dislodge the growing knot, he asked, "Can I ask you something?"

"Sure." She sat down at the table and peered up at him.

"Do you think, after all of this is over, things will be forgotten enough that I could go back to Dalton?" Hillary smiled at him.

"I thought you were planning on moving up here to get a fresh start?"

"I can't decide." His fingers dug into his hair.

"It's the girl, isn't it?" Just the comment made his eyes burn. "I saw how you looked at each other in the hospital."

"She was Dad's last victim, and I happened to be the guy who rescued her."

Hillary nodded. "I know. They showed the story on the news."

"They interviewed me when it happened, but I haven't seen any of the stories. Well, I didn't see mine, I saw Jenna's."

"You are a hero, Cody. You know that, right?" Her face softened. "I am so proud of what you did."

"I don't know so much about that." He took in a deep breath.

"Anyway, Jenna and I kind of got close through it all, then she figured out Dad was the one who attacked her." Cody could feel his nose begin to burn and quickly cast his gaze out at the sunrise. "I don't want her to be haunted every time she sees me and that's—"

"Why in the world would you think that?"

He lifted his mug and blew on his coffee, then sat down at the table. "Well, one, her attacker is my dad, and two, I have lived my whole life basically in his shadow, doing everything he did throughout his life. I am kind of scared I am going to turn out like him."

Hillary sat back in her chair and raised an eyebrow. "You're kidding me, right? You could never be like Dad. I know he desperately wanted to have a son like him, but you were more like Mom than you were ever like him. You have always been so selfless, and have such a soft heart, like her."

She took a sip of her coffee. "Cody, you can't assume how people are going to react to a given situation. That girl may see things very differently than you do, and the only way you are going to know how she feels is if you talk to her." She lifted her cup and drank the last bit of her coffee.

"Now, the other question is, can *you* live in Dalton after everything that has happened? Remember you have to live with the memories too."

His gaze drifted as he thought about it. "I think I could...with Jenna."

Hillary snickered and shook her head. "Oh, young love." She stood and made her way to the sink.

Could he live in Dalton? He continued to mull over the memories. "Thanks for talking to me, Hil." Scooting his chair out, he stood and stretched.

"Let me know what you find out from the sergeant when you talk to him." She picked up her phone, dropped it in her purse, and shut her laptop.

"You are on your own for breakfast. Jack and the kids probably won't be up for a while. There are all kinds of cereals in the cabinet, frozen waffles in the freezer, or a great breakfast taco place I go to all the time around the corner on the left. It's my favorite."

He nodded, and a smile crossed his face. They were more alike than he thought. She gave him a quick hug, picked up her purse, and left.

He checked his phone, then headed out the door to get some tacos.

Chapter Twenty-Three

The air was thick and damp from the early morning rains. Cody sat outside with his second cup of coffee and a pile of wrappers from his tacos and dialed Mitch's number. Joel and Hallie were still in their pajamas playing on the floor just inside the sliding glass door; their hair going every which way. Through this nightmare, there were still small spots of shining lights.

"Cody! Hey, what's up?" Mitch sounded upbeat on the other end of the phone.

"Hey, Mitch. I had a talk with Hillary last night, and I actually think I have come up with a location that needs to be checked out." Cody sat up in his chair rubbing the morning grime from his eyes.

"Great. Let me get a pad and you can tell me about it."

Moving the wrappers out of the way, he set his cup down on the patio table. "Dad had a friend named Mr. Hamilton who had some acreage outside of Montclair. We went hunting out there a handful of times. The only issue is, I was maybe fourteen the last time I went, so I can't remember where it is located."

"That won't be a problem. We can find it. Let me do some research, get things set up, and I will let you know when we can start the search. You said the guy's name is Hamilton?"

"Yes. I think his first name is Darrell."

"I'll make some calls and see what I can find."

"All right. Let me know if there is anything else I can do." Cody sat back in his chair and ran his hand through his hair.

"Will do."

The conversation still played through his head as he walked back inside the house. Joel ran up and hugged his legs, with Hallie not far behind holding her arms up. He bent down to rub Joel's head, and a twinge caught him as he picked Hallie up, but he couldn't stop himself from lifting the giggling toddler into his arms. Somehow, her little hands patting him and her head lying against his neck immediately changed his mood.

"So, what is on the agenda today?" Cody asked, sitting down in one of the dining room chairs across from Jack, who was making his way through a couple of waffles.

Hallie stood in Cody's lap, stared into his eyes, and put her hands on either side of his face. He leaned one way, and then the other, trying to make eye contact with Jack, but it proved futile. Hallie wanted his full attention.

She started into a baby jabber conversation that Cody found hilarious. "Well, Hallie obviously knows what she wants to do today." Her eyes grew big and her hands waved with every unrecognizable word. "Uh, shopping? You want to go shopping?" Hallie's face scrunched. "Oh, not shopping. You're crazy, Uncle Cody." His brows knitted together in confusion and she continued to stare at him and jabber. "Do you want to go to the...playground?" Joel hopped up from playing with his firetruck.

"Yes, playground! Can we go to the playground,

Unca Cody? Please?" Cody diverted his gaze to Jack, who laughed at Hallie bouncing up and down in Cody's lap.

"I don't dare tell Hallie no," Jack said in a quiet voice. "Like Joel said, she can scream really loud. It's kind of ear piercing." Jack squinted one eye indicating how painful it was.

"We have a great playground and splash pad that we can take them to, and I think the temperature should be in the eighties today."

Cody grinned at Hallie. "Well, it sounds like we are going to the playground." Joel clapped his hands and Hallie followed suit. "I can take them if you need to work."

Jack glanced at him from under his brow and donned an evil grin. "Oh, I wouldn't do that to you." Rising from his seat with his plate in hand, he headed into the kitchen. "Actually, I would, if you weren't hurt. I would send you to your doom while I hid and videotaped it. Then I would put it online, watch it go viral, rake in the cash, and retire happy."

Cody laughed. "You know, Jack, there is a dark side to you I did not know about." He pushed his chair back and picked Hallie up off his lap. When he stood, he caught a whiff of a foul odor. "Uh, Jack?" He sniffed at Hallie's clothes and nearly gagged. "I think Miss Hallie umm…"

"Diapers and wipes are in the first drawer under the changing table. Have at it," Jack said, not making eye contact while he scraped his plate and rinsed it in the sink.

Cody didn't know how to respond. Snapping his gaping mouth shut, he returned his gaze to Hallie.

"Oookay," he said, drawing out the word, completely terrified. Hallie gave him a pat on his cheek with her chubby hand. Gently adjusting her in his arms, hoping to not disturb the hot mess in her pants, he stepped around the table and headed up the hall. Jack caught him mid-stride.

"Hand her to me. That's something else I wouldn't do to you...unless, of course, you want to." Cody shook his head and gladly handed Hallie over.

"Yep. Definitely an evil streak, my friend."

****

The park overflowed with little ones running in all different directions. Jack watched Joel play in the sprinklers at the splash pad while Cody took Hallie duty at the slides. He was grateful to Jack for not sending him by himself. It was hard enough keeping up with Hallie, let alone trying to keep up with both wanting to play in different areas. While they were gathering up their belongings to leave, his phone chimed.

"Hey, Mitch." He propped the phone on his shoulder while he sat Joel in his lap to help him with his shoes.

"Hey, Cody. I wanted to let you know, we have everything ready to go for the search."

"I guess you found the Hamilton land?" Grabbing the towels and sunscreen, he shoved them into a bag.

"Yes. I went through the county clerk and she had the information. Anyway, we can start the search two weeks from today. There are about two hundred acres that need to be searched. We have my friend's search dog that we will be using. Didn't you say you had something of your mom's that we would be able to use?"

"Well, it's not hers, but it will certainly have her scent on it.

"Can you mail it to me?"

"I want to be there for the search, so I will bring it by."

Hallie put her arms up and squeezed her hands. He leaned over and lifted her with one arm, trying desperately not to drop the phone, along with the bag he had slung over his shoulder. "Are you going to be in the office on Thursday?"

"I will be here until about five. Can you make it by before then?"

Hallie laid her head on his shoulder and they headed for the car. "Yeah, I should be in town by then."

"All right, I guess I will see you then. Take care."

He hung the phone up and opened the car door where Hallie's car seat sat. Jack slung straps and buckles in record breaking time, locking Joel tight in his car seat. Cody couldn't make heads or tails of how the seat worked. Jack obviously saw the confusion on Cody's face and smirked, then walked around and buckled Hallie in.

When they arrived back at the house, Cody checked the backseat to see both Joel and Hallie sound asleep. "So, do you keep driving until they've had a good nap, or do you take your chances trying to get them into the house without them waking up?" he asked, with a slight smile.

"As much as they played today, we take the chance. We wore them out, so hopefully they will stay asleep." Jack took Joel, and Cody took Hallie. They quietly laid them down in their beds. Cody wondered what it would be like to have his own kids, and again he thought of Jenna. A pink satin-trimmed blanket sat wadded at the end of Hallie's crib. Pulling it up, he brushed a kiss to her forehead.

They strolled back into the kitchen where Jack took out two bottles of beer and cracked them open. They dinked them together and tipped them back, proud of their accomplishment.

The following days gave him a good idea of what it took to be a parent. He had high regard for his sister Hillary and brother-in-law Jack, never realizing how much life changed when kids arrived. His days were filled with keeping the kids entertained and trips to the store for diapers and food. He became an expert at buckling the car seats, and even took his turn changing nasty diapers, and rocking a screaming toddler while trying to get her to go to sleep. Joel didn't lie, she certainly could scream. Although sometimes challenging, he liked the idea of being a dad.

****

The sound of violins and synthesizers filled the cab of the Jeep. Cody pushed the volume, and the bass boomed to one of his favorite songs. Listening for a moment, he tapped his steering wheel, then started to sing along. Time had gone by quickly. He took in the beauty of the landscape along the roads. The colors were changing.

He had to admit, he was in a much better place than when he left. Though he was heading back to face yet another crime his dad may have committed, his attitude had changed. An eerie peacefulness had overtaken him in almost every way. What had happened couldn't be changed. It was time to move forward.

But, regarding Jenna, there was no peace and no answers. She never left his thoughts. Hillary's words, to open up and talk to her, kept ringing in his head. She was right. He had made assumptions.

He would love for things to go back to the way they were, but that couldn't happen. Their lives would never be the same. The whole sleepy little town would never be the same, and he happened to be in the middle of it. Could Mitch be right though, that they see him differently than his dad? Could he and Jenna still have a chance?

He rolled into Dalton, and a surge of nervousness pulsed through him. It seemed like a long time since he had been here, not merely a couple of weeks. The crisp air surprised him when he opened the door of the Jeep after pulling into his apartment complex.

The place was quiet. Nothing had changed. He did a quick scan around the apartment, retrieved a bottled water from the refrigerator, then headed to the bedroom.

The closet was full of boxes and tubs, but he knew exactly where to find what he needed. He dug through a box with his military stuff and quickly found one of his most treasured possessions. After sealing it in a Ziploc bag as Mitch instructed, he placed it inside a grocery bag and walked out.

The police station was only a few blocks away. A feeling of déjà vu crept through him as he killed the engine. Sheri cheerily greeted him and buzzed him through. Mitch's door sat partially open, as usual, but he still knocked.

"Cody!" Mitch stood from his chair and walked around his desk. He gripped his hand and shook it, then patted his back. "It's good to see you."

Cody grinned. "Aw, did you miss me?"

Mitch gave him the side-eye and walked back around his desk. Cody dropped his folder on the desk, sat in his usual chair, and chuckled.

Mitch tipped back in his chair and tucked his hands behind his head. "How are you doing?"

"I'm doing good." He smoothed his hands down his jeans. "I did find out trying to recover from a gunshot wound with a seventeen-month-old and a four-year-old in the house is probably not the best idea. They don't really understand personal space." His eyes kicked open wide and he let out a long breath, but then smiled.

Mitch's head went back in fits of laughter.

"But, honestly, I am glad I went. It was good for me to get away. It gave me a good perspective of what I might be in for later."

Mitch nodded his head. "I remember those days well. Many a sleepless night. But I wouldn't trade them for the world." He rubbed his hand over his head, then sat forward and locked eyes with Cody. "So, have you decided what you want to do in the long run?"

"Not really. Part of me thinks I should come back and deal with the aftermath, and another part of me thinks I should stay away." He shook his head. "Maybe this last piece of the puzzle will help me decide."

"Speaking of which, did you find the item you were talking about?"

Cody's cheeks heated from the wave of embarrassment as he picked up the white plastic bag.

"Now, let me preface this before I hand it to you." Mitch sat up, confused. "When you said you couldn't find anything in the house of my mom's, the only thing I could think of that I had was something I've had since I was a kid. So, don't judge me." Out of the plastic grocery bag, he pulled a large Ziploc bag with what appeared to be a stuffed animal inside. "You said I needed to put it in a zipped bag, right?"

"Yeah, we keep the item in the zip bag so it locks the smell in and intensifies it. That way when the dog sniffs it, it has a stronger odor. The dog is a trained man trailer. They use the scent of the item to locate the person." Mitch turned the bag over and examined it and then bit his lip trying not to smile. "Is that a stuffed dog?"

Cody breathed deep, "Yep," and sighed at Mitch who snickered. "Mitch? Don't do it," he scolded.

Mitch regained his composure and took a breath. "So, tell me the story."

Cody leaned back in his chair. "What do you mean?"

"I mean, tell me why your mom's scent would be on your stuffed animal." Again, clamping his lips together trying to stifle a smile.

Cody rolled his eyes. "Do you have to know that? Can't you trust me?"

The smile that Mitch tried desperately to tamp down now crossed his face. "Well, if I didn't want to know before, I do now."

"Really, Mitch? Really?" Cody could feel the heat intensify in his face and neck and was annoyed at Mitch for pressing the issue. Mitch didn't waver.

Cody sat silent, let out a deep growl, then finally gave in. "When I was little and I did a sleep away, whether it was a friend's house or grandparents, my mom would hug the stuffed dog and then give it to me. That way I would have something that smelled like her, and it kept me from being scared."

"And you still have it?" Mitch was still smiling but more curious.

"She sent it to me when I left for my tour in Afghanistan. While I was there, she disappeared." Mitch's face turned sober. Cody slapped his legs. "So, don't lose my puppy," he said, trying to lighten the mood.

He picked up the white grocery bag and put it on the desk. Mitch put the stuffed animal inside. He saw the folder when Mitch picked the bag up and pushed it to him. "Oh, Hillary signed all the papers."

"Good, thanks. I will get you a copy." Picking up the folder, he tapped it in his hand before putting it in a tray.

"What will happen tomorrow?" Cody asked, sitting forward in his chair.

"We are meeting at eight at FM twenty sixty-eight and two hundred twenty-sixth West Avenue. There is an entrance to the Hamilton property there. Darrell will be there to open the gate." Mitch leaned back. "I will need you there for a short time so the dog can sniff you. That way your scent is ruled out. After that, you can stay or leave.

"We already have part of the property sectioned off in grids, and they will do one section at a time. It's a wait and see game after that. I will stay in contact with you throughout the day if you want to hang out in town."

"I may do that. I need to go by the gym and see how Sam is managing. He has called a few times and may be a little overwhelmed taking over everything. He is great as far as scheduling and making sure the place is clean and operational, but the business side is not his forte."

Mitch shook his head. "I'm with him, I hate crunching numbers." He opened his desk drawer and handed Cody a small brown envelope.

"What is this?" he asked, holding up the envelope.

Mitch pointed to it. "That's the keys to your dad's house, car, and the gym. I had one of the guys put the car in the garage once we processed it."

"Oh, okay. Thanks." He tucked the packet into his jeans. "So, walk me through what will happen if you find her."

"The body will be taken to the medical examiner to try to determine the approximate time of death and how the death occurred. Could take a couple of days. Could take a couple of weeks. Once that is done, the body will be released. You will then be able to decide on what you would like to do burial wise.

"It would be a good idea to appoint an estate lawyer to process the estate. We went through your dad's finances pretty well, so when I get you the copies back, you should have a good list of the insurance, retirement pension, military, real estate, and real money assets there are along with any loans, taxes, and payments owed. The only other thing is household goods."

"And if you don't find her?" He rubbed his hands together.

"Then it's back to square one. You continue to provide locations to search. If the trail goes cold, it becomes a waiting game. The statute is seven years unless the court decides otherwise." Mitch continued. "You can continue to run the gym and you can live in the house. Basically, do what you want to a degree, but you can't sell the house or the business or the car until the court allows."

"Sounds reasonable." He patted the arms of the chair. "Well, I guess I better get out of your hair so you can get back to work." The familiar sting raced through his body when he stood.

"What are your plans for this evening?" Mitch questioned.

"I have no plans. Probably chilling out, watching something on TV with Joe."

"Well, I am pulling a double and will be out on patrol if you want to come."

"I will probably have to take a pass this time. If I sit too long, the wounds get a little crabby, and right now, I am on the edge from the drive."

"All right, just thought I would offer." He patted Cody on the back. They walked out of the office and Mitch hit the button to let him out.

"I will see you out there tomorrow."

"Sounds good."

Chapter Twenty-Four

Cody climbed in his Jeep after meeting with Mitch at Mr. Hamilton's land. Pulling off the dirt road onto the asphalt, he was glad he had somewhere else he was needed. Everything about this morning made his skin crawl. The white plastic bag in the passenger seat made him feel better, at least in part, about the morning's activities. After sharing his embarrassing childhood story about the stuffed animal with Mitch, it turned out they didn't need it after all.

The dog they had at the site was a cadaver dog. It used the smell of decomposition to search for bodies. As much as he didn't want to believe it, he knew his mom was out there. Something in his gut told him. He knew they were going to find her. It was only a matter of when.

Memories flooded back of his mom. Every performance, every game, every award, she was right there cheering, and after each one she would tell him how proud she was of him. Her love was obvious.

No matter what problem he was dealing with, nothing was off-limits to her, she was always there for him with a smile. She was so strong, except for one time. The day he left for Afghanistan, she broke down. It was like she knew it was going to be their last time to see each other. But it wasn't him who didn't come home.

He pulled into the gym parking lot and sat with the motor running, trying to come to grips with what might transpire.

Pulling the stuffed animal from the package, he studied it, then slowly brought it to his nose and breathed deep, trying to remember her scent. A lump tightened in his throat, and he let out a long sigh before setting the stuffed animal down, flipping off the engine, and climbing out.

The chime of the door set him on edge, but Joe's smirk from behind the counter settled it some. "Well, I wasn't expecting to see you this early."

Cody dropped his keys on the counter and pushed his sunglasses on top of his cap. "Is Sam in the office?"

Joe turned on his stool and nodded. "I know this isn't what you want to hear, but he's pissed. He ordered some supplies Monday, and we were supposed to get them yesterday. They didn't arrive, so he e-mailed them. They said they never got his order."

Cody chewed on the corner of his lip. "I'll handle it. He's texted me a few times about issues, so I thought I would stop by to see if I could get some of them cleared up."

"Did you get everything squared away with the sergeant?" Joe's tone was quiet and laced with compassion.

"Yeah, I just came from there. One guy, I think his name was Russ, had a bloodhound who was trained in cadaver recovery. There were several areas sectioned off. I left before they got started." His gaze drifted, revisiting the scene, then he tapped the counter and wandered back to the office.

The door was closed, so Cody knocked a couple of

times then turned the knob. Sam shifted his focus from the computer and began reciting the same story Joe had told him minutes earlier. Cody gazed at the computer screen as Sam found the order. He scrolled to the bottom of the page and found the problem. "You didn't confirm the order." Sam swayed in his chair and let out a long breath.

"I told you, I am not good at the office management stuff. We need to hire an office manager and be done with it. That way we don't have to run from one job to the next."

"You go ahead and head up front to help Joe, and I'll try to get some stuff done. I'm sorry I dumped all this in your lap, Sam. I appreciate everything you have done while I've been gone though." Cody knew Sam was right. He needed someone who had office skills.

Even though he knew how to do most of the computer stuff, whether he decided to stay in Dalton or move, he wasn't going to have the time to do all the paperwork and go to school. From what he could see, there was a bunch of it.

****

Cody sat back in his chair. His eyes darted from the computer to the pile of papers. *I swear the pile grew. Geez, this is ridiculous.* It had taken him hours of sorting through the papers, and there still was hours of paperwork left. Searching the internet for a job hiring website, he plugged in office manager to see what it would cost to add someone to the staff. *Shit, we don't have that kind of money.* He sighed and rubbed his hands down his face. Something had to be done.

His stomach rumbled, and he eyed the clock at the bottom of the computer screen. Almost noon. *I need a break.* He stood and headed out of the office.

Joe glanced up as Cody made his way to the counter.

"I am going to find me some lunch," he called out as he lifted his sunglasses off the brim of his cap and pushed against the glass door. *I wonder how things are going at the site.* His phone chimed.

****

The smell of the deli sandwich sitting on the seat next to her made Jenna's stomach turn. She knew she needed to eat, but April's words came back to her the minute she drove up to the park. Cody's back. At work, her concentration was shot once April dropped the bomb on her. Now her stomach was doing cartwheels, and nothing sounded appealing. Nothing new. Her appetite had taken a nosedive since Cody pushed her out of his life. Everything was off. She wished she could let him go, but he was never far from her thoughts.

Walking along the trail, she crossed the grassy area of the park, then wandered down the secret path to the waterfall. Snapshots of when Cody brought her to the falls the first time tumbled through her thoughts.

Everything had come into focus at that moment. His hands, his eyes, his smile, his voice, had healed every part of her. Jenna felt cherished, like Cody would walk to the ends of the earth for her. She knew then she had fallen for him, hard.

Then it all shattered into a million tiny pieces, and he walked out of her life. All her texts and calls trying to apologize had gone unanswered. All she was left with was silence.

The waterfall came into view. She sat on the flat

rock where they stood and watched the sun come up weeks before.

The conversation with April played over in her head. Mixing with the memories. The realization that Cody had come back because the police had launched a search for his mom, and not for her, pierced Jenna's heart and overwhelmed her. It felt like everything was caving in.

The sound of the rippling water was so peaceful. Jenna had hoped it would ease the tightness that had settled in her chest.

Since Cody left, this was her favorite place to come. Even though the memories were bittersweet, she wanted to remember. Jenna had gotten to the point where she didn't cry every time. But knowing Cody was back brought a fear. What if she did run into him? What would she say? Part of her begged to see him, to touch him, to finally tell him she was sorry and let him know exactly how she felt. But part of her knew she couldn't bear it if he walked away without forgiving her.

Jenna opened the paper around her sandwich and picked it up. Though the sandwich smelled delicious, she couldn't make herself take a bite, and it quickly landed back on the paper. Pulling her knees into her chest, she wrapped her arms around them and laid her head down. The magnitude of April's words consumed her. What in the world would she do now? It had been weeks since she'd spoken to him.

Her arms moved around her waist. The darkness took over. Tears streamed down Jenna's cheeks. Every angry word of their last argument in her truck played through her head. She was the reason Cody left.

The pain in his eyes when she slammed the door shut haunted her. Jenna's heart stopped at that moment, like Cody walked away with it in his hands. She would give anything to make the ache that had wrecked her body go away, to figure out how to stop loving him. The sobs came harder.

The sound of a voice dragged her attention to the path. Fearing someone would see her, she scooted behind some trees and swiped her face, trying to stop the tears. The deep tone of the voice grew louder. A shadowy figure appeared. *It can't be. I know that voice. Cody.* Jenna could barely see him through the trees, but it was definitely him, and he sounded upset.

"Are you sure it's her?" The tremble in his voice was evident. "No. It's okay. Now we know." Walking into the open, Cody stood on the rocks next to the stream where she could see him clearly. "All right. Would later this afternoon work?" His fist bumped up against his mouth. "I just need some time," he said, rubbing his temple. "Thanks, Mitch." Shoving his phone in his pocket, he put his hand over his mouth and squatted down. His shoulders shook, and Jenna could hear the wheeze of his cry.

There was no way she could leave him alone. Quietly, she stepped down off the rock. His body rocked back and forth while he flung rocks into the stream. Her heart pounded, wondering what his reaction would be. The snap of a stick caused Cody to turn.

"Jenna?" His face was wet from his tears.

Her breath stalled when their eyes locked. Before Jenna could speak, Cody stood and crushed her in his arms like she was going to be taken away any minute. He buried his face in her shoulder, and his body quaked as he let go and sobbed. Rubbing her hand up and down his back, she held him like he had with her weeks before.

Trying to regain his composure, Cody backed away, pinched his nose, and exhaled. "I can't believe you're here." The trees rustled with the breeze, and strands of hair fluttered around Jenna's face. Cody lifted his hand slowly and brushed the strands away. His eyes locked on hers.

And then it was like she had suddenly become electrified. Cody lifted his hands off her and stepped away, focusing his gaze on the ground. "They found my mom." His chest heaved and he coughed, trying to fight back the tears. "Something inside me knew they would. But I didn't want it to be true."

Jenna wrapped her arms around her waist. "I am so sorry, Cody." Her throat was so dry her words came out in a whisper. The pain Cody was feeling was written all over his face. But there was also something else she noticed. There was a look in his eyes when he saw her. The feelings were still there, and Jenna wasn't going to let him slip away again before she cleared the air.

She took a chance and slowly wrapped her arms around him again. Cody's arms tightened, and he lowered his head to her shoulder.

"Somehow the scenario of my mom being out there somewhere, living her life, was easier to deal with than believing this." Cody stepped back. The sunlight caused the tears in his eyes to glisten. "She didn't deserve to die." Tears spilled from his eyes and streamed down his face again. "Dammit, that man was such a monster. He has managed to take everything away from me." Jenna's heart ached for him, and all she could do was hold him. His head buried into her shoulder again. She let the silence take over and her hands soothe him.

After several minutes Cody cleared his throat. "But it's over." His voice sounded muffled and Jenna pulled away, her eyes connecting with his.

"Hmm?"

"It's over. He can't hurt anyone anymore. There are no more unanswered questions." Cody studied Jenna's face as if waking from a dream. "Jenna, what are you doing here?"

Glancing back up at her sandwich she answered, "I came over to get away for a little bit and eat lunch."

He continued to search her eyes. "You are not telling me something."

Jenna quickly focused her eyes on the water.

His hand guided her chin back. "Wait. You've been crying."

"Well, yeah, you—"

"Don't lie to me, Jenna."

A lump formed in her throat and words wouldn't come. Turning away, Jenna could still see Cody staring. Tears threatened, so she headed back to the flat rock at the top of the falls and sat down. Cody followed, and Jenna watched as he grimaced trying to get comfortable, sitting across from her. Guilt caused the queasiness in her stomach to grow. She needed to apologize. Wiping her hands across her cheeks, hoping her mascara wasn't smeared everywhere, she tried her best to smile.

"Hi," she whispered. Cody moved to scoot in closer but was hit by another twinge, and the pain filled his face. It was more than Jenna could take, so she turned away. Cody gently took hold of her chin, turned her face back to him, and wiped her tears, but Jenna couldn't bear to see him hurting, so she continued to keep her eyes averted. They sat silently for a minute until she finally heard his voice and set her eyes on him.

A softness filled Cody's face and his tears glistened. "We're a mess, aren't we?"

A small laugh escaped even though tears still streamed down her face.

Cody wiped away more of her tears. "Please tell me this isn't because of me."

The pain quickly reappeared, and Jenna stared out at the waterfall and remained quiet for a long moment. "I can't."

"Jenna, I'm sorry. I honestly never meant to hurt you. I thought it would be—" His words were gentle, but Jenna kept playing the last conversation they had over and over in her head.

Trying to fight off the tears, she closed her eyes then slowly opened them letting the tears spill. "You said you were leaving because of me. Exactly what was I supposed to do with that? I'm the reason you left town. Your dad was right. I screwed up your life."

Cody's jaw clenched. "You didn't screw up my life. I was just so overwhelmed with everything. I couldn't think straight. I'm sorry, I didn't mean—"

"Cody." Jenna's tone became solemn, and suddenly it was hard to breathe. Everything she wanted to say, things she had thought about saying a thousand times if he had called, were now like dust in the wind. Closing her eyes, she took a deep breath hoping it would help her form the words.

"I know you wanted space while you recovered, and I tried to give it to you. When you left, you made it clear you wanted me to forget you. And I tried." Jenna opened her eyes to find Cody staring at her. "But I couldn't. Everywhere I went reminded me of you. I know we haven't known each other that long, but when we met, it was like a voice whispered inside of me saying, 'I finally found you.' It didn't take me long to realize I had fallen in love with you. It wasn't a crush, or infatuation, or some White Knight Syndrome. It was like I found a part of me I was missing. When you left, there was this deep hole. I've tried to move on, but I can't."

The corners of Cody's mouth twitched.

"I kept checking my phone hoping you would call or text, so I could apologize, but you never did." Tears spilled down Jenna's cheeks. "I made a mistake, Cody, and I am so sorry. I, I never meant for you to get hurt. But you didn't even give me a chance to apologize. You shut me completely out and left."

Cody sat back. His eyes narrowed. "What are you talking about? There is nothing you need to apologize for."

Jenna wiped her cheeks and sniffled. "Then why did you leave?"

"No. I want my question answered first. You tell me why you think you need to apologize," Cody said. Irritation laced his tone.

She sat quietly for a moment. "Because I nearly got you killed." Her voice rasped, barely above a whisper.

Cody's forehead wrinkled as his brows pushed up. Gently grasping Jenna's ankles, he scooted in and put her feet on either side of his hips, to where he could wrap his arms around her.

"Why in the world would you think that?" His

fingers moved her hair that was stuck in her tears.

Jenna's lips parted to speak, but her voice caught. The floodgates opened and her tears streamed down her cheeks. "Because..." Her fingers trembled as she pressed them to her lips. "I didn't leave when you told me to, and your dad found me. Then, when he had the gun on me and I escaped, he lost his balance and the gun went off." The words were thick in her mouth, and her chest heaved as Jenna tried to take a breath. "Your dad told Sergeant Gallagher he didn't mean to shoot you. He said I caused him to stumble. It was my fault you got shot." Cody tightened his arms and rocked her as Jenna lowered her head against his chest and wailed.

He brought her chin up and wrapped his hands on either side of her face so her eyes would stay locked on him. "You listen to me." Cody's voice quaked as he fought back his own tears. "You. Had. Nothing to do with him shooting me. You got that?" His jaw pulsed, and tears streamed down his face. "My dad was hellbent on shooting someone, otherwise he wouldn't have had a gun. He was a liar. He said he didn't mean to kill my mom either."

Jenna's brows knitted together. "So, you weren't mad at me?"

"No. You did everything right." The corner of Cody's mouth tucked in revealing a hint of his dimple. "In fact, I was pretty proud of your skills." Cody let the tears roll down his cheeks. A slight smile crossed Jenna's face. "That is what I want to see." He kissed her forehead and tugged her closer. "That was what you were so upset over when I was in the hospital?"

Jenna nodded her head. "Well, yeah. All I could think about when you were lying there were your dad's words. I couldn't stand to see you in that much pain knowing I caused it. When you said you were leaving because of me, it hurt so bad to know you blamed me."

"Oh my God, Jenna. No. I absolutely do not blame you, in any way. That was all on my dad."

Jenna let the words wash over her. He didn't blame her. Leaning against Cody's chest, she closed her eyes and listened to the sound of the rushing water. But, if he didn't blame her, why did he leave? *Why did he say I was the reason?* Jenna opened her eyes and searched his face. Her heart warmed the way he gazed at her. "April told me you came back to search for your mom."

"Yes, I came in yesterday. We met early this morning at some land outside of town that my dad and I went hunting on."

"Did your sister come with you?"

"No, she is too busy with her job, so I told her I would handle it."

Jenna gazed at the water. "Did you enjoy your time with her and her family?" Then her eyes connected with him again.

A smile crossed Cody's face. "Actually, I did. Even though it was kind of crazy."

"Crazy?"

He rubbed his hands up and down her ribs. "I've never been around toddlers. Joel is four and Hallie is a year and a half, and between the two of them, we were going all the time.

"I played cars and superheroes with Joel, and dolls with Hallie." Cody chuckled. "Hallie can't talk, so she had this little language. She kept crawling up in my lap and trying to talk to me. She would put her hands on my face," he mimicked her movement and put his hands on Jenna's face, "and then she would start jabbering." Cody's face became animated as he tried to recreate the moments. "I never had a clue what she was saying but she kept going. It was so funny."

Jenna loved seeing his eyes brighten and the smile on his face talking about the kids. His funny expression made her giggle. "So, you had fun?"

"Yeah. It helped me refocus. I know that sounds weird because it honestly was sheer chaos. I got a real taste of life as a family. They had me doing everything. I can now buckle a car seat without pinching my fingers and change a dirty diaper without puking." He gave her a cheesy grin.

Jenna's eyebrow shot up. "That's impressive."

"But honestly, it took my mind off what I was dealing with enough to where I didn't feel so overwhelmed by it."

"Well, then, I guess my next question is obvious."

Cody dragged his teeth across his bottom lip as Jenna gazed up at him, and then turned away. "Are you going to stay or go back?"

His chin dropped.

Jenna's pulse kicked up. After all of this, could he still choose to leave her?

Cody let out a long breath and his sigh stabbed at her heart. Her face turned solemn. The burn in Jenna's eyes reignited and she gazed at the falls before capturing a glimpse of him. "I'm so confused. Why did you leave? I mean, I know you were overwhelmed, but if you weren't mad at me, why did you push me away and tell me it was because of me?"

Cody sat motionless, staring off into space. "I thought about it quite a bit on the way back, and with what you have just told me, it adds some clarity." His eyes locked on her.

"When you came into my hospital room, I could see the sadness in your eyes. I didn't know why at the time, I thought maybe it was because you were worried about me. But every time you looked at me, I saw the tears, and I knew there was something else going on.

"I wanted to talk to you alone, but Hillary showed up. While we were talking, Hillary made a comment about getting out of town for a while, to get away from the ghosts and memories, and the possibility of people shunning me for what my dad did. Then it hit me.

"Everything happened so fast that I hadn't even processed the fact that my dad attacked you, then tried to kill you." He pressed his hands to his chest. "My. Dad. I was tied to your worst nightmare, and I figured that had to be the reason you were so upset. How could I not remind you of what happened every time you laid eyes on me?"

"So, you left because you thought you would remind me of the attacks?"

Cody nodded.

"You were as much of a victim as I was, remember? And as far as being a reminder, well, to be honest, you are."

Cody's body flinched with her comment, and he took a deep breath and turned away.

"But Cody, you are nothing like your dad. I saw that the first time I met him." She leaned forward and turned his face to hers. "You're the reason I was able to get through the nightmare. Don't you realize that?"

Cody lowered his head in disbelief.

"I remember how scared I was the day of the

attack. No one was around. Then you appeared. You had this comforting way about you. You were so calm and your voice so gentle. When you told me I was safe, I felt it. You taught me wrestling moves to help me fight back, even though I could see how uncomfortable it made you."

Cody's face flushed. "You knew?"

Jenna's eyes darted away, and she gave a sheepish nod.

"And when you found out how much I loved running with Tucker, you ran with me and Tucker to make sure I would be able to get comfortable running in the park again.

"Then you showed me this." She gestured at the waterfall with her hand. "This is my favorite place now. I come here all the time." She smiled.

"Cody, you were willing to lay your life on the line for me, and it nearly got you killed. So yes, you are a constant reminder. You remind me that I had someone watching out for me, making sure I was safe. Someone who wanted to take care of me."

Cody turned away. He tumbled a few rocks between his fingers. "I can't see how you can separate me from what my dad did to you though. I mean, I want nothing more than to have you in my life, but the memories…"

"The only time when I had problems with the bad memories and nightmares was when you weren't there. I need you here because you remind me of the good times. You replaced my bad memories with ones of us. The memories we have made together over the last couple of months have far exceeded any bad memories I might have, and every time I look at you, I remember us."

A glint sparked in Cody's eyes as he glimpsed the falls and a slight smile formed. "Yeah, we have made some pretty great memories." He pulled her close to him again. "So, did you mean what you said earlier?"

"What?" Jenna asked coyly, wrinkling her nose.

The corner of his mouth curved up. "You know what?"

"You mean that part where I said…" Jenna leaned in and gently brushed her lips to his lower lip. "I." A second kiss grazed his cheek. "Love." A third kiss softly touched his neck. "You." Her voice was barely above a whisper in his ear. His body tightened and eyes narrowed locking on hers.

For a split second, she wondered if he was going to break her heart again. Then his mouth found hers. The kiss was heated, aggressive, and hungry. Jenna's lips parted, and Cody plunged deep, tasting her over and over, then backed away and sent kisses down her neck.

"My God, I've missed you," Cody said, his hand pulling at the band in her hair until her curls fell. His fingers laced in her hair, then cupped her face. Her eyes searched his, and his lips pressed against hers again, this time slowing things down. Savoring every kiss.

Jenna's hands tugged his shirt free from his pants, and gently caressed his bare back, her fingers skimming the scar, backing away when he flinched.

"Still a bit sensitive."

She lifted his shirt examining the wounds on his stomach.

Cody made a face. "Pretty rough, huh."

A genuine smile spread across her face. "Battle wounds of a hero." Cody leaned in again to capture her mouth with soft kisses, then pulled away and studied Jenna's face. His fingers pushed her blowing hair away.

"I love you, Jenna." He paused. "I think I've known it since the first time I saw you."

She grimaced, picturing the bruised and bloodied face she saw reflected in the glass doors of the gym the day she was attacked. "Seriously?" she snorted.

Cody chuckled.

Her heart felt like it would explode any minute with each of his words.

"So, you think you would be fine with me being around all the time?"

Jenna's lips trailed kisses down his neck, but she stopped long enough to nod her head.

"I mean, there might be a few people that won't feel the same way. It might get kind of bad you know. What if I get run out of town? Would you go with me?"

Jenna sat back and smirked. "Maybe." Her smile conveyed something different. "I don't like to deal in the 'what ifs' anymore. I mean we both should know by now what can happen in twenty-four hours.

"True."

A buzz startled them both. Jenna studied her phone for a second. "It's my alarm. I need to get back to work."

Cody stood while she wrapped up her sandwich. She stood, but suddenly stumbled and swayed. Cody gripped her arm and steadied her.

"Are you okay?"

"I think so. I got a little dizzy. I must have sat too long." Their fingers laced together, and they walked up the path.

"Do you think you could call in sick? Maybe you

need to lie down." His eyes twinkled.

Jenna turned to him giving him a mischievous smile. Cody stopped on the path and dragged her in his arms, staring down at her. An inferno burned in his eyes.

"What do you want?" she asked, in a smoldering tone.

He leaned in and placed a soft kiss on her lips. "I want to stay."

A word about the author...

DeDe Ramey is a Texas girl transplanted in the heart of Oklahoma. Her vivid imagination and love for people watching gave her a passion to write romance novels filled with swoon-worthy heroes, smart, sassy heroines, unexpected nail-biting suspense, and a good helping of steamy, heart-melting romance.

She grew up in the beautiful historic town of Georgetown, Texas. Her crazy life experiences with family and friends helped develop her rich, colorful imagination. In elementary school she started writing pages of poetry, which transformed in her teen years into writing and performing her own original songs. As an adult she wrote skits and plays, some short stories, and even a script for a TV series.

Before deciding to write full time, DeDe received a degree in sound engineering and broadcast telecommunication but soon realized those jobs were hard to come by. She took a job as an apartment manager, then later settled into the job of domestic affairs manager, raising two amazing kids. Once the kids left home to start their own lives, she revisited her passion for writing.

When she is not reading or writing she enjoys lifting weights at the gym, finding breathtaking waterfalls while exploring the national forests and parks, searching for adventures in new cities, and going to concerts of old rock bands with her husband Keith, her very own devastatingly handsome hero of over 35 years.

CPSIA information can be obtained
at www.ICGtesting.com
Printed in the USA
LVHW022145260121
677570LV00055B/668